THREE STRIKES

ALSO BY ROSS KLAVAN, TIM O'MARA AND CHARLES SALZBERG

Triple Shot

ALSO BY ROSS KLAVAN

Schmuck
Tigerland (screenplay)

ALSO BY TIM O'MARA

Raymond Donne Series
Sacrifice Fly
Crooked Numbers
Dead Red
Nasty Cutter

ALSO BY CHARLES SALZBERG

Henry Swann PI Series
Swann's Last Song
Swann Dives In
Swann's Lake of Despair
Swann's Way Out
Swann's Down (*)

Stand Alone
Devil in the Hole
Second Story Man

(*) Forthcoming in 2019

ROSS KLAVAN,
TIM O'MARA,
CHARLES SALZBERG

THREE STRIKES

THREE CRIME NOVELLAS

Down & Out Books
3959 Van Dyke Road, Suite 265
Lutz, FL 33558
www.DownAndOutBooks.com

Cover design by Dyer Wilk

ISBN: 1-948235-25-0
ISBN-13: 978-1-948235-25-9

I TAKE CARE OF MYSELF IN DREAMLAND

ROSS KLAVAN

To the paintings of Mary Jones

It was a great time for whores.

New York City, 1970, '71 maybe, '72, but, as Bartok was saying, "If nothing else, it's an ace of a time to be a hooker." In fact, he says, maybe it's a lousy time to be anything else. This is what Bartok is telling us he told the whore he's with, standing in the fleabag hotel on Lex across from Grand Central. Something like, "Must be a great time to be turning tricks."

Now, a certain kind of guy won't tell you this but—it doesn't bother me a damn bit that I'm stupid. Plenty of people would mind—I don't. They'd be embarrassed—I'm not. When I was a kid they use to say to me, "You don't have the brains you were born with." And you know what? They were right. Or maybe I did have those brains, maybe I was born this way. Whatever it is, "stupid" is the reason I'm still around.

The way I see it, I'm just smart enough to keep my mouth shut and at this age—I'm an old man now—you get to see that being smart enough to zip the yap is all the smarts you need. If you take the trip and make your way around, what you'll end up with anyway is lots of stories you can tell in a bar when nobody wants to listen. So, it's okay that I'm stupid. Back then, I kept myself dumb except to sometimes say something stupid to make them all laugh. That's all. That's why they let me drive. The smart guys? They didn't last so long. Smart guys or guys trying to be smart. They're always the ones who get it first.

"You're an interesting guy," they said to me. "You're the

only dumb Yid I've ever met." I told them I was proud to show them that it takes all kinds.

So. Bartok. I'm driving, he's in the back seat between Nicky and Ray, and he can't keep his mouth shut, he keeps on chattering like Mr. Happy and he has this strange way of saying things like that he was a guy who "travels the night city, the dark arsenal of bad dreams."

I said, "You're a real poet," and he agreed. I knew he wasn't gonna last too long.

In the back seat, Bartok shoves his voice down into a whisper so that he sounds like he's got some hot, evil secret to get off his chest—that's the way he tells us that he likes hookers except the thing is, they usually don't take to him. I'm thinking that if this is gonna be his confession, then it's his last one. "So you're a guy that even hookers won't go with," I say to him. "Man, you ain't gonna miss much in this world."

"I can't say," Bartok says and it's the only time he gets so agitated that Ray and Nicky hold him back on the seat. "I can tell." And then he goes on about the hotel room and how he's trying to be so cool and charming because, like he says, he's got this thing for hookers. He likes scotch and hookers he says, and that's about everything. That's his entire life. That, and Red River.

"What about it?" I say to him but he only wants to talk more about whores.

"Wow, look at you," this hooker says to him. "You look... uh, well...horrible."

The hooker says this after Bartok takes off his shirt, his pants, and she does a quick, professional appraisal of his body. She can tell a lot from your body: a guess if she's onto a lucrative night because you won't last too long, if you're a disease no-go, if you're clean or if you're gonna give her trouble so she'll have to call gangway-and- look-out-below. "That's some pretty bad...whatever it is, what is it?"

"Scars," Bartok says.

"All that? You look like a melted candle."

Bartok wishes she'd ditch the complaints. There he was, all of twenty-one and on his own thin dime from Disability, trolling around on 5th Avenue and maybe 28th Street shopping the street walkers. It's a parade of tank tops and shoes that have fifteen-inch platforms and hot pants that just about make it to the crotch. This young woman, half-naked on a summer night, steps out of a doorway and says to Bartok, "You looking for a date? I'm working my way through college." Bartok thinks that might even be true, given her not-yet-wrung-out yearbook features. Then she asks if he's a cop and he says "No and I know I can't lie," which is the law, anything else is entrapment, so he follows up with, "It must be a great time to be a hooker."

I mean, this is lower 5th Avenue sporting its cheesy hotels with the girls lolling in the doorways. "And never mind Times Square," Bartok says, "which is just one downbeat carnival in perpetual motion, an in-your-face neon cascade, a bright lighted blister in the night..."

"...all right," I say, "enough."

"...lines of porno theaters, strip clubs, massage parlors, chat rooms, bars sweeping to the horizon line and those signs that advertise Girls, Girls, Girls!"

Although, okay, he's right. Whores in the nighttime, whores in the daytime even when the polluted air is so bad that the inside of your ears go brown after a walk around the block. Like welcome to Hooker City. Steer clear if you don't like it.

I know what it's like now. But back then? Grand Central Station, Lexington Avenue side, the hookers paraded for the Dashing Dan commuters who were out for a quicky before heading home to the wife. The tenements across the street on Lex were transient hotels, mostly whore houses, and likewise at Penn Station, too, same thing, hookers in their cosmic whore uniforms ready for a run for the big hotel on Seventh. "Yeah, a great time for hooking." Stop at a red light with your window open in summer, they'd lean against your car door and ask, where you were headed and if you wanted some company. Or if it's boys you want to do, go up along Third Avenue in the 50s, that's what they called Queens Boulevard with the rent boys in rows, one boy after another, shirtless in the heat, lining the doorways near more massage places and peep shows and anything else you might want.

"Scars? Like that? Jesus," the hooker says. "That's some scars. Good you've got such a pretty face. You're actually sort of beautiful. But that? What about…"

She nods to his crotch, like it's a separate visitor in the eight-dollar threadbare what's-left-of-a-room.

"Everything works," Bartok says. "The plumbing. Sorry. I didn't mean to scare you."

"Not scared. Shocked. Do you mind if I…"

Bartok doesn't mind. He opens his shirt a little more and takes a step closer then does something with his chin that lets her know she can touch him. She does. Her finger makes a tentative slide along the mauled flesh of Bartok's right breast, as if she's picking up some kind of vibrations from the uneven raised and flattened skin that goes from a weird scarlet to a dead man's white.

I saw it when they put him in the back of the car and let me say, it was bad.

"It feels hard," she says. "Strange. It's like a cake decoration."

Bartok thinks he sees a slight shiver fall off her shoulders like she's throwing off a piece of clothing. Then she gives him a shrug, steps back and in one motion pulls the short, thin summer dress over her head and lays it down on the chair, then goes to lie across the bed. She's got a nice body to Bartok's eye, not black-and-blue from a pimp beating or sporting the Dachau look of the heroin-starved, not yet anyway, no oozing sores, no caked dirt, nothing that needs to be lied about and she lets Bartok look at her for a while before she sits up, grabs hold of his ass to pull him closer, and this time runs all of her fingers, one hand, down over his back and then his chest.

"It feels so...what is it? Your skin, it's all lumps and points and melted. Man, I don't know. What happened? You were in the war or something?"

It's not that Bartok's trying to keep any secrets—he's all too ready to shoot off his mouth—it's more that she's got the jitters and doesn't want to hear the answer.

"Feels...holy shit, you're like all..."

"Yeah, I know," Bartok says. "All dead ants and broken bones."

"No, I was gonna say..."

"You're making me feel great."

The bedsprings sing out when Bartok shifts his weight and comes down next to her. "Now, I'm depressed."

The metal springs sing again when she's on her feet. "Look. I don't want to be mean, but I don't think I can do this. I mean, you got one beautiful face, honey bun, that's for sure, but the rest, even if the equipment is all there...look, you want your money back? I'll give you half. Don't cause any trouble, okay? Here's half."

"Keep it," Bartok says. "I'm too sad to take it back." The clothes make him almost look normal again, whatever that means. And, like he told us, this is not the first time he's gotten The Treatment. Not by a long shot. The door's already open and the reeking air from the hallway—all rat poison and dead roaches—slides up his nostrils when her voice behind him says, "Don't tell them down in the lobby. Don't make problems. I know people who'll do you dirty."

"Yeah, yeah I'm sure you do," Bartok says. "Too bad. I kind of liked you."

"If it means anything, like I said, you got a beautiful face."

What a lousy, stinking, dim hotel hallway! That's what Bartok was telling us. It's like the green stained wallpaper that's a hundred years old is dribbling down into the dirt-dark wooden flooring and it's all right there begging him to join in the decay. Then, before he closes the door, one more excuse for a thought pops in. Bartok turns around. "You know, you'd think that with somebody in your line of work you could at least sell me a little bit of kindness or something. I mean, it's not asking much."

The hooker makes a funny motion with her head, this-way-that-way, then shrugs. "Sorry," she says. "I just can't."

"Yeah, okay," he says. "Okay for you."

Like I said, this isn't the first time for Bartok to get this special treatment but that doesn't make it any easier, it's just that this is the last night of his life and he's silently gnawing on that one insulting fact as he wanders back outside onto Twenty Something Street and into the sweetly perfect hooker evening. Okay, okay, calm down (he's telling himself). It's not that bad. It's happened before. Okay, it's bad, yes, but not so bad, it's just that this is the wrong night for it. Awful in a sort of final way. I mean, damn it, Bartok tells himself, if you can't, just for a moment, buy love, then what the hell can you buy?

Okay, so far, the genius plan is just not working. The genius plan is this, Bartok says—go out, find a hooker and get laid, find a bar and shoot back a few pops, maybe find a candy man and get a little high, then push real hard for Red River. Just one more time. Red River and then end it all because he's genuinely had it up to here and wants out.

The search for Red River. Here's what that means. Let's back up two years or so and go into what we laughingly call The World which seems, as it so often does, like it's coming apart or exploding with all the usual horrors running free and easy and dancing happily in a circle with Bartok right there in the path of Bad Luck.

He's nineteen. One minute he's got a gorgeous full-face beard with hair down to his shoulders and his jeans tied with a blue, embroidered cloth guitar strap instead of a belt and the girl that he's hitchhiking with has dark hair down to her shoulders, too, held back with a kind of Indian headband, a dress that gets some men at a gas station to say that her "legs go all the way up" and she's zipping alongside him with this incredible energy, like she's been out to touch some unspeakable knowledge and now she smiles and laughs and says smart things (to Bartok, anyway) and he's convinced himself not that he's lucky, but that this is the way the world is supposed to work.

She calls herself Laverne Love which is probably not her real name but it works just fine for Bartok and he tells her that everything with her, absolutely everything, is always like it's the first time, every moment seems new. He's not sure when he says this to her—maybe at the demonstration in San Francisco when they march against the war, maybe when they hitchhike to Denver, maybe when they spend a couple of days sleeping out with the elements out along the Oregon coast, where Bartok listens to the surf and almost comes to believe in God. Not some vague spiritual jelly, either, he says—he hears the surf, sees the rough, ragged high cliffs of the shoreline, sees that "the whole wide world is made of colors" and he says to Laverne Love, "Why is that so fucking beautiful? That can't just be an accident."

That's to start. It feels like in the next minute, Bartok is having his head shaved in the reception station with the sergeant screaming and he's getting the green uniform thrown at him across the long scuffed-up counter and he's running along with a group of equally terrified kids and he's thinking that, not when he got the letter from the draft board, not when he went down for his physical but there was one moment in the airport on the way to report to base when he priced a ticket to Canada and then paused, looking oh-so thoughtful and considered. Yes? No? And decided he didn't have the guts to make a run for it.

I feel sorry for the kid.

Laverne Love heads for Hawaii where she falls in love with a guy who's been arrested for selling LSD and when he goes to trial she decides to marry the guy's lawyer because not only is he not behind bars but he's also dedicated to The Cause, The Movement, and now she's writing to Bartok that she's tired of the "wild life" and wants to have kids. "If you ever make it home," she writes, "come see me before I become a fat suburban lady."

That's the kick in the privates—in this case, literally because of his rank—that takes Bartok to his knees. She had Dear Johned him. I'm guessing that the lawyer just got a whiff of this Laverne Love and thinks that maybe he'll just happen to lose this case. Bartok has now been in the Army for four weeks. The "Dear John" letter has him deciding that nothing else bad could happen to him, at least not until he gets to the war. He's been love-dumped and he's got a king-sized misery, he says, that winds around him like black ribbon and he's mistaking that misery for something like a supernatural power that cares about checks-and-balances and fairness and somehow will let him personally decide when the cosmos is cleared to attack again. Until he gives the okay—Bartok has spoken!—he's safe from harm or insult. He thinks.

Then, here comes this one particular army afternoon, when Bartok is riding in a truck—a deuce-and-a-half, so called—one of twelve guys sitting six on each side of the truck, butts badly braced to these hard wooden truck slats, their steel pots jangling against their skulls and their rifles up between their crotch. The world sort of rings by, his eyeballs bounce and his brain recoils from every rock, every hole in the gravely ugly red dirt road. Bartok's ass jostles so that his newly formed hemorrhoids ripen with every bump the deuce throws at them. What about the air? He tells us that in the early morning when the company falls out at 4:30 a.m. it's a terrifyingly heartfelt sweet mix of fresh pine and ammonia and his flesh prickles with the morning breeze. Then, later, it smells like a mix of pine and gasoline and gun oil and gunpowder and canvas and the breeze has burned away and it's so hot it stops you in your tracks and the world seems pitted, he says, all dust and flies. Bartok wants to go home. So does everyone else in the deuce. They're headed out to someplace where they'll run around, throw themselves on the ground and then fire their rifles at targets shaped like human beings and Bartok has the thought that the only time he's ever been taught to use a firearm, he's been taught to shoot at other people and kill them. He tells himself this is going too far, he's got to stop complaining and toughen up. Everyone around him feels something of the same. Everyone around him is becoming the same. The army is sending them this message and they read it loud-and-clear, sir, five-by-five: everyone is the same, everyone is easily replaced, and no one will be missed by anyone important. Everyone is there to disappear forever if that's what's ordered from above and the preparation for that order is to accept that you've disappeared already, right here and now, while the body is still capable of knowing and able to march in step. Bartok gets this thought with another jolt of the deuce. He looks at his comrades, numb to all of them. The stupid bastards, no fellow feeling for a single swinging dick, not a goddamned one. He brings to mind an image of the lost Miss Laverne Love, the last time they were in bed together when he saw her against the fireplace in that white peasant's shirt, when she crossed her arms across her breasts and in one movement, stripped. Oh, one other thing: that's when the truck explodes.

Let's dance back in time a little bit here, just by way of explanation. There's the motor pool where the military trucks are housed and cared for. You can see hoards of them, deuce lined up with deuce, rows of jeeps, small communications trucks, repair vehicles, aid trucks, the works. It's like a little boy's toy box come to life, all green with big white stars and US Army stenciled across the green. Just so much *stuff*. And in the motor pool there are GIs whose only job it is to care for and nurse these vehicles and usually they do just that. What else are they going to do? Not much. Maybe fuck-off as much as possible, which is what I used to do, maybe hide and smoke 'em if you got 'em, steal 'em if you don't. I mean, I know what Bartok's saying because, who wants to work? So somebody doesn't do something and you can't really blame him but there's some engine part that maybe should have been replaced or cleaned or tightened or loosened and nobody knows for sure because the officers heading the investigation and the hearing that come afterwards are more concerned with its being over and done and with moving on. But now: Bartok and his buddies. They bounce along under their helmets and it's hold-on-tight, squeezing their rifles between their knees in the back of the deuce. If they're thinking it's about girls back home or it's misery thoughts or it's a body scan of pain. So, it's like from another world when there's this strange sounding *clank*, then another, then a grinding sound that's the music of shredding metal, "a machine's outcry for mercy, a craw of the brakes," Bartok says. Everything changes. The deuce jerks to the left like one side of the earth suddenly dropped away. At the same time, all of the air becomes a noisy plume of thick, velvet smoke so that when you inhale you don't get a thing, your lungs fill up but there's no sense of breathing, "you're living on the blank feed of nothing." Bartok sees flying men. Bartok is suspended in the air. And then there's the swift geyser of flame that only lasts for the quickest, sharpest instant, a giant fire suddenly lit. What else? Bolts. Screws. A butterfly of sharp metal and a wisp of canvas all zap through the air. And there's screaming. Bartok experiences this in a single moment before total shutdown. In one second he's bouncing around on his hemorrhoids thinking of a girl, then in a rapid one-two-three there's smoke, there's a flash of orange and pink, there's that odd, out of joint metal music and he's flying and that's it. Darkness and pain, then darkness and no pain.

Well, not totally, Bartok says. There's something else: Red River.

According to what Bartok tells us, he doesn't yet know he's reached Red River, and he gives the experience this name only later when he's stiff and sweating beneath the rough sheets in the Army hospital and he thinks he might not make it.

Red River is an experience like this: Bartok is hoisted off the ground so that it's like he's falling upwards, twisting in the air, swinging his feet and finding no place to rest and reaching out but grabbing only his palms and then suddenly he's floating, and it's like he's resting comfortably in water and the ground is no longer his reference point and it doesn't matter whether there's ground or not or whether there ever was ground.

A searing, brutal hurt takes over. Bartok's on fire. Every hair, every pore. He can't stand it. He doesn't even know if he's screaming, he hears a child strangling on the line, "Make it go away," but he's not sure what else gets said because the scream is more powerful than he is and it turns into something more than a scream, some kind of "retching primal noise"—those are his words. Bartok feels this weird, nauseating, retching gut sound force its way out of his belly into his throat and he can hear himself making this sound far, far away but then all he knows is that the pain takes over. It's inside his skin, every inch, it takes over his nerves, it becomes his every thought and feeling and the pain announces itself as more important and more permanent than Bartok. He can see only red, a world of red. He resists. He fights. The pain, which Bartok believes can't get worse, now gets worse. It expands beyond what he knows to be himself, Bartok, until it kills off Bartok or whoever it is that Bartok calls Bartok and suddenly...

...nothing.

There's no resistance. Just like that. No fighting. It's not like Bartok is in pain, trying to gut it out, "it's the strangest thing," he was telling us. It's that there's only pain and Bartok is the pain. He becomes pain. He's pain itself. Then everything is perfect. He breathes. He feels the secret. He knows. It's the most remarkable moment of his life.

All of this happens in a matter of seconds.

Another experience of floating but this time, he comes to with the medics carrying him to the back of the aid truck. He hears himself say, "Am I alive?"

"Yeah," the medic answers. The medic's got a purple face and his lips are on his forehead as Bartok stares up from the stretcher. "You're alive and you've still got your balls."

"Do I still have my balls?" Bartok says.

"I just said…"

Bartok passes out again.

The military hospital. He's a mummy, he's a scorched chicken, he's a screaming weave of heated flesh. Bartok doesn't remember much of it, he tells us, only moments like when he's wrapped up in bandages and when they peel the bandages off and when they do some sort of medical procedure that involves rolling small balls of mercury into his burn wounds which is like somebody jamming a chisel into the nerves of his spine. He screams. There are skin grafts. Bartok thinks of them as skin "graphs," like his whole body except for his face is like that graph paper they used back in high school, but each square is a shrieking, pulsing red insult. The doctors tell Bartok that he's going to have a new body now. His skin, the texture and tone, the hair that swept across his forearms and chest, that's all gone forever. In its place has come an ugly, uneven spattering of raised welts and white mounds, the whole thing tinged a sick pink. Like he's been badly poured at birth. Disgusting. He'll be that way for the rest of his life. He cries. He's not dead, true; but the way he sees it, he's been shoved "outside of human consideration, love or concern." Ray, sitting there next to him in the back of the car, rolled his eyes when he heard that. But I know what he meant, I think.

He's as alone as a guy who goes deaf and dumb then loses his feet and hands.

"But my sweet Lord!" Bartok shouts from the back of my car. "There I am scarred and broken and dead, really, that's more what it was, and all I know is this one, slim, strange moment of utterly unimaginable, indescribable…"

"Huh?" I said to him.

Bartok keeps going over that one moment, the most remarkable of his life. He tries to explain the whole experience to one of the nurses, a small, nervous, reedy young woman with quick movements that make Bartok think of Peter Pan. When he's done with his story, she seems—at least for a moment—to gather Bartok into what he calls "her zone of human connection." This, by the way, is the first time she lays eyes on him, it's pity at first sight. And it's only for a moment, because when the instant is over she tells Bartok she's going to see if she can get the hospital psychiatric officer up there in the ward and then she's gone.

The psychiatric officer is a captain named Lemeux. Jesus! Bartok thinks, what an idiotic name and the doctor's also "an old coot, stooped and careworn," with a bald scalp sporting currents of blue veins through what's left of his white hair. Army issue eyeglasses thick as ice cubes so that his big-browns look even larger. Bartok—and this guy knew a lot of words—he tries to tell this doctor what's what, quietly says that he's really not Bartok. He's not Bartok in every way. Not anymore.

"How could I be?" Bartok tells him. "Look at me." But soon all that comes out of his dry mouth is a set of stammers and broken sentences and un-Bartok phrases. He tries to describe what happened to him when he was blown up but he can't. The experience. That moment where everything—and I mean everything—got shaken off its pot.

"It's not unusual for men in your situation to have hallucinations," Capt. Lemeux says.

"With all due respect, sir," Bartok says, "it wasn't like

that. It was, I don't know, some kind of..."

Forget it, don't even try. Even though he says he's convinced that it's the most important thing in the world that he explain what he went through, he can't. Bartok begins to hyperventilate and then he begins to let out a fizzling, pathetic moan.

"Let me be anyone else but me," he says.

Capt. Lemeux gives him back a twitchy shadow of eye movement that makes believe it's understanding, and then he nods three times, either with meaning or with neck cramp, Bartok's not certain. "There's another way to see this," the captain says. "You've still got your gonads. And you've also got your face. Not a bad combination. Plenty of these boys have ended up with less. And I'd say something more—you're a good-looking young man, almost, I guess I'd say, almost beautiful. In a manly way, of course." The captain shrugs. "Maybe when you're able to walk again you can get some work."

"Sir," Bartok says, "look at me. Who'll hire me?"

"Like I said, you're a good looking guy." The Captain shrugs. "Maybe you can model hats. Anyway, you'll be on disability."

The doctor lights up an unfiltered Chesterfield and Bartok passes out. The fluorescents in the burn ward are softer when he awakens, but then he passes out once more and when he comes to again, when his crusted eyes pop open, the ward seems busy with the work and energy of early morning, and soon he's not certain whether the conversation with the psychiatric officer or the nurse actually took place.

For some reason, this makes Bartok uneasy. He'd agree with me—I mean, why should "reality" or what's laughingly called "reality" be the main standard to live by in all cases. All Bartok wants, as he's lying there burned and bandaged in his hospital bed, is to recapture that incredible experience again, that one, single moment that's impossible to name. It's an ache worse than the worst ache he's felt so far in his short life—the hurt of a lost woman, the woman he still loves and will never see again. Bartok and pain; he wants to merge with it, but not ordinary pain. He wants to merge with pain so that there's nothing else, no Bartok, no time, no life, no death, just this incredible union with pain so that there's not even pain, anymore.

Bartok feels exiled. He can't get back to the experience and he can't even talk about it and so get a glimpse, a smattering of how it felt. And when he's not thinking about some return to something he can't name, Bartok's thinking about all the things he should have done, everything from that region of The Great Bygone that he failed to do. Because that failing led him here—to this hospital bed and the torment of flesh. To keep him quiet, they shoot him full of morphine. A haze moves through his consciousness that's the same as if he'd climbed a mountain and lost himself in the thin air and clouds. Things happen around him. The guy in the next bed? He's screaming. Bartok can't raise his palms to his ears so it's like ice picks going into his brain. Bartok wishes that the guy would shut the fuck up and after that he wishes that the guy in the next bed would just die. With that wish, a curtain of standing, moving shadows is pulled across the guy in the next bed and when the lights come back on, when the breakfast trays come around, and when he can smell the sting of ammonia in the air, Bartok sees there is no more guy in the next bed and the mattress has been stripped. Dead. You wished him dead, he's gone.

That sends Bartok back to all the things he should have done. He should have run off with Laverne Love, he should have had the balls to hop a plane to Canada, he should have dodged and gone into hiding in the woods and lived like some wild tribesman. Too late now, you dumb son of a bitch, so this is your life from now on because you couldn't, because you wouldn't, because you didn't...

It's too much. Bartok tells us that he's "stretched between the pleasures of sleep and self-torture," but finally he'll be damned if he's just gonna lie there in his brand new, burned body and let the wild dogs of his mind gleefully feed on his flesh and thought and feeling, no siree. Some other music besides his shrieking is necessary.

So, finally! That's how Bartok found a name for what he wanted. That's how, in the hospital, Bartok had the realization of Red River. That's what he begins to call this experience, the one that has no name. This effort to re-enter a Great Pain so completely that there exists nothing else. In the dark, in his hospital bed, he listens to the strange sounds of rodents rustling in the walls or beneath the beds and the irritating moans of the wounded and every now and then a dreaming kid who calls out to "Mother," or somebody quietly cries. Bartok thinks he's stumbled on his burned legs directly into a new, deeper form of knowledge. Before Bartok, there was the effort to become one with God, one with the Way of the universe. But now? Bartok wants to become one with Pain again. He wants to go back to Red River. And this is why he regards the nameless experience with that particular name...

It happened like this, in a way that I might not personally recommend although it seemed to work for Bartok.

One early evening, the nurses unroll and clatter and set up a movie screen in the ward. Then, they bring in a 16mm projector and show a film to all those too fucked up to stand on their own two feet or get out of bed. The film is *Red River*. Directed by Howard Hawks, written by Borden Chase. Starring John Wayne. And Montgomery Clift. It's a Western that centers on a cattle drive from Texas to Kansas. And to say it's just a cattle drive is to say that Niagara Falls is just a leaky drip.

This thing is a classic. One of the greats. But Bartok doesn't see the film the way you're supposed to see the film, no, he sees this film in his morphine-haze, from inside a pain-killer floating bubble as he feels himself gyrate over and over slowly in space, round and round then head over heels, as the dust rises and the cattle stampede and the cowboys fight or shoot one another. So, the entire film *Red River* isn't really a film for Bartok, it exists for him in a strange, discombobulated, dreamy jangle of memories that glow. For Bartok, there is no story. He couldn't tell you what the film is about. But *Red River* seeps into him with a certain impression. A grand movement. The terrible father who must be defeated. The rise of the son. The moment of cattle drive or fist fight or flogging or shootout where Bartok again gets the hint that only the pulse of the present exists and nothing else. "Images and sounds appear and recede," he tells us. The title creeps into his reptile back brain. It's close—he's sure he's at the door of the same moment that happened to him when he got blown up. It's just about all there. In glowing lights with music. It's the most incredible instant of his life since the truck exploded. Oh, yeah. So now, wrapped up and held quiet in his charred and scarred body, Bartok knows where his life must take him. He wants to go back to Red River.

It's several more months before (at last!) he gets out of the hospital. First, Bartok has to learn to walk again, and dress and move with the bored physical therapist constantly telling him in a flat, dead voice that it's okay to cry. And then one afternoon, Bartok is outfitted in badly chosen clothing—a shirt the color of jaundiced eyes, a rag of some thin, cheap material insulting to the touch, pants that are far too baggy, and now he's sitting in a bus station, his medical discharge still hot off the press and a little bit of disability pay burning in his pocket, waiting to board the bus to another town which has an airport which will fly him back home to New York. He can't come up with anything else to do or anywhere else to go.

He puts on an invisible sign that reads "Freak." He deserves to sit right there. Doesn't matter that he's out of the hospital, freedom is a weight dropped from above in slow motion, right on top of his buzz-cut head. There's release, sure, but that fades the moment he enjoys it. A sudden surrender to the realization that he can go anywhere or do anything or at least no longer be in the death march routine of the hospital—it's like he's getting much, too soon, it's like he hasn't earned the privilege because he's still alive. Bartok sits on the bus station bench and waits. A quick sliver of time passes when he sees everyone in the bus station as some kind of example of suffering humanity, sent to tell him to stop feeling sorry for himself. He thinks of the bus station as the crossroads of the poor.

He lets one bus go by and then another. One bus is cancelled and another bus is late.

The other travelers, old or young, male or female, all look like they've put on their Sunday best but the best is a hand-me-down from several generations. In the dim green light of the bus station, they all look like they had to get used to being cold or learn not to grumble at too-little of everything, from feeling to food. They look tortured. There are faces pushed into just slightly the wrong angle, skin made of old newspaper, teeth missing. Eyes that hold the gaze of Nowhere In Particular or stay occupied with the tobacco and gum stains on the dirty concrete floor. A light breeze offends him with vague and badly mingled smells: sweat, coffee, cheap beer, mothballs, dust and piss. Bartok's glance moves across his fellow travelers like a slow motion slap and he thinks about the experience of Red River and he wants to get out, except that he's not certain what that means.

Look at them, he actually says to himself. Ditch the self-pity. But right after that? Bartok gives them all a big "fuck you" because in a hop-skip-and-jump, Bartok becomes certain that people are staring at him as they walk by. He's positive they can read the "Freak" sign. These throw-away Americans—if they do a quick look-see, they'd spot a beautiful young kid waiting for a ride, but if their eye lingers and gets a gander of his neck, chest or his arms through the short sleeves? Well, then, Jesus! They flinch. Disgusting! They turn away. He hates them all. He doesn't have to put up with it. Bartok has been to Red River. Not them.

There's no reason for Bartok to go home. "I can take it," is what he thinks. There's no reason for him to go anywhere or do anything.

Right around the time he's letting these thoughts tighten his eyeballs and do a kind of Buddy Rich drum solo in his temples, Bartok notices the young woman who's been sort of circling the bus station waiting room, obviously trying to look like she's busy while, at the same time, trying to let anyone interested know that she's ready to be approached. She's got on a puffy little hat. She's way too thin, almost sickly but not quite, her bones breakable and her cotton sundress seems to have fallen onto her after being carried by an indifferent wind. When she notices Bartok noticing her, she slowly and nonchalantly walks over to him.

"Back from the Army?" she says. "I can tell—you got that real short and awful haircut."

"I'm going home."

"Back for good?"

"Good or bad. Can't tell yet."

Her accent is so thick Bartok begins to mimic her. He can't help himself. She gives him a nicotine smile. "Well, while you're deciding..." and here she reaches out and her right hand nearly pirouettes in a practiced coy expression and she lays an index finger on the inside of Bartok's knee. "That bus ain't gonna be by before a few hours and even so, there's another one after that. And you ain't even got a newspaper to read."

"I don't like reading the newspaper," Bartok says. "The people they write about, I don't know them and it means nothing to me. Or I don't know them and even so they're going to cause me some trouble."

"So. What would you rather do?" with that index finger moving in soft, tight little circles.

Bartok would like to say, "I want to go back to Red River," but he knows he can't explain Red River to this woman (or, as he mimics her, "to this gal" he says to himself) and she's just trying to make a living in this one-horse, trashcan town, anyway. So he unbuttons the top three buttons of his charity junkyard shirt and gives her a little peek at what a burned man looks like, what fire can do, a treat of his melted flesh.

"Just so's you know beforehand," Bartok says. "I ran into some real bad luck in the Army and now this is me. This is how I look. And it gets worse. You still up to party?"

She answers, "Sure," a little too quickly and Bartok thinks he catches just a whimper of disgust as the vision of his molten skin pops her in the eye. "There's a hotel. I got a room right around the corner. Come on with me. We'll have us a good time and you'll still be able to catch the next bus home."

Out in the long, dark tunnel of the evening, there's only one building that's walking distance from the bus station. It sits there solid and mournful as an old tombstone. Four crushed stories of a brick squat, a transient hotel, like it won't let go of its own dark cement, plastered together by night sweats and lice. Not even the honor of a neon sign to say "hotel" although there's a buzzing beer ad in one window that's in the last sputtering dances of burn-out. The hint of something like a groan comes out of one window then seems to disappear on the night wind and the air swirling around the building sends a plastic cup bouncing along the street, the kind of cup for a beer, Bartok thinks, or to piss in for a physical. The street gleams—rain, dirty water, the moon glow finding its own sad place. Bartok hears his shoes clap on the pavement, the same sound is coming from the young woman beside him. It seems strange that they're not talking so he asks her name and she says, "That's not necessary." Close to the hotel now and the moon seems to cut in and disappear through a slit in the black sky and it's then with a genuine tensing in his gut, Bartok senses that things are going wrong.

This rides up his spine like a shock from the third rail. It's the sense that some dark spring has come loose in the night, it's given off by some signal in the woman's dull-voiced chat and she starts to remind Bartok of a rabbit standing up on alert. Twitching. Bartok can smell his own medication and her armpits, her laundry, underneath the sheen of dollar store perfume.

"We'll go in through the back," she says. "It's better for everyone that way."

They avoid the front entrance and head around the darkened side of the building. There, jagged lines and Xs are cut in the night near a brooding line of garbage cans and the armored tank shape of a huge dumpster sits in the shadows waiting. Bartok smells orange rinds and spilled whiskey and he shivers, he gets his feelers up—"Some shock-and-spark warning was being hurled through my system," he tells us from the back seat, "and I was feeling every chord of it."

"I know exactly what you're talking about," I say to him, seeing a shadow cut across his face in the rearview. I keep my eyes on the road. He only keeps on talking.

Here's a lesson in how things change. The metal lid of a garbage can becomes something else by magical transformation simply by the act of swinging it at another man's head. It changes once more when it's brought down immediately, repeatedly, swiftly, time and time again, downward like a wild cheer, "like a way to celebrate a man into the earth."

Bartok can't see very much. The man who spins out from behind the dumpster and rushes toward Bartok is a man constructed torso-hip-and-legs out of half-visible black shapes but also out of a series of bad guesses and wrong calculations. One of those misjudgments is that Bartok isn't going to pick up the first thing he can get his hands on and try to kill the man charging at him. Bartok is still weak from the hospital. He doesn't fully trust his body. But his instincts? The circle of darkness tightening around him is all aglow with warnings and long before the attack, Bartok is figuring that something on the foul side of the evening might be heading his way, something where two visions of pain might be fixed on measuring themselves.

The woman is screaming. "Luke! You dumb bastard! Not yet!"

Luke is not Luke but an inky shape that Bartok sees appear out of nothing, suddenly, like a ghost iceberg that a murderous sea offers up in the dark. And even with that, Bartok tells us, he now gets just the edge of a taste of something else: Red River. "It's that same crazy light that was gifted to me when I got blown up and burned, back in the Army," he says, meaning back in those final moments when he was still Bartok. Red River? It's just a taste, a lick. Just the sudden shadow that lifts Bartok into that movement in the alley. He doesn't have to think about anything, doesn't need to consider how to spin away, or think to grab the garbage can top and start swinging. The first swing of the metal connects—satisfying and solid— and then the next movements rip back and forth, up and down, the whole time frame moves without any dead space or stagnation. Red River is coming. And Luke is still not Luke to Bartok. He's a temporary target made of spitting, clawing meat, then another shape that pleads, on his knees with his head bowed, spewing blood and some broken and stained white flakes of teeth until he pitches sideways, the crown of his head drumming dully off another garbage can which rattles in consternation. The angle of Luke's neck seems twisted and weird until he lands on his back on the wet concrete. Then everything straightens out.

"You killed him, you fuck!" the woman is shouting.

She's coming from far away. Something else is more important. Bartok is waiting for that Red River shift but what happens is that the woman's voice gets closer and soon it's screeching from right beside him.

"You killed him dead, you son-of-a-bitch!"

26

"Okay. Maybe I did," Bartok says. "Maybe I should go get a policeman. You want I should go get the law to stop by?"

All the sensations of Red River have gone up the chute. Bartok can feel his lungs doing double-time and there's a pain in the center of his chest that pulses between a lance and a pinprick. But the mist that he was expecting to suddenly descend and protect him? Well, that's headed out to somewhere he doesn't know. Bartok is seeing in a blur, he can make out a man lying flat and stretched on the concrete—who has only now turned into Luke—and the man is still sucking in air, his eyeballs spun to white and his chest roiling up and down like an ocean storm. Bartok takes in the misshapen face and the black hole of the mouth with its broken brown canines. For an instant, he gets that sensation of hurt-animal connection. Then he pushes it away and now Bartok's prediction of this bastard's future is a few solid weeks in some lousy pauper's hospital, all stupidly mummied-up in bandages with his jaw wired shut and locked onto his thin, brown-stained mattress bed, which the son-of-a-bitch richly deserves.

"And you were right the first time," Bartok says "Whoever he is, he's one dumb bastard, he oughta know better," though know better than what or whom Bartok isn't sure.

The woman takes a step that's like she's dipping her toe in blood. Then she devotedly kneels beside Luke, afraid to touch him but willing to brave the bile that's burning her throat. She gets just close enough to lean in and let her brain register the man's bubbling blood and she sees his mouth as an open wound. Then she stands up straight.

"Okay, so he's still alive, the dumb fuck. Jesus, I can choose 'em!" She breathes in hard. "Look. We can still go upstairs," she says. "I wasn't lying about that room. How's ten dollars?"

It was so goddamn near, Red River. That's what Bartok is thinking. He wonders whether this idiot on the pavement felt how close it was when he got clocked. He wonders whether, if he pushed the edge of the garbage can lid into this idiot's windpipe, might both of them get Red River to take them away. Bartok loosens, lets his fingers soften on the garbage can lid, which now drops and gives its metallic assent to the concrete. He kicks it off to the side.

"Shit," Bartok says. Some kind of sensation he can't quite get to or describe leaves him then, like a spirit flying away, and he feels his muscles soften a little bit and relax. He follows the raised lines of scar tissue along his forearms until they seem like he's made out of only these routes of raised flesh. Then he walks away.

Bartok can hear the woman shouting at his back, "Come on, now! Five, how about?!" as the bus station looms closer in his night vision. He tells himself to get her voice out of his head, because now he's talking to himself like a ten-dollar small-town whore. He hears the garbage can lid clatter to the pavement again and there's a flash of replay in his brain where he sees that poor idiot's forehead open up right across the eyebrow as the can lid sweeps across his head. And he feels Red River teasing him as it passes on by.

Then Bartok hears nothing but the moon pulling at the wind and the lights of the bus station tell him to navigate forward like nothing's ever happened. Like he's never left his seat. He floats. He's carried. And so now, back inside, Bartok carefully lets his weight ease down again on the icy wooden bench, and he locks in again on the denizens of bus-land, who haven't given up their afterlife walk, back and forth, back and forth, their shadows widening and shortening on the scuffed up floor; and to Bartok it's like a break in time, like when he was burned and the doctors put him under then woke him up. The first thought that occurred to him was, "This must be what it's like to come back from the dead."

But he's onto something and he's excited.

He gets on a bus. Window seat. Next to him, there's no one. What he'd like to do is sit by himself and keep his eyes on the highway, sort of melt into the rhythm of the ride, get serious with thoughts on where his life has taken him up to now and plot a course back to Red River. But onto the bus, one by one, come the downtrodden, the people who are just slightly superior to Bartok The Freak. Two old ladies in blue hair and flower dresses whose skin is wrinkled in exquisite detail. A pudgy young mother with her bucktoothed son who wears a scruffy, short-sleeved, checkered shirt a size too large. Each of the passengers walks by Bartok and when they get an eyeful of how his flesh runs and peels over on itself, they turn away and try to find a seat somewhere else.

Bartok begins to imagine that he's going to see Luke get on the bus. He sees him running across the street with his stupid face all crushed, climbing up into the aisle, shouting, "That's him! That's the son-of-a-bitch who did this to me!" Then Luke would stop his shouting and catch a shot of how Bartok looks, and even Luke would make that face, that grimace trying to mesh together pity and disgust. And he'd walk away.

But Luke never shows. And Bartok starts to think about the idea that he's the only one on the bus who knows that there's a man, Luke, who's lying half-dead somewhere out there on the pavement with his ugly puss cracked open and that Bartok is the one who laid him out. Bartok, alone knows this and the more he thinks about it, the more he enjoys it.

The pleasure doesn't last long. Soon, Bartok is sitting next to an old man who sports silver hairs poking out from his nose, and when he looks closer Bartok sees the geezer has got a spattering of missed spots from a sloppy shave. A dull white shirt with light, brown stains like a surrender flag. The guy sits a little forward with his back locked in a frozen, upright angle that barely rests against the seat like he's been jammed in place. Also, this old man might not see too well: his eyes seem under water. Everything around this old fella is touched with an atmosphere of toughness and dull disappointment. He's had a hard time.

Maybe Bartok can talk to him. He could talk about what he's searching for. He could say something like, "You ever haul off and just cold-cock a guy? I mean, you're an older fella. You ever have the pleasure of just letting loose on somebody who really had it coming and leaving him on his back to bleed?" He could explain that handing out a beating is not the ultimate but just a taste. After the gray morning floats by for a while and there's been a lot of silence, Bartok says to him, "You ever seen Red River?"

It's like no matter what Bartok says, the words are afraid to crawl in too close and snuggle up to this old man. Bartok feels like he's known the guy like a neighbor in the backyard but even so, the fact that now the old man just sits there without answering seems like an elbow shot to Bartok's chest. Bartok listens to the whir of the tires. The old guy still doesn't answer and Bartok begins to hate him. Maybe you'd like a metal trashcan lid across that old, bald skull, how'd that be? He shakes off the thought and has a few seconds of feeling like he's done something wrong, he'd better pull in the reins, he watches the old man sitting there, thinking, and then the old man finally says, "Cowboy picture." He's chewing on a small, missed hair that grows at the border of his lower lip. "Western movie. Long time ago."

"No, something else," Bartok says.

Still chewing on that single hair, the old man let's this idea run around for a while and then he says, "No. No, I don't think so. John Wayne wasn't it? Yep. Cowboy picture."

"Damn it, I don't mean a movie," Bartok says. "Not just pictures. And not something only in my head."

He can't really describe it beyond saying "Red River" and there are pictures going through his mind—the sky, hurricanes of dust, men shouting.

A couple of nods from the old man whose head suddenly jerks straight. "Holy Jesus! How'd you come by those scars? If you don't mind my asking."

"Too fucking late for me to mind, you just asked," Bartok turns away, and when he turns back, he's got his shirt lifted up in front. "Go ahead, Pop, they're not going away anywhere just 'cause you're staring."

"Christ-on-the-Cross," the old man says quietly, shaking his head. "Lord have mercy."

That's it for any conversation. And anyway, Bartok wants time to think. He wants to think about Red River.

Because back there in the alley, by God, he almost had it. Oh, yeah, he's onto it again, he's sure. He was that close. There was some smooth action back there, that's for certain, but it takes more than a few smooth moves to get to Red River—you have to do something like jackknife dive off the rocks into the crashing surf a million miles below. There was a guy in Second Platoon—he'd already been in the Army once, been in 'Nam, too, plenty of trigger time, got out, couldn't get a job back in the shitty economy, re-upped and asked for Airborne, combat, the whole shebang. You can bet he'd found Red River. Never said as much, but you can bet. "That's why he really went back in," Bartok tells us. "Sure, he couldn't find work, but still." So the way Bartok looks at it is this: he got to Red River once. He's going to get there again. Bartok thinks it must partner up with pain in a major way. Of course, his own pain first. But not just what the common folks think of pain. He'd felt pain and felt it go from one degree to three-sixty until it became every breath, every thought, until there was nothing else because there was only pain and so there was nothing to resist it and so there was...what? Some kind of Original Pain. Not Original Sin and not some kind of Tunnel of Light. Nothing like that. Yeah, okay, but what about back there when that dumb bastard took a few good shots across the skull? Then it was only somebody else's pain. That's right. Bartok eyeballs his own reflection in the bus window. I watch him in the rearview, he's living it all over again. Through the bus window, Bartok sees the road go by through his head and face and it's like he's got the buzz of the flat highway moving through his brain. Bartok nods to himself in the window. He can clearly see the way the rosebush of scars peeks out from the top of his shirt.

Oh, shit. And what if this is all he ever does for the rest of his life? This "going to get back to Red River." Bartok scoots around so that, at an odd angle, he's facing the old man in the seat next to him. "I'm totally out of my mind," Bartok says. "You're the only fella I've ever said that to."

"That movie," the old man answers. "The one you mentioned. *Red River.* I'm trying to think of it. I think it was a good one. Don't remember much, though. Like I said, long time ago."

"No movie. I've been there," Bartok says. "And I'm going back."

Out the bus window, Bartok watches the sky roll gray with clouds so that there's no more light and he thinks: now what's the difference between night and morning? I'm nuts. Because only those of us who're crazy can get even the barest, tiny, sliver of a glimpse of The Great Revolving Swirl and their own part in it. That's something of what you know when you know Red River. That's why this old fart was sent to sit here next to me. To let me in on it. That's why I'm going to follow. My scars, he thinks, are something like a map.

That was before. That's how he got here. Maybe that's why he's in my back seat.

But now, see, we've returned to New York and Bartok's making his sorry way out of the whorehouse hotel. Too bad, because he liked that hooker. Bartok's sorry she was disgusted by him. He's saying to himself, "I wish I looked differently. I wish I looked like somebody else." Bartok feels like he's going to crawl out of his mottled skin. There are plenty of hookers on the sidewalk but this time, when they ask him if he wants a date, he keeps his mouth shut. All he can think about is how horrible he is to look upon, how his flesh is like a thick, uneven, discolored ointment that's been poured and has now hardened over his bones. He heads uptown.

High 40s, low 50s on 3rd Ave. The couple of blocks they called "Queens Boulevard" back then even though Queens Blvd. actually exists in the Borough of Queens. Sure, now it's mostly glass-and-steel high-rise and high-class but back then—maybe you remember—it's where the rent boys would stand in the doorways of the tenements, on sale, one by one. Bartok makes sure his eyes stay on the concrete as he walks by but every few steps he gives them a glance. Everybody seems disconnected. The rent boys seem to be leaning there in pieces. It's like they got blown up and the pieces fell back together but in the wrong way. A cigarette behind an ear which is attached to a forehead. A trail of ripe acne along the jaw line that's too short. Tight T-shirt and hair grease. An arm that's thin as a wire and ripe for needles stuck onto flecks of a beard that's barely grown in.

And it's Bartok who keeps thinking that he wants to look different, he wants to look like somebody else, like somebody who doesn't get insulted by whores. Only whores should be kind enough to put up with him. "Why do I have to think that? Why don't they have to think it?" He stops talking to himself. Hey, it's happened before. Well, okay. But it doesn't have to happen again.

Around the middle of 52nd St., stuck between the peep show, the rap parlor and the massage parlor—all different varieties of whorehouses—there's a half-ways decent hooker bar and Bartok goes inside to (as he thinks of it) drop some scotch on his anger. This could well be, Bartok says to himself, the last drink I ever have. Somewhere between the time he leaves the sidewalk and takes three steps down to the front door of the bar, Bartok decides to kill himself. It doesn't seem like a very important decision. He'd like it to have some kind of soundtrack and maybe a close-up or two, but the thought just sort of enters his head with a comforting slide, like small sip of whiskey. Tonight, he'll make one, final serious attempt to reach Red River and then? That's it. He's had enough.

Bartok's grateful to be inside. The whole place is tinted in pink light so that everyone looks deeply alive and even healthy but it's also swathed in a mist of thick cigarette smoke so that at the same time they all look like they're dead and in Hell.

A bad piano player sings off-key standards. There's a city feel of crossroads: mobsters and undercover cops, hookers and second-rate grifters, commuters and locals, everyone together and everyone alone, everyone lost in their own loneliness and everyone watchful. The piano player goes into a sort of dying dog rendition of the song "Kung Fu Fighting" and from down the bar a scrawny woman gets up and dances by herself, throwing combinations of drunken punches and sloppy kicks at the air. Soon, she slices and pirouettes her way over to Bartok and chops and kicks at him, close enough so that he can feel the air move against the tip of his nose.

"Oooh." She notices the frozen river of scars along the top of Bartok's chest and she sticks out an index finger and pokes at him. "Nice," she says. The piano player keeps up with "Kung Fu Fighting." A few more pokes and the woman goes back to her private version of Kung Fu fighting, spinning along the thin aisle between the bar and the wall, knocking her elbows into the wall twice, wincing, then laughing, before she sits down.

Bartok keeps looking down the bar to see her but she doesn't turn around, she's done with him if she was ever with him in the first place.

He orders his scotch. Another woman, who's a seat away, moves closer.

"Hiya, honey," this one says. "You drinking alone or you feel like conversation?"

"I can't really tell."

"Well, do you want to buy me a drink and chat or do you want I should mind my own business?"

"Even if we chat, you should definitely mind your own business," Bartok says.

"This is a pretty friendly place. Don't tell me I lucked into the only Grade A pain-in-the-ass to wander in."

"She's having what I'm having," Bartok says to the bartender. "And, hey. No pink champagne. Okay. Let's talk. Then I'm planning to set myself on fire and walk uptown a few blocks to see if anyone waters me down and puts me out. I'm on my way to kill myself."

The bartender sets a scotch in front of the woman. For the first time, Bartok takes a close look at her, just as she says, "Is that supposed to make you interesting? Thanks for the drink." And he sees that she's oddly well put together: dark hair cut short and quaffed for what must have been a major expense and make-up done to a T. He wonders how she got her lipstick on so neat.

"I'm not lying. I'm going to have a couple of drinks with you here and then I'm either going off the 59th Street Bridge or I'm throwing myself on the subway tracks."

"At 59th Street?"

"Maybe another stop. I don't know. That's part of why I can't take it anymore. Bullshit comments like that." Bartok drinks and swirls the ice around. "Listen, I'm sorry. I'm in a bad mood."

"Suicide will do that."

"No, that put me back in a good mood," Bartok says. "It's everything else. I got real trouble to pile onto my collection of real trouble and I'm down so far there's doesn't seem to be any point."

"Sweetheart, there wasn't any point before you had trouble."

"Look at me, look at this," he undoes a top button, bares some scars, with a certain flair. "So. What do you know, tell me that, lady."

"I'm not what you think," she says. "Sure, I look like a nice girl. But I got a kid at home, a baby. Maybe you can help me out with the rent."

"Before you start with that line, touch this," and Bartok undoes another button on his shirt, puts her fingers to the wavy scars at the top of his chest. "This is what you're going to get. I'm like that all over. Tell me now if it's too much for you."

In the mirror behind the bar, Bartok sees that the pink lighting makes his scars look even more incredible, riper, more virulent. He's sorry he opened his shirt because the woman, whose name (she says) is Marcy, now gives out a low whistle. "That's a bum deal, honey," she says. "'Specially since you've got such a sweet face. You remind me of Cary Grant. But shorter and all scarred up."

In the mirror, Bartok notices that Marcy has extremely exact and very thick black eyebrows that are mesmerizing. He wants to ask her about this but he's afraid that it'll be too much of a clue that he really is, without a doubt, completely crazy.

"I'm not like this on purpose," Bartok says. "I'm going back to Red River and I'm going to off myself."

"*Red River*? The cowboy picture? That's not playing anywhere. Hey, maybe on TV but then you've got all the commercials."

"Goddamn it, not the movie. Look at me, you can see why I'm on my way to end it. Right after this drink."

"I sure can," she says. "So, maybe you're no help with the rent, how about you just help me out a little with the groceries?"

Bartok reaches into his pants pocket, takes out the wad of everything he's got left and presses the folded bills into her hand. "For you. If you promise me you won't take me to see your kid and you won't say anything else." He rebuttons his shirt.

"Not here," she pushes the money back at him.

Right about then, the woman who'd been doing the Kung Fu dance gets up again and starts another, slower, more languid and sensual number, running her hands over any man at the bar while the piano player goes into his terrible rendition of Joni Mitchell's "Blue." Bartok thinks it's an insult to just about everything human and it's another reason to go off the side of a bridge or subway platform. He's not going to stand for it—or, rather, he is going to stand for it because he gets to his feet to go say something to this tone-deaf idiot who calls himself a musician, when suddenly it's his turn with the Kung Fu woman.

She runs her hands down his arms and back up again, then presses a finger onto his chin so that his head is angled down, then she sees the top of his chest, touches his scars and gives him a boozy, "Hey, don't we know each other?"

Bartok is about to answer when the Kung Fu woman pulls away from his chest like she's touched a welding torch and lets her hand drop down to the bar so that her rings and bracelets clatter on the metal. That startles her. She jerks away. It's an unfortunate move. The weight of the alcohol-imbued hand goes smack into a wine glass on the bar and beneath the piano player's leaden fingers and his horrible cover of the black-and-blue "Blue" there's added the crack-and-ringing of shattering glass and the Kung Fu woman holds up her hand, gazing at it as she says, "Ho-leee shit."

She's accidentally slashed her right wrist. The great favor, though, is that this doesn't bother her at all. Hey, maybe it's not so much of an accident. It's sort of like she's in the mood to make a kind of offering. Or maybe she's showing off. She simply holds out her wrist as it pumps lines of bright blood all over Bartok and she reaches out once more and sticks her finger on his scarred chest, which is now not only scarred but also soaked in what looks like dark ink from a fish.

The place goes wild. The bartender yells, "Shit!" everyone at the bar shouts or grunts or whispers a different version of "Whoa!" and jumps up and takes a few steps away from the bleeding Kung Fu woman so that "Blue" slows down and ends with "…a song of…" as the piano players gets an inkling of the action. Besides the drunken salad of voices-in-surprise there's only the sound of bar stools scraping along the floor. Only Bartok moves in.

He takes her finger off his bloody, wounded chest and grabs her wounded, blood-shooting wrist, puts pressure on the cut and holds her arm up in the air. She's goes limp. She's so weak in the knees that she begins to collapse like some kind of cheap toy and she's about to make her way in a faint to the floor. Bartok eases her down. He keeps his hand on the cut and the arm elevated and he says very, very calmly to the bartender, "Call an ambulance."

But right after that, it occurs to him that here's a chance to learn something. To the woman, he quietly says, "Red River? Have you reached it? You know what I mean, I know you do."

What's the point, she's half out of it. "Montgomery Clift," she says, "Shit. No. For me, I was doing Kung Fu fighting."

Bartok keeps pressing his thumb down so that her hanging flesh stays shut up but he recoils a little at her answer. He remembers the old man on the bus, the guy who was like a telegram from the universe, like the universe thought enough of Bartok to send him a message. This woman was sent to him, too, could be, anyway. Bartok begins to wonder whether this woman is talking in code. Maybe he's hooked into some sort of code from the Great Beyond or even the Great Here-and-Now. Bartok deems himself lucky—that's what he told us. These things just sort of come to him.

See, there's the possibility that this is how it works. That's what crosses Bartok's mind. He can be calm, efficient, he knows what to do when the proverbial chips are proverbially down, but with all that—even with the booze and the blood all over the place and the sheer absurd wackiness of it— there's no Red River. Not for him. But who knows what it is for her? Kung Fu fighting? For Bartok, here in the hooker bar, there's still Time and Space and whatever tags along with

Time and Space—I can't tell you and you'd have to ask some-body smarter than Bartok, that's the guy who can help you out. Here, Bartok knows what to do. But that's as far as it goes.

Pressure on the wound. Arm elevated. Soothing talk. The Kung Fu woman is on the third rung of a stepladder into the deep end, anyway, going down into the coma-pool. She lolls on the floor while two waiters start to mop up the blood de-signs all over the floor and sweep up all the blood-damp ciga-rette butts and the bartender takes a cloth to the bar.

"It's okay everybody," the bartender calls out. "Help's on the way," like he's in some television show re-run.

After the ambulance leaves and things go back to their normal level of lousy, Marcy says to Bartok, "You're a saint. Or maybe a doctor."

"They put us through a lot of first aid training in the Army," Bartok says. "Right before they blew me up."

"I figured it was something like that. Don't tell me you're a patriot or something. Don't tell me you got caught up in that shit. Guy in here a couple of weeks ago, left most of one arm over there."

"I got blown up before the war," Bartok says. "But there was something else. Red River…"

"That money you were going to give me…"

"Yeah, sure," and Bartok takes what's left of his cash and slaps it in her hand.

This time she puts the wad of cash into her purse. That's when the bartender says to Marcy, "I told you not here, god-damnit, you're gonna have the fucking cops down on me, like, in lickety-split. There's a fucking table of them right over there," and he makes a pretty obvious come-hither head ges-ture. To somebody. A guy comes up behind Bartok and Mar-cy from what seems like "downstairs" and Bartok gets a whiff of an unfortunately too-enthusiastic aftershave, as if some-body mixed together all the rotten berries in the world and squeezed. The pink light somehow makes it even worse. It's like this guy behind them is big and long reaching as a construction crane and when he takes Marcy by the elbow with some kind of pincer grip in his whale hand she winces, arches off the stool and goes up a little on her toes, before he jolts her in an off-kilter walk to the door.

Marcy is wincing and giggling and then grimacing and giggling and to Bartok she says, "No mun, no fun, hun. Good luck killing yourself, kill yourself one good one for me," and after that, she's outside on the street.

"And you," the bartender says to Bartok, as he sets a free drink down on the bar in front of him. "So. Hey. Many thanks for your help." Before Bartok can say anything, the bartender goes on with, "I mean, you look like you've been through some kind of shit, right?"

"I'm sorry she had to leave. Not too many people will talk to me. Women, I mean."

"You know that was a guy, right?"

"I know what?"

"Well, not quite. Like that Christine Jorgensen. You know. She used to be a guy and then she had that operation."

"Look at me," Bartok says, showing off his scars. "You think I think that's a problem?"

"Don't make me no never-mind, either," the bartender says. "Just I can't have people breaking the law in here and passing around shitloads of money or even looking like it. She came in when she was a he and now she comes in when she's a she and I like her better now, at least when she doesn't fuck up." The bartender smiles. "You a cop?"

"Do I look like a cop?"

"Do I look like a bartender?"

Bartok splays his hands in a little I-don't-know gesture and the bartender moves to answer the phone at the other end, near the piano player. That's when Bartok stands up and gets out of there quick, heel-toeing away on the sidewalk so fast that it pulls at his hamstrings.

* * *

So, let's just say, it's not exactly a night of shit-and-giggles for Bartok. He probably should have figured on a way to get big-hearted and spring for more green for the hookers—I know a couple who would have been happy to fuck him scars and all, but obviously for the right price. Too bad he didn't meet me before. But here's what set him off on this final, ultimate, showdown with Red River and death. At least, I think so. He tells us that writing "The End" to his particular story seemed like an idea that just sort of slipped into his mind but, actually, it sounded to me like there was plenty behind it. Plenty that, along with everything else, pushed him over the top.

A day before all this, Bartok is lying down skinny, scarred and naked on his unmade-for-six-months bed, thinking that he looks like a piece of broiled fish, thinking about Red River and thinking also that it might be time to take the sheets to the laundromat since he never has and the room is getting a mite ripe. Instead, he does that unbalanced newborn-deer-walk to the mirror in the kitchen, near the bathtub, in a room with a single bulb that hangs down showing off the walls which are painted the color of a toad, and here he examines his face and thinks what a waste of a good lookin' guy. The world is lousy. Then he slides on his clothes and walks out into the yellow light and permanent shadow of his crummy apartment building, past the walk-up stairs that look like they were chipped by machine gun fire and down the scruffy hall of the ground floor to the battery of little dented mailboxes in the foyer. That's where he finds that the Veterans Administration has some bad news for him.

Apparently, according to the VA, Bartok doesn't really need the disability pay he's been drawing because he's not really disabled. Obviously, the VA hasn't interviewed any hookers or any women at all, for that matter, who might have once considered Bartok a catch. His case has been reviewed and it's been determined that although he's been caused "cosmetic harm" he's fully capable of work. Don't agree? Make an appointment with a supervisor. Come in and have a chat.

"Of course I don't agree, you fucking batch of third-rate midgets," Bartok says out loud, just before he catches himself in a deep, grief quilted sob. "Oh, God!"

The VA supervisor is a heavyset black man with "Former NCO" written all over him. A great guy to have your back in a foxhole, but not so good to have your front sitting at a crappy metal desk in a VA cubicle. He's got his Combat Infantryman's Badge pinned to the pocket of his threadbare sports jacket, which Bartok notes should be invited to accompany his sheets to the laundromat. Hair cut down to the scalp. Also, he's missing the little finger on his right hand, which is run rough with raised scars. Bartok clumsily takes the man's hand in a shake, feeling the absence of the finger, a grip that gives off a heavy vibe of "no sympathy for you." The supervisor's name is Mr. Hughes.

"Well, like I say," Mr. Hughes begins tapping a paperclip on his desk after he looks through Bartok's file and after Bartok talks straight, then jokes, then pleads and finally lies for a half hour. "You've had no further hospitalizations, no doctor's visits, you're on no medication, so there's no reason you can't join the rest of us who don't get to hang off Uncle's tit."

"Look at this," Bartok does his usual thing with his shirt, "who the fuck wants this walking around his office?"

"It's a rotten deal, sir, I'm on your side. Between you, me and the four walls? It's tough times where the federal dime is concerned and you know what tough times call for."

"Yeah, crapping on anyone who can't fight back." Bartok motions towards the damaged hand. "How'd that happen?"

Mr. Hughes picks up the solid, square, some kind of glass paperweight that was near his pencil holder, pops it up and down a few times and then gives it a toss across the desk. "Nice catch."

Bartok turns it over in his hands, looking at the photo of Mr. Hughes with a wife and two little boys, all seated beside a Christmas tree. "Your Christmas tree blew up?"

Mr. Hughes does a hand-winding signal so he doesn't have to actually say, "Turn over the cube, genius." On the other side is a black-and-white photo of Hughes in his helmet and jungle fatigues smiling in front of a roll of barbed wire. Bartok turns the cube again. On the other side is a black-and-white photo of a squad of helmeted, rifle-toting GIs all smiling, standing behind a small pile of dead Asian men wearing black. Professionally printed across this photo is the message, "Killing is our business and business is good."

"Sixty-eight, the Mekong Delta," Mr. Hughes says. "And you know what? It could have been a lot worse," Mr. Hughes shakes his head, unbends his paperclip and tosses it with a small clatter into the trash. Bartok keeps turning over the paperweight, bounces it in his hand. "About your case. I wish I could be more positive."

"No, you don't. You're just thinking about what to have for dinner."

"No, I was thinking about when I damn near lost my arm," Mr. Hughes says. "But instead it was just my finger. So. Our time is about up. Anything else I can help you with?"

"You didn't help me at all." Bartok is already on his feet walking out of the little cubicle when Mr. Hughes says, "Excuse me, but..." and he motions to the paperweight.

"Oh, right, this..." Bartok says and suddenly he snaps. "THIS!" as he begins to rip at the glass with his fingernails, digs his fingers into the smooth, cool surface or tries and then, growling he puts the paperweight to his mouth and goes at it with his teeth, "THIS!" now garbled, comes out with a moan.

Mr. Hughes sits there. "It's sealed," he says. "You can't get inside."

Out of breath, Bartok does a frantic look around the cubicle to see where he can fastball the paperweight and then he decides that right at the fucking head of Mr. Hughes is the very spot. Perfect. He draws back his hand.

"You know, besides the scarring you're a very good-looking young dude..."

One more windup. Then? To hell with it. And Bartok puts the paperweight back on the desk. "When you were blown up, did you get to Red River?"

"What the fuck are you talking about?" Mr. Hughes adjusts the paperweight to just exactly where he likes it. "It knocked me cold. Stansfield—he hit it and got off clean—he said he never heard anyone scream like I was screaming. But I don't remember. I woke up in the hospital with nine fingers."

"Too bad," Bartok says. "You don't know what you missed," and he takes off, keeps on walking as he hears, "Thanks for stopping by..." fading out behind him.

But that was the day before. And the day after (and the day after that) will be days of no money. So, now, it's a trip to the river for a last splash. Not Red River, he's not that lucky. Only the East River. Bartok walks crazily like a man going the wrong way on a moving stair in a strong wind—or like a man who's been drinking all night while contemplating suicide and murder. The city pops up around him. It's got a satisfying, pointed, deep breathing grimness like it's out to prove that everything really is as bad as you think. Grimy and dark. He comes out of the moving metal tattoo of the subway, the walls snaked with graffiti, names and scraggy, penned images of penises spurting, of huge female breasts, and once on the street Bartok is in the glorious neon mushroom cloud of Times Square, not knowing exactly why he's there. It seems like he wants to travel in the Heart of Things, the Center. This, he figures, is the secret central chakra of the city—that's what Laverne Love would say—he floats through streets planted with every kind of whore and rent boy and grifter and lonely crowd. Bums and alkies shuffle by demanding change. A man walks up to Bartok and asks to give him a blow job. There's a man on a pay phone—two other men come up behind him, grab him around the throat and take his wallet. Another man—older, a tourist with his wife—takes out his wallet to offer some charity and from a doorway another man rushes out, slaps the wallet out of his hand, grabs it and runs. Somewhere near the small empty abandoned patch of Bryant Park, three young men in a drug war run crouched behind a row of parked cars with drawn revolvers down by their hips. Somewhere nearby, somebody breaks a bottle for a fight. Somewhere nearby, the cops push a handcuffed suspect onto the back seat of an unmarked car and then jump in after him to pound at his nuts, his kidneys while he curls up and pulls his knees to his stomach in a useless defense.

Somewhere, somebody who's down on their luck and without a roof over their head squats hidden between two cars with his pants around his ankles. Bartok lurches. His eyes trace the neon scrawl for rap parlors, topless clubs, massage parlors, crappy electronics stores that are out to cheat you, food stands out to poison you, dogs out to bite you and every breath is salted with the rank smell of cheap booze and human piss. He's broke. He'll probably step in dog shit. The evening is plunging downhill. It's madness.

Bartok's not even certain where he is, anymore. He's not even sure whether he feels himself present on the street or whether he's flying high above the city, seeing himself as a small burned-body-dot who's crookedly pushing his way among the crowds of The Beautiful and Healthy or whether he sees everyone else is just like him, burned badly but still with a face and a crotch that works. Does it matter? He's not sure. Bartok follows the energy of the city out from Times Square as it radiates towards the river, not so much weakening as it travels, but taking on a fancy disguise.

He imagines himself looking into the East River wishing it

was the Red River and hoping that when he takes the plunge it'll turn out to be both. This is the finish line.

When he can see the dark, grand slash of the 59th St. Bridge, nearly a shadow, Bartok stops and tries to figure out the best way to get to the middle section so he can jump. As he looks and thinks and wonders about the best way to propel himself into a fall, a group of three people moves in front of him blocking his view. Two young men and a young woman, all in long hair which is now shifting slightly like water in the breeze and all in wrinkled, patched checkered shirts and jeans that are also worn through. Two of them—maybe all three—are apparently lovers, whatever that means. How they fit together is tough to tell. They pass around a joint. Bartok can smell it. Bartok is listening. They begin to talk about the bridge, the vast expanse of it and one of them—the woman—mentions *The Great Gatsby* and how F. Scott Fitzgerald wrote about the lights like diamonds and then the two men begin to discuss how strange it is that when you're having trouble pissing, if you turn on a faucet, the sound of water will draw you out.

"It's like the body is going back to the rhythm of nature," the young man says, "you know, like, we're mostly made of water and so when we hear the, you know, rush of water we want to, like, join with it, join in."

Bartok steps forward towards them. "So, is that what's happening if you jump?" he says.

This gets him the quizzical eye.

"I'm going to jump off the bridge in a few minutes, so does that mean all I'm doing is rejoining the water—which is what I'm mostly made of?"

"It's just a rap," the young man says. "We were talking about pissing. Maybe you should take a piss, not a plunge."

This gets them all laughing, the woman a little too into the joy so that she's holding her gut and bending over, grimacing so that she looks like Lee Harvey Oswald at his shooting. Bartok takes a good, deep sailor's breath of the marijuana hoping for a contact high. One of the young men offers him a toke on the joint, saying, "Have a hit. Then if you want to jump, we'll applaud for you."

"What's that funny shit on your chest?" from the young woman. And when Bartok answers, "Burn scars," she says, "Cool," and then starts giggling again.

"Good shit," Bartok rasps, complimenting the dope. And he tells them about Red River, everything he can think of, like he's listening to himself on a form of cosmic radio.

"I'm going to kill somebody tonight," Bartok says.

"Not cool, man," says one of the young men. "No, not cool. Here. Have another hit." Bartok can feel the smoke like airborne gravel swirling in his lungs. He begins to float. He thinks he might be approaching Red River.

"I'll kill somebody," Bartok says. "Me or somebody else."

One of the guys slips two fingers in a shirt pocket and out pops what looks like a small piece of cardboard. "Give this a lick. That'll take you where you want to go."

A lick is what he gives it, but that's it. "Last time I did acid I fucked my mother," Bartok says. And it's true, almost. With Laverne Love, his Dear John writing ex-girlfriend, an acid-enthused night of visions and balling had her kneeling on top of him as her face melted into the face of his mother and all Bartok could think was, "I drop acid and end up in Psychology 101? No thanks."

Bartok's about to let loose on these three idiots and explain to them that he's been a failure at most of the central actions of this generation—drugs, war, free floating love, finding Nirvana, he's screwed them all up. But when his attention returns to the street and the bridge he sees that his three fast friends are now far, far away, heading to another locale, back into their own lives if they'd ever left their lives behind in the first place.

So, now he's alone. Maybe he blacked out or maybe the people he was talking with could fly or maybe they were never there at all—Bartok now lives with memories that might as well have been scenes in a book or movie. After a while, he thinks, I'd have been better off just reading the book. He's thinking about this as he goes climbing out towards the middle of the bridge, the traffic's metal rapids crashing all around him, but the funny thing is that he can't see the bridge anymore, it's not under his feet. Then, he's back on the pavement looking at the bridge and he doesn't remember whether he'd ever really been up there, maybe he was just thinking about it and thinking about it made it real. He's back on a street, like he wakes up walking. The experience is nowhere near Red River, it's more like a Red River imitation, a trick, it reminds him of The Monkees doing The Beatles or those guys who dress up like Elvis. He can still walk straight and tell time.

There's a bar on the corner. Not sure which corner, somewhere on York near the bridge. A good hooker bar, high class, it's got that reputation.

Inside, first thing, he walks right into the atmosphere, no one could convince you that you were anywhere else. Live jazz. Bartok sees the trio on the small stage, he sees the empty seat at the bar next to the woman who's beckoning him to come on over.

"You're in the right place, big guy, sit down," she says. "Let's have a drink." A scotch appears before Bartok. The jazz soars, snakes a rhythm into his ears until it sort of rattles at the base of his skull and he's afraid he's going to black out. He'd better confess. "I don't have any money," but when she gets this info all she says is, "You look like you could use a stiff one. So could I, if you know what I mean. Get a load off, have a seat. I've been waiting for you all night."

She stretches out her legs to indicate the empty seat beside her and that gets a loud throat clearing from the man behind the bar.

"Hey, do you mind," she says to him. "I'm showing the man my legs."

Florette is her name, she says, which is interesting because her words scratch along with the brassy crowing of a Manhattan accent. "Sit," she says. "If nothing else you'll hear some music." Why does she keep staring at him? Bartok knows why. But why do I keep staring...where? Somewhere else.

This could be tricky. Bartok isn't certain he wants to take a chance at attempting to use language since speaking will probably mean slurred words and idiot sentences. Language is a pain in the ass, anyway, is what he's thinking. And that's another reason that right now he's back to yearning, expecting, hoping for Red River. Damn it but he was right at the edge! Even an imitation doesn't seem too bad. Now it's nowhere, there's only music and lights and smoke from Florette's very long, slim lady cigar.

"What do you mean Red River?" Florette says. "Like the cowboy film?"

"You know about Red River?" Bartok says. "Who told you about Red River?"

"You did, you just said it."

Uh oh. A black out is well on its way. Well, if that's how it's going to be, if he's going to be swept away, dancing like a puppet, then he might as well throw in with it. He tells her as best he can about Red River, all the details, while he undoes the top two buttons of his shirt so she can take a look at his scars. He takes a long drag off her lady cigar and blows a few smoke rings.

"I tell you what," she says. "You got a real talent for nicotine."

"Everybody's good at something," Bartok says with an attempted smile. "Also, I don't know what you're talking about."

She directs his eyes down at the ashtray on the bar where Bartok sees an uneven war-like pile of half-smoked skinny, broken sticks of her cigars. "That's a lot of smoke. You oughta think about slowing down. Also, consider how you'll get me another pack, is what I'm thinking."

Bartok is about to say that he didn't smoke any of them, that he doesn't smoke at all but when he opens his mouth to speak one of her little cigars, perched on his lips, falls out and hits the bar. There's a small explosion of ash.

"I'm not completely sure where I am," he says. "Why is the ceiling getting lower?"

"Well, somebody's ready to go out on a date," she says. "Or are you telling the truth about no money?"

Bartok's stumped for an answer. The music and the small stage of musicians passes by like it's on a riverboat, floating back and forth at the end of the bar, way back there beyond the tables. People shouldn't applaud so loudly, Bartok is thinking. There are too many people in here who have large teeth. And someone—who is it?—is wearing a perfume that gives off a floral aroma like a bathroom aerosol. God, I hate this place. Then for just a tiny slice of a minute, Bartok gets another inkling of Red River, this time an airy welling in his gut that links up with a small shiver across the shoulders. He may have cooked his brain to the point where it's at the doorway.

"Paris," she says. "You said you were going to take me to Paris."

Bartok thinks he might have popped a blood vessel in his eye trying to remember whether he said this. Somehow, some-where, he's been unlinked from the chain of events that make up any kind of understanding, even in fantasy. Now, moments are just happening in the way that flashbulbs go off when somebody famous comes to town.

"I don't believe you," she says, "I'd know if you were."

"Were what?"

"Famous," she says.

Right around then, A Regular Guy breaks in. Bartok is thinking of him exactly in those terms—not even The Regular Guy because there's nothing standout. He's only A Regular

Guy in Bartok's fevered mind. Medium-sized, wrinkled gray suit, white shirt, tie, but a genuine type. In five years—if he doesn't have a coronary—he'll have a gut that hangs over his belt like an escaping elephant. But now it just sort of edges out like a personal secret and he uses it to thrust a randy self-assurance in front of him so that it runs interference. His head twists around and his huge face swivels towards Bartok, who begins to count skin marks and hair follicles. What's left of A Regular Guy's hair is slicked back over a scalp that's dappled like an oil-stained tarp. But he's not all that bad looking, not his face, anyway. In five years he'll be a mess but right now he's got a kind of ordinary good looks. You could bring him to a party without blushing but nobody's gonna get jealous. All this clicks detail by detail through the foggy territory of Bartok's noodle as A Regular Guy pushes in between Florette and Bartok and then jacknifes in on the bar with what Bartok called "an angle of architectural collapse."

Bartok was very clear about all this. He had no plans to stop talking.

When A Regular Guy leans in, well, that's when Bartok is positive that—all things considered—A Regular Guy looks a lot like him, Bartok. Same size? Not sure. There's something "the same" about him. Okay, he's not a mass of horrible scar tissue but Bartok has this mystical sense that he's standing there with his double. He knows for a fact this observation is popping up because his mind's all fucked up but he's having the observation all the same.

"No, he doesn't," Florette laughs, pushes A Regular Guy on the shoulder as he squeezes out a grin. "He's handsome. You're the mess."

Bartok hears A Regular Guy say, "Yeah, yeah, I know, I see him," and then he leans in further and whispers something into Florette's ear. She pulls away nodding and saying something like, "Uh huh, uh huh" not in agreement but slowly and deadpan and more like she knew this was on its way and she had it scoped out from a mile down the road. She whispers something back to him. A Regular Guy turns around and that's like a whale breaking to the surface and rolling. Facing Bartok, he says, "That's some set of designs on you, boy." His fingers are already at the top of Bartok's shirt. He unbuttons one button. He lightly puts his fingertips—oddly cool—on Bartok's chest. "Fire can really do a job." Then he reaches up and runs the back of his fingers down Bartok's cheek. "Very pretty. That fire had an appreciation of the good things."

"Why do you say that?"

"Jesus, you been talking about it all night," Florette says.

But A Regular Guy, where did he go? That same possibility: Bartok isn't sure whether he's imagined him. He buttons the top of his shirt but that's not easy to do when your fingers don't totally belong to you.

"Don't worry if you're really broke," Florette says and puts her fingers to Bartok's lips as he's about to ask a question. "Our boy, there, he just picked up the tab."

"I don't want him to do that."

Bartok pulls away from her stare. It's a searchlight beam off a cruiser. He begins blinking.

"We can make us a dime or two," Florette says. "From that horny guy."

"I'm gonna need more than a dime."

"He's good for it," she says. "He just doesn't know it."

"What did he say? What did he want? When he leaned in like that?"

"What the hell you think he wants," Florette crosses her arms in her lap and blows smoke like she's taking direction in a film. "He said he wants to fuck me and suck you."

"That's not good."

"Well, you think I don't know it's not good, you little idiot? We're not going to really do it. I mean, I could just go with him alone, maybe, but that's not the way I do things. I'm the type that always thinks up the biggest idea." She does the smoke thing again and Bartok is entranced by it for some reason, he likes the feeling that he's in a film and what settles on him now is that this may be the surest way to get back to Red River.

"Of course we're not going to do it," Florette says. "We're going to roll him."

Bartok's not sure he heard that right. But the booze, the dope, the cigarette smoke, the general malaise and the time of year and the city and the war and the economy and his memory of Laverne Love and, of course, the death of God and higher mathematics and, most importantly, his looking for Red River, it all makes for this big chunk of time where he just stands there at the bar and stares with the music going through his head and a feeling like he should get the hell out of there and pronto.

Bartok doesn't remember much anymore. A lot of what happened to him is more like a ringing in his ears or an irritated nerve than a memory. Images? Maybe. Sometimes. A helmet flies up in the air, a rifle. He flies. Nothing special. It's all still a miracle. Celebration. Just keep in mind the lesson: History doesn't love you.

"He's a little pisher," Florette says, "but you can take him. While his attention's on me, you do the dirty and we grab what we can get. And by the way, doll, I know we can get plenty."

Bartok is letting this sink in while he remembers that he's not really much of a fighter. "I've never actually hit anybody," he says. "Not like that. Okay, once, in the Army. And then they beat the living crap out of me."

This isn't totally true. There was Luke, who got trashcanned in the alley behind the whorehouse hotel but to Bartok that now seems like somebody else might have told him the story. Bartok had seen a couple of genuinely bad fights in the service because if you put a lot of young men together with a lot time and with the idea that they're supposed to be killing people, eventually—war or no—somebody is just bound to get their head handed to them. But in those circumstances, Bartok always talked his way out of it or stepped aside. Except this once.

Somebody had scored a bottle of Robitussin from sick bay and somebody else had scored a bottle of very bad wine by paying off an NCO. So, now there were four guys—Bartok is one of them—who'd skipped out on duty on a Sunday and were hiding by a garbage dump, drinking and talking and jokingly insulting one another and then finally, arguing and threatening for real. A few days before, the hand-to-hand combat instructor had taught them how to use pieces of their equipment or a rock or a stick to hit someone and kill them. Here, the argument which led to threats now led to one of the guys smashing the wine bottle across the face of another guy and of Bartok standing up and, drunkenly swaying, shouting out, "Holy shit! What's the matter with you!" then hauling off and connecting with a pretty well-thrown straight right fist that popped onto the cheekbone of the wine bottle wielder and made the guy's head wiggle back like a bobble toy. The recipient of the wine bottle was crawling around on his hands and knees moaning and bleeding into the ground but the other guy spun Bartok around and as Bartok pulled back for another shot, this guy got in maybe three, maybe four, expert shots so that Bartok had to watch the grass and the earth itself rush upwards at him roaring truck style. He lay there unconscious.

And that turned out to be good luck. When the wine-bottle-wounded-guy reported what had happened, the wine-bottle-wielder was hauled up on charges and so was the guy who'd clobbered Bartok only...nobody knew who Bartok was—they reported to the First Sergeant that Barton from C Company had been with them, too, and he should get charged, too, but nobody knew it was Bartok of A Company. So Barton of C Company would have to do some explaining while Bartok (of A Company) would only have to stop the ringing in his ears. But that was his foray into unarmed combat.

Back in the club, with Florette, Bartok remembers the incident so well that he now isn't certain who he is, either, Bartok, Barton, Barman, it doesn't matter. What about Luke, what was poor ol' Luke doing now? Bartok sees A Regular Guy at the other end of the club putting his arm around another man's neck and with a big smile, dragging him in close, buddy-buddy style, while the other man looks like his eyeballs might pop.

"It doesn't matter," Florette says, "you can do it, I know you can." And she gives him first a funny little squeeze on the bicep, testing his strength, and then yanks on the pectoral where his tit joins his shoulder, maybe testing his nerve, and after that a slight nudge with the point of her high heel. "Look at that horse's patoot. I hate him, and if he don't deserve a good shot across the bow, then I ask you, who does?"

"You know him?"

"That guy? He's got some ideas. And by the way, he's one of the richest men in the world."

"That sounds like pure, unadulterated bullshit for sure."

"Okay. One of the richest men in the city, I don't know. He's richest somewhere," Florette does another toe tap on Bartok's shin with her pointy black shoe as she directs him with her eyes to look at her knees. He does. Her hand lays in her lap and, partly hidden, she's holding something that looks like a small candy bar. Bartok can't figure out why.

"Don't just stare at it, stupid, take it," she grabs his wrist. The candy bar shifts to his hand and, of course, the candy bar turns out to be a small sap, a professionally made blackjack, black leather with a piece of steel inside. "Bop him with that when you get the chance," she says. "Just hit him once, though. Don't go to town on him. Just give him a solid zotz right on the back of the head."

"What if I kill him? By accident, I mean."

"Kill him? Jesus. Don't make me laugh. You'll be lucky he doesn't turn around and shove that thing right up your keester.

That one's got a noggin like poured concrete."

"I hope you know what you're doing," Bartok says. He hopes somebody knows, anyway. He looks over towards A Regular Guy. "Funny thing is, I don't like rich people. That's the whole problem with the world—it's just a lot of money being pushed around by well-groomed nutcases."

"Now, see, that's what I call bullshit," Florette says. "Who're you trying to con? And the word is: psycho-neurotic. Well-groomed psycho-neurotics. Who cares as long as he goes out quick."

The strange thing is, Bartok feels deeply comfortable with Florette like he's known her all his life and like the two of them are locked together, inseparable pals, well-oiled in each other's foibles and triumphs and most importantly, joyful in each other's illusions and gracious about each trip-up and fall.

Why the hell do I feel this way? This is what Bartok is wondering. Also, he's wondering just exactly how did he come to be with a woman who says her name is Florette, walking down the hallway of some very posh hotel with his right hand cupped around a blackjack, playing like he knows how to use it. One second he's ready to go off a bridge—then there's some music and a lot of colors and then? What a place, this hotel! Fleshy in a lemon colored light. Somebody's idea of class was to decorate so that this hallway has a Versailles ring to it, mottled in curlicues and leaves and ribbons. Bartok keeps trying to put together how he was in the bar with Florette in one moment and then suddenly walking with Florette and A Regular Guy down this hallway with everything in between gone away on the ark with the animals. A blank. And he's thinking back to when he downed some son-of-a-bitch in an alleyway with a garbage can and when he watched a guy get clobbered with a wine bottle and he's wondering whether this is the way to Red River.

Next, Bartok's in a quietly deadpan examination of how A Regular Guy is splaying the cottage cheese cheeks of his hairy ass on the edge of the bed, in a kind of backward leaning sit, eyes rolled white. There's Florette, on her knees with her head in his lap and her feet spread out at an odd angle. Bartok is standing nearby, nailed in place. Florette's calves are smoother, whiter and thinner than Bartok remembers until he remembers that he's never seen them before. Her hair keeps pushing and squeezing against A Regular Guy's future gut, mingling with the sandy hairs spreading across the weak flesh of his chest and Bartok thinks he sees Florette momentarily take her hand off A Regular Guy's boxy thigh and make some kind of motion towards him, Bartok. Now. Hit him. Now. Do it. But Bartok doesn't budge. A Regular Guy's head shakes just a little bit and he turn his eyes to Bartok and when his head's not lolling back, he gives that two-fingered direction signal, pointing at Bartok, then pointing at Florette as in, "Watch."

Bartok takes in a lungful of old cigarette smoke and hotel soap and through the windows he can hear the city ignoring the hell out of him because it's so set on its own bubbling grumble, all metal and rubber-on-the-road.

Then A Regular Guy smiles and makes a motion that invites Bartok to undress but Bartok doesn't want to undress because then he'll be not only naked, but naked with his hideous body of uneven, rivulet red scars gleaming there like frozen lava and not only that, he'll be naked with his scars and with this blackjack in his hand. How could he have been such an idiot as to get himself involved with this? Bartok gets an image of himself like that: a scared, scarred, stupid man, naked with a blackjack. A man totally unsure of himself who's ready to become a murderous clown.

Maybe he should walk across the ceiling. Hey, now there's a way to escape! Just walk up the side of the hotel wall, walk right across the ceiling and then back down to the door. Red River is on its way, oh yeah, it sure is. Bartok goes after himself with a bullhorn of How-Stupid-Can-You-Get. Who else would be stuck here imagining the whole idea of the ceiling walk?

There's something about being on the edge of Red River that's a world class tease and tantalizer, it whirls every point of his being into an incredible web of here-I-am-where-I-shouldn't-be. He wants to stand there, that's all. He wants to watch it crumble. Everything. He wants to be present at the Fall, if there's going to be one, it's worth the ultimate price.

While Bartok has been lost in philosophy, A Regular Guy has climbed on top of Florette, who's now making hand signs of "What the hell of are you waiting for, NOW?!" He watches A Regular Guy fucking. Some other time, maybe, that would get his motor going but right now it's just another reason to give himself a smack on the head. The grunting, too. A Regular Guy does a lot of it.

Also, Bartok watches Florette signaling. And she's not wrong, Bartok thinks, now would be the perfect time to step in and wallop this lug right across the skull with this black-jack, knock him cold and take his loot. Bartok senses he's talking to himself like he's in an old movie. The room smell changes to the odor of dying roses, Bartok pinches his nose and then snorts. Maybe it's him, Bartok, maybe this is what Bartok smells like when fear spills out of his pores. Bartok's never quite been afraid like this. Oh, sure, he's been afraid before but only Mondays through Sundays, 6 a.m. to 6 a.m. and this is a different quality of fear. Not greater or less—but definitely different, it creates its own day of the week, call it Fear Day, so that it can come into being as a part of the week. This fear has a very strange edge, it's telling Bartok you might be able to survive death but then afterwards you'll find something much worse and live there forever. Something that'll make you wish there really is a Hell.

An electric quiver whizzes through his stomach and Bartok stares as A Regular Guy, making sounds like a goat, turns his head slowly to the side so that he can lock eyes with Bartok, almost like they're picking up on one another's brain waves and then A Regular Guy purses his lips and with his eyes half-lidded, he blows Bartok a kiss.

Florette has her thighs and knees locked around A Regular Guy and her painted-red toenails are perfect, not a chip, her feet small as a child's. Bartok is suddenly suffused with the feeling that he's ecstatic to be here with her and with her feet. Who knows why? As Florette signals with her gaze this time, she actually mouths the words, "NOW! You idiot! NOW!"

For the first time, Bartok notices that A Regular Guy has a perfectly tiny, round, brown beauty mark to the left side of face, not far from his nose where the nostrils are billowing in slow motion, a wild pig. He wonders why he didn't notice any of this before. He connects to the perfectly even little spaces between A Regular Guy's teeth, unusually small and straight. What will it be like, he's wondering, when he swings the weighted blackjack against that head bone or might he hit A Regular Guy smack in the teeth and see them shatter? So many possibilities. For just an instant, that feeling flutters by: I'm gonna put a round right through your chest, motherfucker, I'm gonna take you out. You know why? For everything. For Everything. That's why.

It's a sign that Red River is coming. The breeze of a spring day, sunshine on the ocean in the early morning, mountain air, a million other postcard feelings take Bartok into a moment so deeply sensual that he lets his head tilt backwards. Oh, God, life is good, so good. Red River is almost here. Bartok is in love with the moment. The moment expands until it's willing to last forever. Bartok breathes deeply and smiles. Red River. He actually says the words, "Red river."

"Take off your pants," A Regular Guy says.

He's maybe two, three feet away.

This is not good. Bartok thinks about what to say and comes up with, "Huh?" A Regular Guy takes another step closer, his chapped, square naked foot dully gleaming in the hotel room light as the heel hits, as the toes follow, as Florette's face pops up over his shoulder like a little zoo balloon and then there's the sound of a branch snapping, *WHAP!*

"Shit," A Regular Guy says. His palm becomes a little prayer hat on top of his head like he's the Pope of Naked Men. And his neck sinks into his chest as he inches around to see what Florette's got in her hand. The blackjack. She's going to hit him again. All Bartok can see is A Regular Guy's shivering white ass with the trimming of black hair across the back, the blood that's dripping down between his shoulder blades and when Bartok looks down at his own right hand, he sees that it's empty. Where's the blackjack? Florette's got it, goddamnit, I dropped it, he thinks, or in some other dimension she took it away or never gave it to me. How could I be so...

This is cut short by a second sound, something like the sound a woman makes when she's knocked backwards into a small hotel table.

"Son of a bitch!" which is Florette's voice as she tries to get back on her feet and Bartok wants to ask if she's all right but he can't because his own voice is now sounding like a cheap washing machine on the fritz. That's because A Regular Guy has his hands on Bartok's throat, thumbs pressing right where they should be pressing if you want a man to sink to his knees and die quick.

Bartok's world goes off-air. Dark. When everything comes back on, A Regular Guy is on his knees with his head bowed forward and Florette is standing behind him with the blackjack about to slam him again.

"Cocksucker hit me," she says, panting, growling, going pop-eyed at Bartok. "Nobody hits me." Then she waggles her face and says, "What the fuck are you still doing here?"

"Doing where?" Bartok says.

But there comes this glimpse again—*hello!*—a few drops of Red River. Bartok knows that for sure. That's what he's thinking and why he's fingering the worm-like scar tissue that crawls up towards his throat when A Regular Guy raises his chin.

Bruiser's eyes to Bartok's eyes and then Bartok gets a gander that A Regular Guy's on his way out, his gaze is like a misted windshield. *We're all together, driving in the rain,* Bartok thinks. Very wise, he tells himself, because now he's feeling generous towards all of humanity. Except that doesn't seem to stop A Regular Guy from getting up to his feet.

"Hit me? Hit me? I'll kill you!" Florette is on him. She swings the blackjack. When that flies out of her hand she hauls up the chair that's near the hotel room desk but that turns out to be a waste of time and energy because Bartok wants everyone to know he's doing his part and he's sent out a solid, thundering right hand, the fist popping into the nape of A Regular Guy's neck which makes A Regular Guy do something that should be impossible: he swings around backwards towards Bartok with his arms open wide and, in the very same motion, he steps forward twice and then he combines the two motions—like ballet—by doing a little dance until he wheezes loudly and collapses on the floor right next to the bed.

Bartok wants to applaud. It's very quiet. Bartok hears himself breathe. He hears Florette, too. And then there's the comforting always-to-be-counted-upon sound of traffic from the street below.

"Look at that piece of shit," Florette says.

"Is he dead?"

"He better be. You promised me you'd waste that slob, you better not just be flapping your gums."

"Me? Why me? When did I say that?"

"I hope he's dead, son-of-a-bitch. Hit me you piece of shit?" she's down on one knee feeling for a pulse along the damp gray seaweed of curly hairs that cover A Regular Guy's neck. "Okay. Oh, great. He's still cooking. Barely."

She's got an ass like a dancer is what Bartok is thinking. How old is Florette? Bartok compares her face with her breasts which seem tired and stringy as she bends forward in this kneeling position. "What?"

"I said, he's still kicking but I don't think he'll last too long. Go into his stuff, he's gotta be toting a wad of bread."

This is when Bartok makes a note of her pubic hair, which is very neatly trimmed and he wonders whether this is some kind of professional necessity.

"What the hell are you waiting for? Jesus!"

"Maybe we should just go."

"This is a rich man who had it coming," Florette says. "I told you about it before."

"I don't know when that was," Bartok says. "Stop trying to make me nuts."

"Go! Now!" Florette can't re-hook her bra with her hands behind her back and so she curses and pulls the hooks to the front so she can see what she's doing.

A Regular Guy's suit jacket bursts apart in Bartok's grip. It's like his nerves, skittering through his hands, dissolving the threads. He throws the torn jacket down. Now, a wedding ring pops out of A Regular Guy's pants pocket when Bartok shakes the crumbled up garment. It's the same as when, in the comics, a poor guy turns his pockets inside out and flies buzz out of them but here, it's a wedding ring which is A Regular Guy's way of pretending that *I ain't got nothing to worry about or go home to*. Then, along with the ring, comes a faded silver Zippo lighter with the engraving "Gun Bunny '69" and some military division crest. And then finally, a money clip. A thick one, too, gold with a silver dollar on it.

"Don't stand there like a jackass, grab that cash," Florette says, "and help me get this piece of crap into bed," as she throws back the sheets.

The air conditioner sounds a little bit like a plane landing. Bartok listens to it for a while and then he says, "Maybe we should just leave," wondering now, *just what the hell happened to Red River?* Something about the entire situation has a heavy dose of *shouldn't be*. Bartok starts musing to himself with a silent voice saying that this may be a perfect time just to make a run for it but he's also in that trance which holds on tight to the closest Bad Idea.

"The cash, come on! Give it here! And now get a hold of his fucking shoulders," Florette says.

If you've ever lifted dead weight you know that each person becomes his or her own complete, weary world—that's how heavy people are when they're out cold. It's like lifting a world. A world with hips that buckle and a head that lolls back and a stretched out naked back and belly that you can barely get to clear the floor let alone raise high enough to throw on a bed. Sometimes, like with A Regular Guy, there's a thin, streaming stink like the air has morphed into a dead dog and it's coming through the pores and right up to tickle the hair in your nostrils and it's tough to keep hold of the shoulders because your hands keep sliding down on the sweat. A small tuft of this guy's back hair might come off in your fingers because it gets caught when the body slips down.

"Look at this piece of crap. You're not such a tough guy now, are you, you hunk of pig shit! Just think how he'll be when he's dead," Florette's got his big, cracked feet and his ivory calves and she's puffing and straining and turning her face to one side to avoid looking directly at the start of a balloon gut and the balls hanging down like two deflated flesh bags.

"I'm doing my best," Bartok says and a moment later he wonders why he said it.

When A Regular Guy's on the bed, Florette covers him with the blanket. "Somebody will just find him. It'll look like he banged his head, hit the sheets and died in his sleep. We hope, anyway. This turned out to be kind of sloppy. That's because you didn't move when you should move! Wait. I gotta make a call." She snorts out a laugh. "You can't even use a blackjack. Jesus, we gotta get outta here."

Bartok starts to shiver. One finger goes along the sweating, solid flesh of a scar line near the top of his chest and the other runs through his hair. A couple of hard blinks because he can't quite see straight and everything's got that look when you think you're the life of the party but you've discovered you're really at the bottom of an aquarium.

"What's wrong with you?" Florette says. "Hey. Hey, hey." She snaps her fingers in his face.

Bartok is still on his feet but he's tottering and pretty much gone. Into Red River? Not quite, really, but into the search for what he thinks of as "the Red River state." Why didn't it happen? He seemed so close. He remembers back when he was in the Army, the alleyway, the moment when he swung the garbage can lid against the skull of his attacker and WHAM! no Red River, but close there, too. Damn, but he feels terrible, he feels like his skin is drying out and pulling so tight he'll strangle. This is the same, he's thinking, he clobbered this son-of-a-bitch and he got close, but no Red River.

"You know what it is? It's that nobody got killed."

"What do you mean?" Florette says, "Half the time I don't know what the hell you're talking about."

"How long do you think A Regular Guy will last?"

"Who's A Regular Guy?" Florette says. Then, "Oh. I get it. What do I look like, a doctor? Maybe he's gone before we leave the room and maybe he hangs on a while. Hey. Maybe he collects Social Security, but he better not. Hey, what do I know?" She's dressed now, sitting on the edge of the bed, pulling on her right shoe and getting one finger slightly stuck against the heel, which makes her quietly curse. "Here, take this," and the vision of a small, brownish pill with a tiny star of light shining on it passes before Bartok's sight and then he's tasting the little orb as a tiny bitter stone on his tongue. He swallows.

"Give it a minute. That'll set you up fine," Florette says. "Then we're going to walk out of here like we're best of friends and then we're going down to the street. We gotta meet a guy."

Bartok is suddenly made of air. He can walk through walls. It isn't Red River, true, but it's not Bartok, either, or it's not who he usually takes to be Bartok—ugly, skin-sculpted, terrified, he's so tired of himself that he bores even the bored, a corpse who hasn't the good sense to call it quits. Florette says something about "I can see that little pill is doing the trick," and her huge face floats up so that she can peer right into his eyes. Bartok starts to take off his shirt and let the mucus-like curlicues of his mottled flesh breathe, let them have the life they really want. So then, everything that's gone wrong goes even wronger.

"Shit," Florette says. "Who is it?"

"It's Bartok," Bartok says, "I've been here all along only not this way."

"Not you, you horse's ass," she says, and then Bartok hears it again: someone's knocking at the hotel room door.

There's a voice that's liquid cotton but it dies out before it can get through the door and enter the room. When Florette calls out again, "Who is it?" her voice grinds like a buzz saw.

"Room service," the far off voice says

"Shit," Florette says to Bartok. A Regular Guy, before he went pants-off-lights-out, called the desk for champagne and "a little snack." Bartok tries to remember but it makes his head hurt. "You were in the bathroom," Florette says. "Remember? You were hiding, we had to talk you out."

"Room service," the voice says again.

Bartok doesn't remember and it's as if somebody else now owns his life or at least this moment of his life. "It's not fair," he says out loud.

"Room service isn't fair?" she's at the bedside, throwing the covers over A Regular Guy and making sure his head with its ripe, encrusting blood patch, is nicely hidden. The chair they used to help A Regular Guy into unconsciousness if not into The Promised Land—that has to be set right, too, and put back near the little hotel desk. Florette heads to the door.

"I'll sign for it. I'll sign this idiot's name."

"He might wake up."

"More likely he'll snap into the rigor mortis and we'll both be fucked," she says.

The man who wheels in room service is small-boned and the size of a jockey and he almost dances into the room with the rattling glasses playing their own little musical accompaniment. His white jacket hangs off his shoulders like he's wearing his father's clothing and he's a full tank of professional joy out for a tip. Bartok thinks he's pretty much the same size as Bartok, maybe a little smaller. No scars, though. Just a small mustache that tops off a South-of-the-Border bandito feel. Ice bucket, champagne, a beaker of martinis and three martini glasses, a plate of crackers and cheese and olives and little pickles. "Here you go," he says, and then he comes up short. The tray rattles. He does a double-take at the bed. "I see Mr. Poltoon had a good time, again. How are you, Mr. Poltoon?"

"Nap time," Florette smiles, patting her hair. "Don't wake him. Don't worry, I'm good for the tip."

The room service man does a kind of counting-off gaze, his eyes riveting back and forth from the big mound in the bed to Florette and to Bartok all of it with a kind of what's-going-on-here-oh-I-get-it grin.

"Looks like he had loads of fun-fun-fun," he says. "I'm surprised he's still alive."

"Me, too," Florette says.

"He must really like his sleep." One short, grunting laugh to demonstrate that he's a man of the world and he says to Bartok, "You want I should pop the cork or do you want to do the honors?" But this time, he doesn't exactly stop—he slows down. "Hey, wait a minute. What's that on his head? Hey, Mr. Poltoon..." But then he gets a gander of Bartok's chest and even though he'd like to, he can't pull away from the damaged, pink lined 3-D map of Bartok's flesh—nobody

can turn away from those goddamned scars. He stares so hard
that to Bartok it's like a scraping fingernail gritting against the
skin, chipping at the hard, raised lines.

"I got hurt in the service," Bartok says.

"Yeah, you sure did. Sorry to hear it," says room service.
"Man oh man. Sign here."

"I'll take that," Florette steps closer with the numbers end
of a folded one hundred dollar bill showing sharp and green
in her closed hand and she places herself protectively between
room service and Bartok. But in that movement, she's gawk-
ing at Bartok's wounds, too, and with just as much open disgust. "Cover yourself," she says.

"You sure Mr. Poltoon's okay? He sure looks awful quiet."

What is it about getting somebody's—anybody's—
attention that nails Bartok in place? The room service guy is
still staring at Bartok and only at Bartok, who doesn't move.
His shirt is the theater curtain opened onto the grand ugly
scene of his wormy chest. And as he stands still, taking its
own time, he feels some kind of magic light come off him, a
creeping touch of Red River that glows around him like a halo.
Florette might not see it—she may be blind to the energy field
that shines off anybody's—everybody's—private unknown
scars and pain but the room service man is practically in a
cartoon jaw-drop.

This is what Bartok told us in the car, anyway.

"Never seen nothing like that on anybody," the room service man says. You'd think he was going to reach out and
touch Bartok's chest or sweep his fingers over the halo of
light. It's almost like he's in the presence of some kind of
ghost body that's announcing in public, "The world is nothing like you think it is."

"Saw a bad bus accident once but everyone was dead, lying
out there by the side of the road.," says room service. "The
people were all covered so you couldn't see their faces. But
there was lots of dead. Maybe eighteen. Gives you a pretty

lousy feeling, I'll tell you. You folks must play pretty hard."

"It's not polite to stare," Florette has a light grip on the room service man's white sleeve as she tries to turn him towards the door. "We'll leave the tray outside," she says. "I'll ask for you by name if we need anything else." Which is good for another fifty dollars. Florette pushes the bill into his upper chest pocket.

"The weird thing is," the room service man keeps chattering, neck craning in a big, dumb can't-turn-away, both looking at Bartok and fighting Florette's grip. He backs into his cart. The wheels catch and rattle. He pushes back and maneuvers away. "Getting burned like that, I'll bet that hurt like a son-of-a-bitch. If you'll pardon my French. But your face. You're a gorgeous guy with kind of a gorgeous glow. Of some kind."

"It didn't really hurt so bad," Bartok's now ogling at the reflection of his scarred chest in the mirror where everything always appears flatter, harsher and closer. "Afterwards, then it did. Hurt. But when it happened? I just sort of flew out of my body. I mean, it wasn't that way exactly but it's the only way I know how to say it."

"You can take this up later with your new friend," Florette says. "Maybe down in the bar. Not in the room."

"Did you die and come back? I'd like to know about it."

"Not now," Florette says.

"I have to sit down," Bartok says. "I think I'm going to be sick."

Florette rushes over to grab the cheap, theatrically ornate chair from the little desk and drags it over to Bartok as he makes a motion that's part old-man-bends-into-a-sit and part legs-don't-work-and-are-gonna-give-way. He slumps in the chair. Florette lets loose a quick glance to the room service man. "He'll be fine. We just had a—how do you say it?—very playful session. A little slap-and-tickle, that's all, sweetheart. Look, call me sometime. I think we can work something out.

If you know what I mean."

"There's something happening here that I need to learn," says the room service man.

It's at about that moment that A Regular Guy, in his bed, begins to make sounds.

They're not really human sounds, not words certainly, but also not even moans or groans. The sounds come from deep in his chest or deeper, like he's sucking something greasy and rotten up through the mattress, through the floor, through the entire hotel. It's all glottal air and collapsing diaphragm and the sounds come along with an odor like somebody's sliced open a bloated, sheep that's been dead for days. Then A Regular Guy's head perks up. Just a little. A sideways movement. And the blanket shifts enough so that what's in plain sight is the back of A Regular Guy's head, with its large circle of crusted blood and torn skin. Also, what Bartok can see through his nausea and drugged haze—there seems to be an indentation in A Regular Guy's cranium, a cracked-through spot. Florette must have really whacked him.

"Hey," the room service man says. "Hey."

What he was going to say next was probably something like "What's going on here?" or "What's with that guy?" or maybe some shocked stuttering and then a threat to call the police. What he says instead is closer to "Wha..." because Florette lays the blackjack across his small, beautifully coiffed jet black hair and the haircut that he was justifiably proud to sport and his face now does a small snapping motion as he drops almost in place not like he's been clocked from above but more like he's lost all support from below. His knees buckle, he twists around, he drops. That's it.

Bartok slams a hand over his mouth and it's like the coach has taken him off the bench but sent him running for the bathroom and those four or five unsteady, lurching steps ram him sideways into the bathroom doorjamb and then he careens onto the tiled floor near the toilet where he vomits.

"Oh, that's just great, just great, nice move, Sherlock," Bartok can sense Florette walking towards him like he's picking up vibrations though his ear, pressed against the cold bathroom tiles. It's as if he's listening for some message from something cold and solid and instead of words, he's getting the vibe. Lying on bathroom tiles, the trail becomes cold, literally. "Nice. Very nice. Look at yourself. It's your fault, you know, if you hadn't put the whammy on that dumb bastard and just let him leave, we'd be out of here and on our way to..."

Bartok is waiting for the finish. The answer...

"Wherever he was going, anyway," Florette says.

Something cool slides into his hand. Bartok's not in the best position to make judgments but he's sure his first and second fingers are moving without any conscious intent and so he turns his head just-so to watch in amazement. Like a blackout revelation, he now sees with surprise that his right fingers are grasping Florette's blackjack, his fingertips pressing into the shiny leather and he thinks Florette is saying, "You didn't need to hit him so goddamn hard," as she pulls away and straightens up again. In the empty space she leaves behind, there's a faint whiff of her scent—jasmine, maybe, the flowers from a funeral—tinged with some odor of too-much-strain, a touch of her sweat. And he can smell himself, his own sharp sickness on the floor nearby.

The emptiness around Bartok is now an immense sac that swells and becomes heavier. He hears Florette's voice saying, "I'm not lying," and then, "I know that wasn't the plan," and then "Look, what do you want from me," and finally, "Don't, don't even joke about that. Yes, you are. Don't joke."

After that, Bartok picks up on a different sound somewhere, very far off, the hotel door squealing open and shutting with a faint, hollow click. The emptiness rings now with a silence that's as weighty as a world of its own, the special weight of a room where the dead have been lying, the way that a room that's borne a body is tinged forever. Bartok shifts his legs. For Christ's sake, when is Red River coming? Bartok moves his lips and feels his cheek squall against the icy white tiles. He knows that it's ridiculous to call out for Florette because she's gone away (far, far away he sings to himself) and then he wonders whether she was ever really there in the first place.

And what about the dead men lying in the other room? Maybe they were never there in the first place, either, just a little touch of too much scotch, smoke, those little pills that he ingested, the other little pill that Florette slipped him, some other little pills and a grand imagination. He makes the big mistake of thinking profound thoughts: mourning is the life-line the dead throw to us only so they can stick around for a little while longer, even as shadows. But once that's through, the dead, too, are gone, gone, gone (Bartok sings this to him-self) gone not to nothing (because "nothing" is a word that exists) but gone even more than that. Bartok knows he's alone.

Around here is where I said to him, "Yeah, but what about Red River?"

There on the bathroom floor, Bartok goes back to waiting for Red River, for the magic to crash through. Thinking pro-foundly while lying beside the sizable nutty acid spill of his own vomit. Bartok feels the beginning twinge of Red River, the rising surge, and he remembers that one, single, solitary time long ago when he, Bartok, became pain—not felt pain, but became pain—and now it's like those old silent movies except that he's tied down on his own rusted, all-too-well-used rail tracks while Fear barrels towards him with its on-coming light striking him blind. There's nothing he's not afraid of. Death, dismemberment, sure, but also hangnails, paper cuts, a runny nose, it's all the same. This isn't some vague idea of fear—it isn't a wise talk "about fear"—Bartok is too smart for that. And it's not simply the anxiety heat-in-the-head turned on high with his heartbeat running wild and his breath chasing after it in little puffs. This is more like if you put your eye to the lens of the world's largest telescope and what you see—all that you see—is Fear. And that's it. Bartok becomes fear. In the same way that once and only that one time he'd become pain, now he becomes fear.

Everything goes white.

All he can see are the tiles.

It's like a million spiders are crawling around in his head. He can't get ahold of it, can't settle down. "Red River," Bartok says out loud and then? Bartok becomes a holy man. Why not? Small, sick, terribly scarred, lying in his own abuse—who better to believe? Who could yearn more than Bartok? No one. He's king of the yearners. You think you could do better when it comes to reaching the Magic Mountain or whatever you call the top? He was halfway there already and now he knows he's crossed over into the Promised Land or, at least, he's close enough so that the call's not long distance. Bartok tells us he "has an inchoate sense of this" and because he can't find a way to explain it to himself, he can't hear his own voice say it, he knows that he's at the border line of Red River and getting ready to move in there for real and forever.

He gets that sense that Red River is very, very near.

Slightly dizzy with a cannonade going off inside his skull, Bartok uncurls and rises to his feet like some creature from a Japanese horror film stepping out from the sea. More slowly, of course. More wobbly. But as he lurches toward the bathroom doorway, he feels himself enveloped in some kind of protective Cloud of Knowing and all of the fear that had dogged him all of his life has vanished. Now, he's free to give thanks to the fear because the fear is what brought him to this place. It was the fear that came for him like the horrible head in a jack-in-the-box, springing up from under every wish and thought. No, that's not true (Bartok told us that he thinks this as he leans against the door frame) the thought of Death was

72

permitted. Death, disease, poverty, and fear itself but when he ventured too far from that home? Then, soon, the crank got turned too far, the top flipped open and fear popped up right in his face, wagging at him man-to-man.

But now he's holy, imbued with holiness, that's what Bartok is thinking. Something terrific has happened but he isn't sure what. Something fantastic. Bartok is completely confident in the imminent arrival of Red River but even more deliciously, he's rippled by sensations of fantastic calm. Even his flesh seems poured on him like syrup. All is well. This is great. Incredible. That's when he feels the blackjack weighted in his hand and somewhat stupidly looks down at his fingers pressing into the gleaming leather surface. And that's when he stares into the main room.

The room service man is spread out on the floor with his unlit eyes wide open and A Regular Guy is lying coffin-still on the bed with one hand raised to his heart.

"Oh, no." Bartok actually says this out loud.

I've killed two men, is what he thinks. How the hell is that possible? Then, again, he actually says out loud: "This is real trouble."

The path to Red River has seemed somehow linked to death. Preferably, the death of somebody else, but that doesn't seem to work. So, okay, Bartok has always known that eventually he'd kill somebody or (as it seems here) more than one somebody but he always imagined that his reaction would be a style of ruthless, cold, unfeeling indifference. Like an old French crime movie. He never calculated on the way he feels now which is like his entire body is one high-strung, high note, so tight and high that only dogs can hear it. He tries to catch his breath but it's very difficult because every pore and follicle and inch of his flesh is shrinking and tightening to the point of strangling his bones. And he puts the back of his right hand in his mouth and bites down on it while actually repeating, "No, no, no." He's afraid he might cry and wet himself all at the same time.

Bartok tries to recall what took place before the killing and was the killing necessary like in self-defense or did he do it for the hell of it or did he do it at all. He walks unsteadily into the room and circles the room service man then moves to A Regular Guy's bedside. Somewhere in his mind, he'd expected to be more squeamish about dead bodies but he feels nothing like that, only that they have an odd, distorted expression frozen on their faces which instinctively tells Bartok that no one's home and again there's that weird silence in the room that only the presence of the dead can bring about.

Then he thinks he remembers Florette. He's not sure she really existed. Bartok can't bring her back fully in his brain because there's so many fleas and bats flying around in there. He was holding the blackjack, that much he knows because it's still in his hand and there on the bed and floor are two dead bodies who very much appear to have had the life beaten out of them. This is not good. In the kangaroo court of his own head, he takes the roll call and comes up with "guilty."

Bartok sails into a panic so intense that it settles him down. It's a new world. In this new panic world, he feels even closer to Red River and it's like somebody's voice in his head—some stranger—saying to him, "What the fuck's wrong with you? RUN!" It's an honest, clear vision of himself as a fool, an idiot—and trust me, I know all about that. So Bartok drops the blackjack which makes a little *chuck!* sound as it hits the rug and then standing at the hotel door, with the knob cold against his palm, he scares himself by looking down, his hairy eyeball traveling along his torso and he realizes that his shirt and pants are discolored and blotched and covered in puke and maybe—the darker stuff—blood. It's not a great look for someone who's running away. Not in a five star hotel.

This is a real problem, another one. It's topped off when he looks at his own flesh peeking out from behind his mottled, ruined shirt. There's his own skin, himself—like his shaped and frozen wounds, he's finished, he's human garbage. Bartok comes up with the easiest, obvious answer to all this, which is: kill himself. He's going back into the bathroom to find the sharpest object he can and he's going to open a vein and let it all hang out because what's the use? He's done for, anyway. Wasn't that the plan? But when you're really up against it, pal, you change your tune, that's it, isn't it? But then, he's thinking, maybe the window-to-the-street is the best route to eternal escape because they've got to be around seven floors up. At least.

But that's where A Regular Guy comes in. The room service man, also.

Between the two of them, there's enough clothes to dress one man. A Regular Guy has the pants and maybe the shirt and the room service man has the jacket even though it's a hotel uniform jacket. Somebody has shoes, but so what, so what, it's all fine, it's going to work.

With A Regular Guy it's not so bad. All his clothes are on the floor like some stripper tossed them there and only the jacket is useless and in shreds because of Bartok's trembling hands. Going through all those clothes, it must have been like playing the piano, you had to have a light touch. The room service guy is a little different. He's dead and Bartok has to move him to get the jacket off. So now, Bartok finds out three revelations: dead people are really heavy to move, they give you no help at all and it's almost like they're already buried, already attached to the ground. Also, that when you move them sometimes they fart and a lot of times they've already shit themselves and their heads loll back sometimes so that their eyes roll white like monster marbles. Being alive really is better. And finally, Bartok learns that he's going to have to wear a truly ugly jacket.

Sick. On the verge, anyway. That moment where your deepest inner gut is squeezing in on itself and ready to toss and you're begging it not to. Bartok gets dressed. Fast. I bet he doesn't spare a look at his scars right now and also, he's probably so goddamned relieved that he's got new clothes that he gets a rush: Red River is coming, he knows it's close. Bartok rushes into the bathroom, washes off his face and mouth and wets down his hair and takes a hundred-mile stare at himself in the bathroom mirror. Dressed like that—in parts of the suit and parts of the hotel uniform—he looks like a circus clown. It's almost as bad as wearing the blood-and-vomit outfit but not quite. But I'm guessing here that Bartok gets one weird moment when Red River seems so nearby it can blow in his ear and tease him and, at the exact same time, he looks like he's had his ass kicked in the middle of hosting a kids TV show. How the hell is he going to make his way out?

This is when, I think, Bartok talks to Bartok and says to himself that he's got to fall back on sheer guts. Red River will come to him, he trusts it. But for now, he'll actually have to use the difficult hard-knocks lessons that he's learned in his more than difficult ill-spent life: Keep moving, smart guy, he tells himself, and make your choices without a map. He likes the sound of it. It's exactly what I'd have told him myself.

Bartok opens the hotel room door and parades into the hallway which is not the way he remembers it. First, it's in focus. Not like when he first entered and was half-carried to his room. Also, it's now got the dead flower smell of disinfectant mixed with the acid aroma of nausea and as Bartok walks along the rug and looks at his shoes—he realizes he's forgotten to put on socks. Doesn't matter. He only has to get to the elevator. Then to the lobby. Then to the street. And then he has to decide what the fuck to do…

The elevator bank is ahead of him like a glimpse of the Emerald City except they're more a series of doors that seem to be made out of old doilies, like the yellowish wallpaper that ends with the white of the room doors. Apparently, he's on the ninth floor because as Bartok stumbles along he can read the room numbers—9003, 9002, 9001—and he has a quick mind flash that when he gets caught and locked up, one of those numbers could be his new name. When he hits the turn in the hallway he goes to the left and there, in front of him, is the bank of elevators. One opens with that elevator door sound that to Bartok is a little like a medieval torture device and the timing is almost too perfect. As soon as it opens, a room service man comes out with two uniformed police officers and they all hustle past. Bartok is thinking—like me—about Marx Brothers movies.

Bartok twists out of the way, so that he has to catch his balance and then too loud and friendly he says, "Hello there!" The room service man turns around. Maybe he's responding to Bartok's jacket. Maybe to the hearty hello. He squints, wants to say something but whatever he's doing doesn't really matter because Bartok does a comic big step into the elevator just as the doors close and it pauses, clatters, makes some kind of electric sound, then begins its descent to the lobby. Bartok begins to giggle. He's giggling in a hundred different images of himself because the elevator is lined with mirrors. When he finally calms down, Bartok gets a funhouse full view of himself in a million different angles, like he's already been torn limb-from-limb and he stops without thinking of stopping and then sees a million Bartoks who giggle then snivel, then make funny faces as he looks at all these clown-dressed, badly scarred, doomed man reflections. For some reason, just standing there, he knows he's fucked.

That was how he looked the first time I saw him.

A sleepwalker with bumblebee eyes, he stepped out of the hotel and into the street like he was cutting through a wheat field. He didn't know where he was situated and he didn't really care. Maybe the noise got to him. The lights, maybe, that'll do it to you if you've been inside too long. You shrink into yourself and your skin gets all quiet and your ears start to hum and then suddenly you're in the land of barking horns and taxis and streetlights and headlights like the marks after a whipping. It's a total hoot, if you're up for it but if not, then you're a short order for the doctor's little white pills or shock treatment. That was Bartok. The first time I saw him.

There was that one uncomfortable moment down there on the street when Florette yelled, "Yeah! Yeah! That's him! That's who did it!" and one of the boys, either Nick or Ray, said, "Are you sure, Florette? 'Cause this guy here, he looks like he'd pop himself off by accident before anybody fucking else." It was funny because later we heard on the radio that the cops were looking for a guy in a clown suit.

"I did like they said, this wasn't my idea," Florette was saying, but this guy Bartok didn't seem to hear any of it and I said to her, "Mazel tov, pumpkin, you got a third eye for finding suckers."

"It was him, not me," she said.

"Well, I think you might have fucked it up just a bit," I said and gave her a little pat on the tush. Somebody moved Florette away and got her into a car and later I heard she made out okay, they only got a little pissed off.

The boys took Bartok into my car without a fight. One had one arm, one had his other arm, Ray and Nicky bent him into the back of the limo so that he was sitting between them. The thing I remember most is that from the very first moment, Bartok really did look like he'd wandered out of some circus that had left town without him and also that up close, any part of his skin was roughed up permanently and big-time. Pink like melted candy. His face was something special, though, handsome even, actually more than handsome. I wondered whether it hurt to live that way. And I was sorry— and I was only sorry sometimes—that we had to drive this poor, dumb fucker over the bridge to Jersey where the last thing he'd see would be that empty marsh that smelled like you'd been sitting in a sewer and the city all around in the background like haunted lights.

They didn't have to do anything to him in the car. He didn't even seem frightened. That was the weird thing. He sat there sort of like he was waiting for the movie to begin and then as we headed towards the bridge he started talking about "Red River" which none of us understood until I said, "You mean the cowboy movie?"

Then he really started talking. Nonstop. He talked every solid minute of the whole long, smooth trip. That's how I found out about Bartok and Red River and how I made up the parts I'm guessing about—and all of it's got me wondering how Bartok was when it all ended for him, finally. See, I like to listen to the guys we take in the car because really, when you come to think of it, there's not much else to do. You sit, you drive, you listen and you take them where they're going. No return trip, maybe, but you meet a lot of interesting people. After a while, you don't try to catch the meaning of the words, you're not rummaging around for anything too smart. You hear them talk and pretty soon, it's just like turning on the radio and listening to music.

"Maybe if I hadn't been me, it would be easier to be me," Bartok said. He was staring out the window, which was funny, I guess, 'cause we'd had the windows tinted dark.

We got over the bridge and found our usual spot and I watched from the car as they took Bartok away into the marsh and he was still talking and talking and probably—Red River, poor jerk, can you believe it?—probably he was talking all the way to the end, even after I couldn't hear him anymore and I guess he didn't see the point in shutting up, not then, not for a moment. Bartok was heading into the marsh with all his scars. I can say this much—he seemed like an all right guy. I liked him. It got real quiet. I was thinking that it was something like the quiet Bartok was describing to us, like when you're in a room with the dead. Then I heard two shots. Well, okay. That's that. And I'm thinking that, just like the rest of us, he probably never knew what hit him.

JAMMED

TIM D'MARA

For my in-laws,
Les and Cynthia Bushmann

"I oughta shoot you where you stand."

I know, but I swear to God, that's exactly what he said. With all I'd been through in the past day and a half, I almost laughed, and I woulda, except he had this huge-ass gun pointed at my face. I guess all guns look big when they're pointed at you. Forget about it being the biggest cliché in the world, but I was *sitting* at the time. In his pickup truck. A beautiful red pickup truck. I tell ya, if ya ever commit a crime in the Midwest, make sure your getaway vehicle's a red pickup truck. Soon as you hit the highway, you'll blend in like a sore thumb in a podiatrist's office. A sore toe is more like it, but I don't know what they call hand doctors, so...whatever. You know what I mean.

Truth be told, I was surprised he said anything to me at all. If I was him, *I'da* shot my ass before I got into his truck. Make sure I didn't get any blood on the seats. That's if I was him. Me? I couldn't shoot someone who wasn't trying to shoot me. Or maybe trying to hurt a loved one, I guess, y'know? I especially couldn't shoot someone who comes to a gunfight with a set of keys, which is all I had on me when I got in his truck. That, my driver's license, and an expired credit card. I think back on it, if I *did* laugh, it woulda been more than likely my last laugh. My momma used to say, "He who laughs last, laughs best."

She'da been wrong this time, though. He who laughed last mighta got his ass blown all the way to hell.

Anyway, that was Cook talking, the guy I got my meth from. I screwed up trying to go big league with him. I shoulda learned my lesson and stayed small time and just kept on going with the flow. Sitting next to Cook, in the back seat of the pickup, was that guy Robert who owned the ranch, and was gonna pay me, Elmore, and Mickey to drive those illegal cigarettes to Illinois. You know things are going to shit when three guys ride out and only two ride back. Somebody wrote a song like that a buncha years ago. The Byrds? The Eagles, maybe?

So, there I am in the back of a pickup, sitting across from Cook and Robert, and I very slowly reach behind me and pull out the money I owed them. What I had left of it, anyway. Robert took it and did that thing like he was weighing it in his hands, letting me know that had the deal gone the way it was supposed to, he'd be holding a lot more money than I'd just given him, we'd be talking about the next deal, and I wouldn't have a gun sticking in my face.

Nobody talked for a few minutes and I sure as shit wasn't gonna be the first one to strike up a conversation. I could tell they were both deciding what to do with me and none of the things I came up with in my head were good. Next thing I know, they both take out their phones and start texting. That confused the shit out of me, but after a little while it dawned on me—the way Cook texted and then Robert's phone would ding and then he'd text and Cook's phone would ding—that they were texting each other. *More than likely about me.* Here we are, sitting in the parking lot of a rundown rummy joint and they're sending messages up to space that ricochet off the satellites back down to earth just so they can talk about me *in private* three feet front of me. I guess once they had me in the van, they didn't want to let me out of their sight. Can't say I blame them, as every time I *was* outta their sight the last two days, the proverbial poop hit the blades.

After a few minutes of this, they both put their phones away and Robert says to me, "Boy, you musta been born under a lucky star because this is your fortunate day." He and Cook grin and shake their heads.

I take a deep swallow before I can speak and then I say, "How's that?"

"Turns out," Cook says, "we are one driver short tonight and we don't have the time to find a decent replacement at this hour." It was almost eleven on Saturday night, in case I didn't mention that.

I felt my heart start to slow down a bit and I was able to control my breathing somewhat. Again, I took a little time before talking. Sometimes I say things when I'm excitable and they come out wrong and get me in trouble. I wanted to be real careful this time around. I did that breathing thing my ex taught me before I spoke.

"I can drive," I said.

They both laughed. I thought I was in trouble again for a few seconds. "We know you can drive, boy," Robert said. Then he looked at me and said, "What's your name again? Aggie?"

I nodded, deciding to go along with the nickname I'd acquired over the past two days. I figured the fewer things I talked about, the better.

"We know you can drive, *Aggie*," Robert said again. "It's what happens when you get out of your vehicle that concerns us."

"None of that was my fault," I blurted out, and right away wished I hadn't. I sounded like a middle-school kid making excuses.

Cook leans forward, his gun on his lap, but still pointed at me. "We lost a whole shipment of smokes when you decided to pull over into that rest area." (That was not my idea, but I kept my mouth shut.) "Then," Cook says, "Mickey gets himself killed when you get to the drop off outside Chicago." (Again, not my fault, but these guys were not in the mood for excuses.) "Finally," Cook goes on, "you get back here and it turns out your new partner is working with the feds, and we lose out on what was supposed to be a nice payoff all around." He looked at his gun again and started slapping it against his thigh. I was scared as shit that it was gonna go off accidentally on purpose if you know what I mean. I closed my eyes and waited for one of them to start talking again. It was Robert.

"So, here's the new deal, Aggie," he says. "You're gonna get what most people never do: a second chance." Then he gets this look on his face and says, "Who was it who said there are no second acts in America? Was that Steinbeck? Anyway, if it was up to me and my friend here, we'd just as soon shoot you and dump your body into the river and let the fish have at ya. But..." And here's where he does that dramatic pause 'cause he's in complete control at the moment. I got the feeling this guy watched a lot of movies—obviously he read books or how else would he know what Steinbeck said, right?—which made me think we'd be friends under other circumstances. He ends the pause by saying, "...we need a driver right now and you're our only choice."

Again, they were silent for a bit, but not as long this time.

"You got your license on you?" Cook asked.

I told him I did and I patted my front right pocket.

"And it says you can drive a truck, right?"

I nodded and said, "I got a CDL. A commercial driver's license. It's good for any state in the United. Had it renewed last year." I was about to tell him I needed it for the construction gig I had on the side, but he interrupted me.

"Least you're good for something," he said.

Now, a lotta times a comment like that would sound like an insult, but when it comes from a guy pointing a small cannon at ya? It comes across like a compliment. At that point Robert leans forward, over my shoulder, and taps on the glass. The Mexican turns around and Robert says *Avanza,* which I think means "drive" because that's what the Mexican does and we're back out on the road.

I was curious as to where we were going, but I was clearly

in no position to ask, so I just kept shut. Cook and Robert went back to texting, but this time it wasn't to each other 'cause I didn't hear their phones going off. After about five minutes of this, Robert turns to Cook and says, "Fitzgerald" and Cook says who the fuck's Fitzgerald, and Robert says that's the guy who said that thing about there being no second acts in America. I guess he Googled it. He gets back to business by saying, "Our guys are expecting us. Just over the bridge by the golf course."

Cook nodded. "New York's ready. I told him to expect a new guy." He turned his phone, aimed it me, and took my picture. Then he pressed some buttons and said, "Now they know what he looks like."

"New York?" I said. "The city?" I asked that because New York's a big state. You say New York and you could mean the part that touches Canada or you could mean the city. They both nod and I say, "I haven't been there since my dad took us to see the Christmas show at Radio City."

"Yeah, well," Robert said. "You're not gonna be there long enough to take in a show this time, Aggie. You'll be lucky if you get a chance to pick up a hoagie—excuse me, a *hero*—and then head on back." He looked at his watch. "The drive'll take you sixteen and a half hours. Let's round that up to seventeen, so you can take a pee break or two and account for any traffic. It's just over a thousand miles, so watch your speed and drive accordingly. Last thing we need is a repeat of what happened with the smokes at that rest area or you getting pulled over for speeding."

I wanted to remind him that "what happened with the smokes at that rest area" was his fault for giving us a truck to move bootleg cigarettes that also was used to transport ammonium nitrate. That's a fertilizer that's also used to make homemade explosives. *Oklahoma City, anybody?* That's what the cop dog smelled, not the cigs. But I didn't say it. What I did say was, "When do you expect me back?"

Robert looked at his watch again and said, "You'll be on the road by midnight." He closed his eyes and moved his lips, but I couldn't hear anything. After about a minute, he said, "Seventeen hours to get there, four or five hours to unload and then reload, seventeen hours back, that's thirty-nine hours. We can round that up to forty and say you have to be back here...at four o'clock Monday afternoon."

I looked over at Cook, who was working the buttons on his phone, nodded, and said, "That's good. Four o'clock, Monday. P.M."

That's when I started doing the math in my head—which I'm good at if it's below triple digits and doesn't involve division or fractions—and it seemed pretty tight to me. Cook musta been able to read my face, because he says, "That a problem, Aggie?"

I took another big swallow and said basically that forty hours didn't seem like a lot of time, especially with all that can go wrong on a round trip to New York City.

He looks at me and smiles. So does Robert. Then Robert leans forward and says, "Why don't you think of it as forty extra hours we're giving you to breathe, huh, Aggie. Unless you wanna say no right now and our business with you will be concluded? No second act for you."

"Nah, nah, nah" I say. "I can do it." Then I take a chance and say, "Can we work in a couple of hours for me to sleep?" I thought back over the last two days where I hadn't even come close to a bed, and then added in the next forty hours, and say, "With the past couple of days, it's gonna be about four days with me getting no sleep, is what I'm saying. Kinda dangerous me being on the road behind the wheel of a truck all sleep deprived and all. That's how most truck-related accidents happen," I add, sounding like I knew this for a fact. "Sleep deprivation."

We had just made the turn onto the bridge when Cook said, "We'll give ya something to help you stay awake. Sorta like that NoDoz crap they sell in the stores, except this stuff isn't over-the-counter." He tapped his nose with his index finger. "If ya know what I mean."

I did, and I was not happy with it. Not like I was in any position to bargain here, but I hadn't put anything up my nose except for decongestants in about three years. But, like they say, "When the guy holding the gun tells you to do something, do it." I don't know who said it, *exactly*, but I'm sure someone did. Maybe it was Fitzgerald.

At this point, we're almost off the bridge and I start thinking about my daughter Brooklyn, my ex, and my ex's new guy Elmore, or whatever his name really is. If everything worked out, by this time they shoulda been under the protection of the feds and that Witness Protection Program they got. That made me feel a lot better about this whole thing, and now that I had the possibility of making it through this shit storm alive, I counted it as a blessing.

Lucky me, huh?

So we cross the bridge and head over in the direction of the river access and the bike trail. We make the right toward the golf course and pull over to where a couple of semis are sitting side-by-side. "Out," Robert says, and I get out. He and Cook get out behind me and I notice Cook slips his gun behind his back. That's when he gives me a weird look and says, "C'mere."

I step over to him and he spins me around, and starts running his hands up and down my body. They'd forgotten to frisk me the whole time I was in their ride. Not that I thought of packing a piece, but it's not like Cook to miss a detail like that. Anyway, after I come up clean and he relieves me of my cell phone, he pushes me in the direction of the first semi. There's a guy behind it, twirling a set of keys, giving me the once-over.

"This," he says to Cook and Robert, "is the other driver?" Like he's done evaluating me after looking at me for all of five seconds. Cook says, yeah, and the guy with the keys clocks me and says, "He's a fucking pot dealer. He sold to me when I was over at the college."

Then this guy with the keys steps up to me and gets about as close as he can to my face without actually kissing me. He's got this weird combination coming out of his mouth; it's like cigarette, spearmint, and coffee. Three things I like separately, but when you put them together like that, in a guy's mouth, not so much. Keys then reaches behind himself like he's about to pull something out—I'm thinking gun at this point, judging by how the evening's gone so far—but he just leaves his hand back there. I take a slow step back.

Now, I'm pretty good with faces, but I've sold to hundreds of smokers over at the colleges the past five or so years. I look at this guy and I do not remember his face. But after all, I've had hundreds of customers in my job, how many dealers has he had?

"Well," Robert says, "for the next coupla days and nights, he's a pot dealer who's driving to pay off a debt. And at this hour, we can't be choosy."

Any other time, I tell ya, my feelings mighta been hurt. But if all I had to do was haul their truck to New York City, unload and reload, and bring it back by Monday afternoon, I was not going to question the situation. Keys gives me a look and shakes his head like, "Whatever." Screw him, right? From where I was standing, we both were doing the same job that night. And he's gonna judge me? Shit.

So Robert dangles a set of keys in front of my face and asks me again if I'm sure I can handle the rig. "I've driven bigger," I say, which may or may not have been true—more likely not—but what the hell? A truck's a truck, right? It's a bit bigger than the one I was hauling the cigarettes in, but if I could handle that one, this one didn't seem to pose any new problems. Just to show him how confident I am, I hold out my hand, flat like this. He looks at it for a few seconds and then drops the keys into it.

Then Cook speaks up again. He reaches out his hand and says, "Here," and gives me my cell phone back, only it ain't my cell phone. It's much lighter and shinier. It somehow didn't look as smart as the one he'd taken from me. He points to the phone and says, "That's how you communicate with us." He then goes on to tell me that I'm expected to check in every three hours on the way there and every three hours on the way back. He also tells me the phone's equipped with GPS so they know where I am at all times. So the phone, like my dad once said about me, was smarter than it looked. If they know where I am at all times, I'm thinking, why do I hafta call in all the time? I don't ask, in case you wanna know. I'm also expected to turn that phone over to the guy in New York, and he's gonna give me a new one. These guys are smart, I tell ya. Anyone's tracking the phone on the way there is gonna be shit outta luck tracking it on the way back. It'll probably end up in the Hudson River after I'm done with it.

After I put the phone in my pocket, Robert brings me around to the back of the truck and signals the other driver to raise the door. He unlocks it and lifts it up like he's some kinda game show host showing me what I've won. I take a look inside and my eyes can't make out shit in the light, just a whole lotta white, but when they adjust I see barrels. White barrels and they're stacked three high and go all the way to the front of the trailer. I figure there's three rows, stacked three high, and they go back maybe ten in each row, that makes ninety barrels.

Of what? I wanna know. But again, I don't ask. If they wanted me to know, they woulda told me. I'm thinking oil or maybe one of the ingredients that goes into making crystal meth: battery acid, acetone, antifreeze. I'm hoping it's not ammonium nitrate because that's one of the main reasons I'm in this position.

Cook looks at me and says, "Maple syrup." Then he smiles

and says, like he's talking about cocaine or something, "Pure grade, straight from Canada." That's when I remember reading in the paper about some Canadian trucks that were supposed to deliver a buncha maple syrup to a refinery up in Minnesota that never made it. I remember thinking that's a dumbass thing to steal, pancake syrup, except when the article says that a barrel of this real maple shit is worth about fifteen hundred to eighteen hundred bucks. So I'm looking at—and here's where my mental math skills come in handy—about one-hundred-and-thirty-five to a hundred-fifty thousand dollars of that sweet stuff.

Shit, right? First I'm dragging cigarettes across state lines because of the excise tax profit, and now I'm bringing Canada's Finest one thousand miles to the east. And it hits me again that there is a boatload of money to be made in *legal* shit.

Between the Marlboro Man, Mrs. Butterworth, and Aunt Jemima, I could forget about pot and meth and make a fortune with these guys. Except, I'm not. Making a fortune. I'm just moving shit from here to there, helping *these guys* make a fortune. Made me wonder what I'd be bringing back from the great state of New York—maybe pancake mix—but I figure if they wanted me to know, they'da told me.

Robert takes back the phone he gave me, punches a few buttons, and then hands it back to me. Now I'm looking at a map. "That's where you're going," he says. "The west side of New York City." I look closer at the map and do that two-finger thing that lets me zoom in and out, and sure enough, there's the Hudson River and there's a big old red pin. He takes the phone again, presses another button and says, "And here's the route you'll be taking. No diversions, no short cuts, no visits to your cousin in Pennsylvania." I'm about to ask him how he knew about my cousin in Altoona, but he says, "Forty hours. There and back." Then he gets this grin on his face and says, "If you're late, Aggie, you're gonna be the *late* Aggie."

Well, he and Cook think that's the funniest thing ever and even Keys starts to join in, so I figure, why not, and I start laughing a bit. That's when Cook reaches into his pocket and pulls out a buncha bills. "For gas and tolls and shit," he says. I count it out and it's ten hundreds. A thousand bucks for the round trip. I have no idea what kind of mileage this rig gets, but I'm guessing they do, because they seem to have all this figured out. So, I pocket the bills and say, "Is the tank full?"

Keys says to me, "Of the course the tank is full, *Aggie*. You'll refuel when I do. In fact, you don't piss until I do." He then goes over to his truck and comes back with a walkie-talkie. He throws it to me and says, "That's how *you and I* are gonna keep in touch on the road. Just like a couple of Boy Scouts."

I look at the thing and it's a helluva lot more impressive than the one I had in high school when I was doing that bird watching thing so I could hang around that Lottie chick. She liked birds and I figured if I could get her in the woods…never happened. This one's got like four channels and one for the weather. I ask him what happens if we're outta range of each other.

"That happens?" Keys says, "Then you ain't keeping up with me and that's gonna pose a problem. You don't wanna pose no problems."

What if I did pose a problem? I'm thinking. I mean, what if I gotta take a big old piss and can't reach Keys on the walkie and we get separated? What're they gonna do? Kill me? It's just me and him, and I'm assuming we both gotta get to New York 'n back in the same forty hours, based on what Keys just told me. Not for nothin', but if they off me, then they're back to being one driver short with a truckload of maple syrup sitting somewhere, and all this's been for shit. It's not like they can kill me on the road, either. If they had the manpower for that, they wouldn'ta needed me in the first place.

See, all this shit is going through my mind, but I don't say anything. Let them think I'm just some dumb hillbilly living on the Redneck Riviera in his dad's house with barely a thought in my head. I'm not saying that I planned on fuckin' up, but if I did, even I can see that their opportunities to punish me were limited. At least at this point. I guess they could always make me pay for any transgressions when I got back, but for the next forty hours—like Robert said—they had to keep me breathing to drive.

After Keys makes his little threat, Cook makes a big deal outta looking at his watch and says, "Time to hit the road, boys." Then he reaches into his other pocket and pulls out what looks like a dime bag to me. He steps over and hands it to me and I see it's a buncha pills. Blue ones. I give him a look, like "What's up?" and he explains to me that those are the extra-pharmaceuticals he was telling me about that'll keep me from falling asleep on the job. He shakes the bag a bit and says, "There's ten of 'em."

"So I don't gotta put any shit up my nose?" I ask. That makes him laugh and he says that that was just an expression. He also tells me not to take more than one every four hours. "You do that and you better make sure you got your seatbelt on," he says and laughs like now *that's* the funniest thing anyone ever said. This guy loves to laugh, I tell you that? I just stick the bag in my shirt pocket and tell him I'm cool.

Robert comes over to me and gives me an envelope. He says, "Here's your billa laden." Now, I'm so tired and still a bit scared, and I think he says, "Osama bin Laden." So I open up the envelope and there's one sheet of paper. I scan it for a few seconds and realize he'd said it's the *bill of lading*, which is just a piece of paperwork saying what I'm carrying and how much of it I'm carrying. I look at the paper more closely and it clearly says I'm hauling maple syrup. Robert musta seen the look on my face 'cause then he says, "It's gotta say maple syrup, Aggie. If you get pulled over and the bill says you're carrying...I don't know...custom-made furniture, and they decide they wanna check out the back, and they find maple syrup, you're gonna have some serious explaining to do. This way it looks as legit as it can get. Those are my barrels back there. It may not be my syrup, but they're my barrels, and possession is nine-tenths of the law, as they say." I heard that nine-tenths thing very recently and it reminded me of how much I hate fractions. Anyway...

Robert says again that it's time to go, and what with it being ten minutes to midnight, I mighta just bought myself an extra piss stop on the way. Again, lucky me, right? So they walk me to the cab of the truck, tell me that the registration is attached to the visor, and remind me to stick to no more than five miles over the speed limit.

"Nice cab," I say. And it is. Plenty of room for two folks up front and what looks like a decent-size space to sleep in the back. Hadda a friend back in high school whose parents drove an eighteen-wheeler cross-country. They told him that him and his three siblings were all conceived in truck stops somewhere between Los Angeles and Pittsburgh. (Which explains why their names were Reno, Cheyenne, Lincoln, and Cleveland.) Too much information, if you ask me, but it does go to show how much room those sleepers got. Robert must've read my mind because he tells me not to even think about checking out the sleeper section. "You do that and you're gonna get ideas about using it and you don't wanna get those ideas, Aggie."

"Y'also don't wanna get pulled over for speeding with all that sweet stuff in the back now," he says. "Y'also might wanna know that we checked and the weather between here and the Big Apple is supposed to be uneventful the next coupla days. So make sure you stick to the plan, keep calling us every three hours, and watch the pills and the clock and the road. No excuses."

"What about weigh stations?" I ask. And he nods like that was a smart question. "Don't worry about them none," he says. "Most states don't require them and I've only had a few drivers get pulled over for not stopping at them. Ask ten highway cops about weigh stations and you're bound to get ten different answers. You just drive right on by and stick to our schedule."

I tell him I understand and he reminds me I seemed to understand the last time we had a deal and that's what led to this time. I stick out my hand and tell him—I swear these were my exact words—"You can count on me." He grips my hand tight and pulls me in to him, real close. "This ain't no job interview, boy. This is you beginning to make it up to me, and maybe you making it through the week." I didn't like that word *beginning* but I kept quiet about that. I just assumed this was a one-time thing, but you know what my dad used to say about assuming. And I was in no position to make an ass outta anyone. Then he really squeezes my hand and says, "We clear about this?"

I try not to show that my hand is hurting and I take a deep breath and give him my best Tom Cruise smile. "Crystal," I say to him, just like Tom did in that movie with Jack Nicholson. Well, he gives me a look like he's wondering what my nose might taste like, lets go a my hand and says, "Get the fuck going."

So I do.

I wait until Keys gets in his truck and watch as he pulls off the dirt road onto the asphalt. He's done this before, I can tell. I don't do it as smooth as he does, but I pull out and I follow him out onto the route that's gonna take us to the Interstate. I'm rather familiar with this road 'cause it's the one I used to take to Fulton, which has two colleges, and therefore, lots of people who were in need of my drug-procuring services. Students and professors. Now I remember Keys. He was a janitor at one of those schools. One of them colleges is the one where Winston Churchill gave his "Iron Curtain" speech back in the day. There's a big monument and museum there.

It was such a big deal because that was when we *really* started to hate the Russians and Communism, and we had all that Cold War stuff. They had the big bomb, we had the big bomb. Enough fire power to blow up the world about ten times. Shit, it's amazing we're all still here, ya think about it.

There's also a pretty cool used bookstore in that town and a place that sells the best pizza I've ever had except for that time we went to New York City. That got me thinking about my daughter Brooklyn again. She's so used to the crap in this town calling itself pizza, I make sure I take her—took her, I guess—a coupla times a year to taste what real pizza should taste like. I didn't think I'd be getting to visit any of that stuff this time around.

Ya got a napkin? I think I got something in my eye. Thanks. Yeah, that's it. Anyway...

It takes us a half hour to get to the Interstate and there's this truck stop there that always makes me think Las Vegas and Atlantic City had an illegitimate baby. You can probably see it from space it's so bright. They got like four gas stations and the biggest bull crap tourist shop between St. Louis and Kansas City. It's called Ozarkland and they sell all this shit like T-shirts, candy on a stick, snow globes with mountains in them. I've been in there before and for a place with a real American-sounding name, there wasn't one piece of crap that was made here in the U.S. Like we gotta outsource our crap-making to other countries. That's what this guy in the White House should be saying. "We can make touristy crap right here in America!" They also got a buncha bathrooms at this stop, which reminded me I shoulda gone before we got in the trucks, but now I'm gonna have to hold it until Mr. Keys up in fronta me decides he's gotta go.

On top of that, I realize I'm also starving. I can't remember the last time I ate, but I know it wasn't in the last twenty-four. I have had a few drinks, though. And here we are, passing by one of America's monuments to pissing, eating, and buying crap, and I gotta do two outta three of them things. I hope to God that Keys feels the same way, but apparently not, because we just cruise on by and hit the Interstate. Less than two hours to St. Louis if we keep to five miles over the speed limit, which I'm sure we're gonna do after getting that speech 'bout not getting pulled over.

So I figure I gotta keep my mind on other things. I hope to God again that this rig's got a radio in it and, brother, I am not disappointed. It's not only got one, it's got a satellite one. This is gonna work. So, I spend about five minutes flicking around and I find some Johnny Cash and I leave it there. He's singing about shooting a guy in Reno just to watch him die and I'm thinking, "I know how that feels, Johnny." 'Cause I can think of three men I'd like to shoot right now and one a them's driving about a hundred yards in fronta me. I probably wouldn't watch 'em die, though. I'd probably just shoot 'em just enough where they'd agree to leave me the fuck alone 'cause I really just wanna get on with my life.

I really am doin' the best I can. All this shit just seems to find me, y'know?

Anyways, that song ends and on comes "Ring of Fire," and I figure I landed on the all Johnny Cash channel, 'cept when that finishes they play "On the Road Again." Now is that funny, or what? Seems to me you can take any of life's situations and apply them to most country and western songs. Ya look at the last twenty-four hours of my life up to that point and tell me that wouldn't make some country star richer than he already is. If he sat down and wrote a song about it.

My ex-wife disappears into the Witness Protection Program with my daughter, my truck and her new boyfriend, who stole my crystal meth; my dog don't wanna speak to me anymore; I owe a couple of tough guys a buncha money I got no way of payin' back; they stick a gun in my face; and now I'm driving a semi full of product that don't belong to me one-third a the way across the United States of America.

I mean if that ain't worthy of the Grand Ole Opry, I don't know what is. I mean, what the hell else can happen, right?

And that's when the curtain to the sleeper area opens and I hear the sweetest little voice say, "Hey, Mister. Who the hell are you?"

Well, I doubt you ever done it—no offense—but trying to drive one a them big rigs is tough enough without getting the shit scared outta you when you're going seventy-five miles an hour on the Interstate. It was all I could do to keep all eighteen wheels on the road. After the initial shock, the voice behind me says, "Really. Who are you?" And I'm keeping my eyes on the road and tracking Keys in his truck in fronta me and I say, "Who the fuck are you?"

That's when the owner of the voice decides to crawl outta the sleeper and climb into the passenger seat. She had to be all of sixteen, blonde hair all over the place, and looking like she'd just waked up. She rubs her eyes and says, "Watch the language, Mister. My daddy doesn't like people to speak to me like that."

She pushed her hair back and I take a quick look at her and notice she's got these amazing blue eyes. She looks a bit familiar, but I got no idea why. She's too young to be one of my ex's friends and too old to be one of Brooklyn's play-mates, y'know? I take another look and then get my eyes back on the road.

"Who's your daddy?" I ask, and then realize how funny that sounds. I don't laugh, but the girl does. "Rigger, please" she says. "My daddy is your boss. So be nice."

I take a few seconds and think on that and say, "I don't have a boss, Sweetheart. I'm a"—and it takes me a bit to come up with the right words—"I'm an independent contractor." I liked the way that sounded and decided I'll use it again someday. I hoped.

Well, the girl starts laughing again and says, "Then whatchoo doin' driving one of my daddy's trucks, Mister Independent Contractor?"

Her daddy's truck? I'm thinking, Holy Shit, and say, "Robert is your father?"

She leans back into a stretch and says, "Yep. All my life. So ya might wanna be careful how you talk to the boss's daughter."

I look at her again and realize she's wearing a Lynyrd Skynyrd T-shirt and shorts that are cut so low they have their pockets showing. So now I'm thinking this is great: not only am I riding around with a bunch of smuggled syrup, I also got a minor girl in the cab with me. I'm about to pull over when I realize I've been instructed not to do exactly that. And the bridge is coming up. If I pull over now, I'm gonna lose Keys's truck for I don't know how long. Then, like she's reading my mind, the girl tells me to keep driving.

"Over the bridge," she says. "I love to look down at the Missouri River."

Now, before I go on, I wanna point out that just before the river is this casino I used to go to. Right on the water. I think it's some kinda law that casinos out here have to be along a river or actually *on the water*. Like on a riverboat, or something. Anyway, I used to go to this one a lot because it was close, and I could sell some product in the parking lot to help pay for my losses, but most of all because I had a serious crush on this blackjack dealer. She was about the prettiest female I have ever laid eyes on. She had this long dark hair, skin like a cup of coffee with half-and-half, and brown eyes that I know distracted their share of card players. My guess was that she was Native American, but looking back she mighta been Hispanic 'cause her name was Corazon, which means "heart" in Spanish.

Well, I'll tell ya, Corazon was named right. She was the Queen of Hearts in my book and that's where the ironic—no, not ironic, more paradoxical, coincidental, something like that—part comes in. I was way ahead one night after weeks of losing. I mean I was so up, one more winning hand woulda erased all my losses for the year and put me up a couple hundred. So I'm at her table—I was always at her table—and I get a king and a deuce. The worst. Now I'm thinking about sticking 'cause Corazon's showing a jack and a five, which means she's got to hit, y'know, anything under sixteen and she has to draw another card. So I figure the odds are in my favor. Then I'm thinking, not so much, because twelve's such a shitty number and it's an unlucky number for me in particular, if you wanna know the truth.

I'm not a superstitious guy by nature, but when I look back on my life, twelve just ain't been all that kind to me. The guy I was pitching to when I blew out my arm and my chances for a baseball scholarship? Wore number twelve on his jersey. My mom died when I was twelve on December twelfth, which is twelve/twelve when you write it out. There's a coupla other examples, but I won't bore ya. Just take my word for it: twelve and me do not get along.

So, after some deliberation, I decide to hit on twelve. I shut my eyes I was so nervous and when I opened them back up, there was a queen sitting on my king's face, and not in the good way. And wouldn't ya know it, it was the queen of diamonds, which is from my favorite Eagles song, *Desperado*. Where the guy's warning you about don't draw the queen of diamonds 'cause she'll beat you if she's able. Well, she was able and she beat me like an unwanted puppy. Corazon looks at me with those big beautiful brown eyes and says something I'll never forget. "Better luck next time, sir." It wasn't the "better luck next time" that got me. It was the "sir" part. She forgot—or never cared to remember—my name. I took that as a sign from above to quit gambling and haven't been back inside a casino since. I still sell some product outside in the parking lots sometimes, but I don't go in anymore. Too many bad memories.

Well, back to more recent history, I just keep driving and

we're over the river. In fact, I got so lost in thought, we were now crossing over the Mississippi and it really is an impressive thing to see and think about all its history, Mark Twain and that stuff—and, just like that, we're in Illinois.

The girl leans forward into another stretch and says to the floor, "Now we've crossed state lines, Mister Indie Contractor. How familiar are you with the law about that?"

Now I feel my stomach starting to try and climb up my esophagus. I do not know the law about this, but I got the feeling this girl does and I'm about to get schooled.

"Interstate transportation with intent to engage in criminal sexual activity," she says. She lets that hang in the air for about fifteen seconds, and then I say, "How old are you, anyway?"

She says, "I'm gonna be sixteen in three months."

Now that's another thing I hate. I specifically asked her how old *she was* not how old *she's gonna be* in three months. Just say, "I'm fifteen," right? I mean you ask someone how much money they got on them, they don't say, "If I had five more dollars, I'd have twenty bucks." They say they have fifteen dollars. Jesus.

Well, I gotta tell ya, for the first time in a long time, I am speechless. One time was the first time I laid eyes on my ex-wife and another was when I watched Brooklyn being born. There was also that time in Kansas City when I shook Dale Earnhardt's hand, but those were all good things, y'know? Now, I'm like speechless 'cause I literally don't know what to say. Well, she does.

"I know, I know," she says. "You didn't know I was in the back of the cab and you surely had no intention of having criminal sex with me. And that's a good, true story. But who's the victim here? The older guy driving some stolen maple syrup across state lines—that's another federal offense, by the way—or is it the fifteen-year-old, blonde-haired, blue-eyed farm girl? I know who the cops are gonna believe and I sure as shit know who my daddy's gonna hold responsible." And then she adds in her innocent little voice, "Excuse my language."

Man, I thought things were bad an hour ago. I don't remember ever being in this kinda situation before. I mean, I am jammed up, brother. Before I can even think what to say, the girl looks over at me and says, "I'm Charlene. What's your name, mister?"

I tell her Aggie and she asks if that's my real name. I tell her no and she says, "Well, what's your real name?"

"If it's all the same to you," I say, "just call me Aggie." With all else that's going on, I do not need this girl knowing my legal name.

"Okay, Aggie," she says. "Keep driving. You're doing great so far."

So we're like that for a few miles and then I finally get myself together enough to speak. "Whatta you want, Charlene?" I ask her.

She laughs and says, "I thought it was obvious, Aggie. I want a free ride to New York City. And thanks to you and my daddy, I'm gettin' it."

Lucky me *again*, right? Not only do I get to be a syrup smuggler, I'm now also an eighteen-wheel Uber driver. Charlene settles in, makes herself comfy in the big passenger seat, even kicks off her shoes and puts her bare feet up on the dash. She looks at me and says, "When're we gonna stop for food? I'm like starving over here."

"Ya see that guy way up there?" I said, pointing at the truck Keys is driving. "It's all up to him. Your daddy says I gotta do exactly what he does, exactly when he does it."

Charlene seems to take that in and after a few seconds says, "You must have screwed up bad there, Aggie." I ask her what she means by that and she says, "My daddy's treating you like his slave." She tells me there's another word she coulda used, but she doesn't like that word, but it rhymes with itch. "I've seen him do this before. Somebody he hires messes up and he makes them do what he likes to call 'penance.'" She looks up ahead at the other truck and says, "Is that Cornell up there?"

I tell her I don't know the other guy's name and she says it's probably Cornell. "He screwed Daddy a coupla years ago on a cattle deal. Daddy turned him into a driver and now that's what he does."

"A couple of years ago?" I ask. "How long does your daddy make people do this penance thing?" She tells me about a year or so, but some of them work out so good where they start working for him regular. So now I start thinking maybe this'll work out for me. If I don't screw this trip up—and that's not gonna happen—maybe I can start working with Robert. He's got his fingers in a lot of pies, right?

I look over at Charlene and say, "Why New York?" She says, "Supposed to be the greatest city in the world, right? I mean that's what you hear people on TV say, and I bet those people haven't even been to every city in the world, so where do they come off saying New York's the greatest? It's like all those people my daddy knows who voted for this orange guy we got for president, saying America is the greatest country in the world. How the hell do they know? Have they ever been to France? Italy? Morocco? Probably not, but they keep saying it like they know what they're talking about."

I tell ya, this kid may've been only fifteen, but she had some real strong opinions about stuff. But she really didn't answer my question. So I ask her again, "Why New York City?"

She gives me a big old grin, rubs her hands across her thighs, and says, "You're taking me to meet my boyfriend."

Now I'm thinking, *Oh shit, this is exactly the definition of screwing up.* I'm driving an underage girl across state lines to meet her boyfriend in New York. Now, I don't know this family all that much, but from what I do know about her daddy, somehow I know this ain't gonna earn me bonus pay.

"How do you have a boyfriend from New York?" I ask

her. She laughs. "I didn't say he's *from* New York, Aggie. I said I'm gonna meet him in New York."

Great, right? So now we're playing word games. "Where's he from?" I ask. She tells me he's from Florida, so again, I ask how she met a boyfriend from Florida. I'm expecting her to say they met on a family trip at Disney or Epcot or something. But, no. She says, "I never said I *met* him. I said I'm *gonna* meet him." And I'm like, What? How the hell can he be her boyfriend if they never met, right?

"We met online," she says. "On a website that people who really love riding horses go on and talk about horse stuff. Their favorite breeds, favorite styles of riding, stuff like that. It's called Hot To Trot dot com." Then she looks at me and says, "Pretty clever, huh?"

Oh, yeah, I'm thinking. Pretty fuckin' clever. She doesn't even know what "hot to trot" means, and I am not gonna be the one who schools her on that particular point.

"So," I say, just to keep the conversation going, "what's your boyfriend's name?"

"Moe," she says. And I'm like, "*Moe*? You mean like from the Three Stooges Moe?" And she looks at me like I'm speaking French. "Who the hell are the Three Stooges?" she says. "A rock group old people listen to?"

I'm not in the mood at this point to explain who the Three Stooges are, so I just say, "This kid's parents named him Moe?"

I get this look like I'm the slow one now. "No, Aggie," she says. "His real name's Mohammed. He calls himself Moe for short."

"Mohammed?" I say and before I can even get another word in she's all like "Don't get started on the Muslim thing. They're people just like us. His family's been in America for a long time and they're real Americans just like the Christians, the Jews, the Mormons." She pauses and adds, "Maybe the Mormons."

We're quiet for about a half minute, I check out the exit sign and make sure I've still got Keys in my line of sight. I do. Then I say, "Let me guess. Your parents don't know about Moe?"

She laughs. "Oh, yeah. They know all about my Muslim boyfriend from Florida that I met online. You think I'm crazy, Aggie? If they knew about him, they'd lock me in my room and homeschool me until I was outta college. My daddy thinks all Muslims are terrorists, even though he doesn't know any personally. Except maybe that guy who owns the liquor store in town."

Now, I know the guy who owns the liquor store, and he's not a Muslim. He's from India and he's a Hindu. I tell Charlene that and she shrugs and says, "Whatever."

I tell her I'm guessing Moe's family doesn't know about her, either, and she says I'm right about that. "How's he getting to New York?" I ask. "Is he hiding in the back of some truck, too?" She gives me a fake laugh and says that he's taking the train up. They've been texting and he's already in Carolina. I ask her which one, and she says, "There's more than one?" Then she gives me a look to let me know she's kidding and says, "North. He's got about fifteen hours to go." I look at the clock on the dashboard and say, "That's about what we got, too."

Which reminds me that I should probably take one of those pills Cook gave me but I'm not real tired yet. I'm thinking I still gotta pee—worse than before, but I've been distracted, y'know—and I could really go for some food. I look down at the walkie-talkie in between me and Charlene and start visualizing it coming to life with Keys's voice telling me it's time to pull over. And, damn, it does.

Keys comes on and says, "*Next service area, Aggie. We're gonna make a pit stop. You're gonna get ten minutes to do what you gotta do in the men's room and get yourself something to eat. We'll gas up later. Ten minutes. No more, no less.*"

We pull in together, we pull out together."

Those last words crack Charlene up. The teenage mind, y'know?

So I'm looking at the dashboard clock and it's been almost three hours since we left, so I gotta call in. I tell Keys I hear him and I pull out the phone Robert gave me. Now Charlene gets all upset and asks me who I'm calling. I tell her that I have to call her dad every three hours.

"You're not gonna tell him about me, are ya?" she wants to know. "You do and I'll scream my head off at the truck stop and you'll be in big trouble."

Right. Like this girl knows what big trouble is. I ask her doesn't she think her father and mother are worried about her. Not being home and it's almost three. She tells me that they think she's sleeping over her friend Missy's house and they won't know she's gone until she's already in New York.

So I ask her, "Are you running away? Are you and Moe gonna live together in New York or something?" She tells me they haven't thought that part through yet and they'll figure it out when they meet up.

I pull into a spot a few places away from Keys and tell the girl she needs to get back in the sleeper. She says she has to pee and she's hungry. Damn. "Okay," I tell her. "Wait until Keys—Cornell—is inside and then go to the restroom." I ask her if he knows what she looks like and she says, yeah, he's seen her around the ranch a couple of times. So I tell her to be real careful and not let him see her.

"This mean you're not gonna tell Daddy about me?" she asks. I tell her I don't know what I'm gonna do about that, but I'm not gonna tell him anything now, except that we pulled over for a break and will be back on the road in ten. "I'm taking off in ten minutes," I tell her. "So you better be back in the sleeper by then." Although I'm honestly hoping she's not, and then I'll just play dumb about why she ended up in a truck stop two hundred miles from home. My word against hers and I'll take that chance.

I get outta the truck, call Robert, and he picks up after two rings. I was half expecting someone else besides the boss would answer at this hour, but he's a hands-on kinda guy. I tell him everything's fine, he says he's heard the same from Cornell and he'll speak to me in another three hours. We hang up, I go inside and pee, and then hit the Mickey D's for some food. I see Cornell over at the vending machine and give him a wave. He ignores me, but then raises his hand to show me five fingers, meaning we got five minutes. I give him the thumbs up and I see Charlene on the other side of the place heading to what I assume is the girls' room. I remember she says she's hungry so I double my order, hoping Cornell doesn't notice or bother to ask.

He leaves—I guess he brought his own food with him, as he had more time to plan for this trip than I did—and I wait for my meal. It comes pretty quick, I guess, because there's not a lot of people here at this hour. I take my time getting to the truck, figuring I'm not gonna get another chance for a while to stretch my legs. Anyway, I end up running into Cornell outside. I guess he had the same idea I did.

"We'll gas up in a few hours, Aggie," he says to me. "How's the rig handling?" I tell him okay. He looks at my bags of food and says, "You angry with your intestines?" I tell him I'm starving and remind him it's been over a day since I ate anything. He shrugs and says, "Whatever. Let's hit the road."

I head back to my truck, put the bags of food on the passenger seat and the drinks in the drink holders, and start it up. If Charlene's back in the sleeper, she ain't talking. I ask if she's back there, and I get no answer. I figure maybe I dodged a bullet here and she can explain to her daddy how she made it so far, but like I said, I'm planning on denying everything and anything.

That's when I see her coming out of the rest stop and running toward the truck. She might as well be holding a sign saying, "Hey, look at me! I'm running away from home!" I hope to God Cornell doesn't see her, but there's nothing I can do at this point. She opens the door, climbs in, almost knocking the food all over the place, and says, "Let's go, Aggie!" I tell her there's no hurry, I gotta wait for the other truck to pull out, and she says, "No, really. Let's go." She reaches into her back pocket and pulls out a road map. I'm about to ask where she got that from and she says, "I stole this." And I'm like, why the hell did you steal a road map and she says, "I gotta problem. I'm kinda klepto and this was the only thing I could slip into my shorts."

That's when I see a guy come out of the stop, acting like he's looking for someone. Most likely a kleptomaniac who steals roadmaps. I put the truck into gear, tell her to keep her head down and pull away. Luckily, that's just when Cornell pulls out so I follow him and we're back on the Interstate. I'm guessing that he didn't see anything or else he'da not gotten back on the road, or he woulda radioed me or something.

Charlene tells me she was afraid I'd leave without her. I denied even having the idea and said, "I brought you food, didn't I?" She thanks me for that and starts to dig in. With a mouthful of quarter pounder, she says, "You got a girlfriend, Aggie?" I tell her no, I got an ex-wife and a daughter, but I leave out the part about probably never seeing them again because of the whole witness protection thing.

Then she says, "Why's my dad so mad at you? What'd you do?"

"I screwed up a deal with him," I said. "I lost him and his friend some money and this is my way of paying him back."

She chews and nods like this isn't the first time she's heard this story. I eat a coupla fries and I swear I can feel the grease and salt going through my veins. I hate being this hungry, but what the hell? I'm alive to tell the story, right?

I ask Charlene how she and Moe are gonna survive in the

big city and she reaches back into the sleeper and pulls out a knapsack. She opens it up and pulls out a wad of bills big enough to choke a horse. "How much is that?" I ask, and she says, "Four thousand seven hundred and fifty-five dollars." And before I can ask where she got it, she says, "I've been saving up for a while. I have my own ATM card and Daddy got me a credit card last Christmas." She then tells me she's been withdrawing money a little bit at a time for almost a year.

"So you've been planning this for a year?" I ask. She says she wasn't planning *this exactly* but she kinda thought there'd come a time when she was gonna need some cash to get outta town. Now I obviously don't agree with her methods, or the way she pulled me into her plans, but I gotta say, a lot of teenagers don't think that far ahead. I was kinda impressed.

"What about Moe?" I said. "Is he coming with a buncha cash, too?" She says he told her he's got about five thousand also and that makes almost ten grand between the two, and that should hold them for a while. Maybe they'll get jobs, she says, a small apartment. I'm thinking I don't know about all that. I mean I know what it takes to make it in this world and it's tough enough for grown-ups, let alone a couple of lovey-dovey teenagers. I don't tell her all this 'cause I don't wanna be that guy who tells her what's wrong with her plans and shit. She ain't gonna listen to me anyway, right? I mean, here she is, a runaway stowing away in one of her daddy's trucks. She probably thinks she knows everything, and here I am, working off a bad decision on my own, who the hell am I to tell anyone what to do?

We finish up our meals and she's nice enough to put all the garbage into one bag and then puts it down by her feet. I feel better for eating, but Mickey D's on an empty stomach would not've been my first choice.

We're driving for a bit, not talking, just listening to Patsy Cline sing about why she thinks she got some serious psychological issues, when Charlene says, "You mind if I change the channel? This hillbilly shit's gonna make me slit my wrists." I tell her to go ahead and she ends up finding a channel with eighties' music—the stuff I used to listen to back in the day. I say, "You like this?" And she's all like, "Yeah. Retro's cool." So, I'm thinking, great, I'm pushing fifty and without even knowing it, I'm retro. Lots of good stuff comes on and it turns out we both know most of the words and we spend about an hour or so singing along with the retro eighties. Anybody looking in would not have seen a guy smuggling maple syrup and a fifteen-year-old running away to New York City to meet her boyfriend she'd never met. I bet we looked like a father/daughter truck-driving team, transporting goods across this great country. And that's when her phone rings.

I'm about to shit a loaf of bread now, 'cause I got it in my mind that it's her dad and the gig's up. Again, not that any of this is my fault, but I can see where Robert would think I shoulda called him as soon as I realized I had his daughter in my truck. And he'd be right. If some grown-up had Brooklyn and didn't let me know about it, I'd wanna piece of that guy.

Anyway, she looks at the screen, shows me a picture of a dark-haired guy and gets all excited. "It's Moe," she tells me and answers the call. She starts gabbing away, but now she's talking real low so I can barely hear her. I can make out a few words like "truck" and "Illinois" and "I love you, too," but the rest just sounds like teenage stuff, so I keep my eyes on the road, hoping that Cornell up in fronta me doesn't decide this would be a good time to radio and check in on me.

And, damn it, wouldn't you know, it's exactly what happens. I look over at Charlene and put my finger to my lips, telling her to keep it down. She lowers her voice even more and I pick up the walkie and say, "What's up?"

"What's up?" Cornell says. "What's up is we're gonna pull off in about fifteen minutes and fill up." I look at the dashboard and see that I'm down below an eighth of a tank. We musta been driving longer than I thought. Cornell tells me there's a gas stop coming up and we're just gonna pull in, gas up, and pull out. No bathroom, food, coffee or anything. It seems we're five minutes behind schedule, and I'm like, Jesus, this guy reminds me of my ex-father-in-law, who knew down to the penny what the expenses were on a thousand-dollar job. Here we got a seventeen-hour drive and we're off by five minutes? Shit. I tell him cool 'cause I know the five-minute delay ain't my fault, as I'm following him, right? He over-and-outs me just as Charlene ends her phone call.

She's quiet for a bit and I say, "What's up with Moe?" She's quiet for a bit and then lets out a big breath of air like teenagers do when they think the whole world's against them and says, "He's running late. Some kinda train trouble. I might have to wait for him in New York."

Now here's where, under other circumstances, I could be expected to say something like, "That's okay. I'll wait with you." But these are not those circumstances. I'm on a tight schedule—and five minutes behind, apparently—so I can't be babysitting a love-struck teenager in New York City while she waits for her beloved. I ask her if she knows anyone else in New York.

"I live on a ranch in the middle of Podunk County," she says. "Who the fuck am I gonna know in New York City?" Never fails, right? A teenager is pissed off at the world and whoever's closest becomes the target of their anger. I guess it's like that with grown-ups, too, but with teens? Look out!

I say, "What kinda train trouble?" and she gives me a stare and says, "I look like a fucking conductor, Aggie? *Train* train trouble, I don't know. Maybe they ran outta coal." Now I know that trains don't run on coal anymore, but I've learned from the last minute of conversation to keep my mouth shut about that. In fact, I decide to keep my mouth shut until she speaks again. Which she seems to not want to do and by the time I pull over into the gas station, she hasn't said another word.

I pull in next to a pump, away from Cornell, but close enough where he can see me. Without saying a word, Charlene climbs into the sleeper. Maybe she'll fall asleep for a few hours, I think. That's what teenagers like to do when things don't go their way. I'm just glad I didn't have to tell her to make herself invisible just in case Cornell decides to come over. I hook up the nozzle to the gas tank and settle in for a spell. This thing holds about two hundred gallons and filling 'er up is gonna take a while. I figure that's the reason Cornell *does* decide to take a stroll over to me and bust my balls. Except he's got his cell phone up to his ear and says, "Gotcha," and hangs up.

"That was the boss," he says. "Problem back at the ranch." "We're not turning around, are we?" I say and he's says, "No, we are not turning around." He pauses for a bit and takes out a cigarette. Doesn't offer me one, even though I don't smoke much anymore, but it woulda been nice to be offered. He lights it and says, "The boss don't know where his daughter's at." "Whatta ya mean?" I say, and he says, "Just what I said, Aggie. Girl was supposed to be sleeping at a friend's, and the friend's mother calls up asking Robert because she's thinking her kid's over there, and there's some sort of emergency at home, and Robert goes and checks his girl's room, and neither one of them is there."

I let that sit for a bit and then say, "Does he want us to do anything about it?" "Like what?" Cornell says. "Keep an eye out for them on the road? Check our trucks and see if they're stowaways?" That thought almost made me choke. I said I guess not and he says, "He just wanted me to know in case he's out of pocket for the next day or so while they figure out what's up with the girls. Apparently, this ain't the first time Charlene—that's his daughter—has pulled something like this." He took a drag from his cigarette and said, "This doesn't change anything on our part. We still make the drop-off, load up and get back by four tomorrow."

We both stand there in silence for a bit, me thinking how screwed I'm gonna be if anybody *did* get the idea to check my truck for Charlene, and Cornell taking long hits from his smoke and looking like he's all pensive and shit. I just wanna get back on the road at this point, get my mind back on the task at hand, so to speak, and I mention that. Cornell gives me a look like I shouldn't be talking unless I'm spoken to, but then he looks at his watch, and like it's his idea says, "Let's hit the road, Aggie." He takes one last drag off the cigarette, drops it to the ground and crushes it with his boot, and he walks off to his truck. As he's walking away, he says, "Next time you call into Robert, don't mention anything about the girl. If he wants you to know, he'll tell ya himself."

Like I had any idea of bringing up that subject. I get back in the truck and follow the same procedure: I wait for Cornell to pull away and then follow him when he does. Charlene comes back outta the sleeper and says, "You guys were talking about me. I heard the whole thing." Yeah, I said, we were talking about her. I ask her how long she thought she'd be able to get away with this whole running away thing.

"A lot longer than this," she says. "I don't know what kind of emergency Mrs. Williams had at the house, but Missy told me she does have a habit of checking on her when she can't sleep." Then she adds, "I wonder where Missy is." All I can think of at this point is why the hell would you use a girl in a lie whose mother has a habit of checking in on her? This was not as well thought out as I had previously thought, but whatta you expect from a girl who's gonna be sixteen in a few months? "Does she have a boyfriend?" I ask. And Charlene tells me that Missy—that's more of a name for a cat, don'tcha think?—just broke up with the boy she thought she was gonna marry and she's been kinda depressed lately. Marry? I'm thinking. These kids are in their first year of high school and they're thinking marriage? Damn, times have changed. Then again, Charlene here is talking about moving in with Moe and getting jobs and shit. Sounds close to married life to me.

I also don't like the way these teenagers throw around that word "depressed" these days. They get sad for about fifteen minutes and all of a sudden they're diagnosing themselves with a clinical mental illness. Then, fifteen minutes later they're all happy and going to the mall. Let me tell ya—and not a lot of people know this—I've been depressed. And I mean going-to-the-psychiatrist-and-getting-a-prescription depressed. I couldn't leave the house for days sometimes. Couldn't eat, couldn't sleep, didn't pick up the phone for almost a week. I lost a lot of business that week, I tell you that. So whenever I hear one of these young kids telling me how depressed they are, I just keep my mouth shut and go about my business.

And, by the way, I don't sell to anybody I think's under eighteen. I wouldn't do that. That's too young to be messing with your brain. And it's not like I haven't had the chance to sell to them. I mean, they're *depressed,* right? Jesus, if I didn't have the ethics I got, I could make a fortune with the younger demographic; but I do have ethics. I also know that they'll be around when they're eighteen, and then I got no problem selling to them.

So there I am thinking about all this and I hear, "Aggie, you ain't been listening to me." I turn to face her and realize she's right. She's been yammering about something for a bit and I'm thinking about other shit and keeping Cornell's tail-lights in sight. So she goes on telling me she's real worried about her friend and what she might do and I'm thinking what's the worst that could happen. Like she's reading my mind, she says, "Missy has a thing when she breaks up with boys. She has sex with the next boy she sees." Man, where were these girls when I was in high school? I'da gladly screwed a few that needed some consoling. It's like those teachers who get arrested for having sex with a student and they make the papers and TV. I woulda slept with a coupla my high school teachers, especially the one who taught us keyboarding—what my dad used say was just a fancy way of saying "typing." I used to hang around her room at lunch and we'd do the *New York Times* crossword together, sitting real close, and the whole time I'm thinking of a six-letter word for a person in a cage, I've got this six-letter word in my pants: hardon. Maybe that's two words, I don't know. And I gotta tell ya, I'm not so sure she didn't have some of the same ideas I had. But back then, teachers didn't do shit like that. Or at least it didn't make the papers. Anyway...

I watched as Charlene reached back into the sleeper and got her bag. She pulls out her phone and starts punching buttons. I ask her who she's calling and she says to me she's gonna try and reach her friend Missy. She's real worried about her. I grab the phone out of her hands and almost lose control of the rig. She's all like, "What the hell, Aggie?" and I tell her that her dad's got GPS on my phone, what makes her think he doesn't have it on hers. "He did," she says. But a friend of hers from the tech crew at school showed her how to disable it. I tell ya, the nerds are this close to taking over the world.

I give her back the phone and she listens for a bit and says that it went right to voice mail, which means Missy either turned it off or it's dead. Now she's really worried. I tell her she's probably fine, probably over at some guy's house if that's her habit and she'll be home—and in trouble—in the morning. She thinks about that and after about a half-minute of silence, she agrees that I'm probably right and she thanks me. Which was weird 'cause it's the first time I've felt like a father in while, y'know, what with all the stuff that's been going on between me and my ex, and her new guy and my daughter.

That's when I think about that old writing assignment: "If you could have any super-power in the world, what would it be?" Right then, I'm thinking I wish I had the power to go back in time. Even if only for two days. I never woulda broke into my ex's (and used-to-be-mine) house to get my stash;

never shoulda gotten involved with her new guy and tried to step up a level in my business. I'd be home right now, I thought, sleeping in my own bed and not driving across one-third of the U.S. with ill-gotten maple syrup and an under-age girl.

Ya ever think of stuff like that? How it's the littlest events or decisions—life choices my parole officer calls them—that lead to the biggest changes and obstacles in our lives? Even if I did decide to break into the house, if Elmore hadn'ta been there, I coulda been in and out with my stash and gone about my business. Or if the cops hadn'ta shown up a coupla nights ago at that trailer and busted all of Mickey's guys. If Mickey wouldn'ta pulled a gun on those guys we were delivering the cigarettes to. Shit, man. Shoulda, coulda, woulda, my grand-dad would say. But here we are.

So, we're driving like that for about a half-hour: she's quiet, I'm quiet, we got the eighties blasting from the radio. I'm whispering along with Springsteen, singing about better days and being able to throw fastballs and I'm relating to that. All this time I'm sure to keep my eyes on Keys's taillights ahead of me, and I watch as he almost goes off the road. I'm like "What the hell? This guy's supposed to be a pro, right?" Then he rights himself and a few seconds later he calls me on the walkie.

"Aggie," he says. "We got a problem." *We?* I'm thinking. *You got a frog in your pocket or something?* I radio back, "What's up?" and he tells me we gotta pull over as soon as we can. I ask him if he's got truck trouble and he says, "Not exactly." I ask him what the problem is and he says he'll explain when we pull over. Now I know it's not good 'cause not only does he sound all shook up, he's talking to me with something verging on respect. I roger that and in about five minutes we pass a sign that says, "Weigh Station Two Miles." The sign also says it's closed, but up ahead of me I see that Keys has put his right blinker on so I figure this is where we're pulling over. And we do.

He parks all the way to the right, and this time I pull up in front of him so as to keep the front of my rig and my forbidden passenger as far from him as possible without seeming too obvious about it. We meet between the trucks and I can see he's all upset about something, so I go, "What's up?" And he's like, "You're not gonna believe this shit." "Try me," I say. After what I've gone through the past coupla days, I had a hard time thinking of something I would have trouble believing.

"There's a girl in my truck," he says. I wait a few beats and say, "You pick her up at the last stop?" And he's like, "No, jackass. I didn't pick her up at the last stop. You and I are under strict directions not to do anything stupid like that." Then how'd she get in your truck? I ask him. Here's where he gets quiet again and then says, "She snuck in back at the ranch." I say to him he must be shitting me and he says he is shitting me not. "What's her name?" I ask. And he gives me a look like that's not the first question he expected me to be asking, but then he says, "Missy," and I'm like Holy Shit! "Why you wanna know her name?" he asks.

Well, I look at him and say, "*You* are not going to believe *this*." I walk back to my truck and ask Charlene to come out. She says, "What? I thought you didn't want Cornell to see me." I tell her that the narrative has changed and would she please come out. She does, and we walk over to Cornell, who clearly cannot believe what he is seeing and says, "Charlene?" Then he looks at me and says, "What the fuck, Aggie?"

And then I tell him my story, which at this point I'm sure sounds quite believable to him because he's got the same one. Charlene's all like, "What's going on here?" and I yell out, "Missy? Come on out here, girl." The passenger side door of Cornell's truck opens up real slow and out crawls a girl who could pass for Charlene's sister. She's got the exact same blond hair, cut-off denim shorts, but instead of Lynyrd Skynyrd she's wearing a Led Zeppelin T-shirt. As soon as she

120

walks over to us, she and Charlene start screaming like they hadn't seen each other for years. They're both jumping up and down, going "Oh my god! Oh my god!" which is funny 'cause that's clearly what Cornell and I are both thinking.

So as they're jumping up and down, Cornell pulls me off to the side and says, "God dammit, Aggie. You had Charlene in your truck this whole time and you knew the boss was shitting bricks back at the ranch and you didn't say anything to me? What the hell were you thinking?" I give him a few seconds to process the words that had just come outta his mouth and say, "What were you thinking when you realized you had Missy in your truck, Cornell? Did you immediately think 'Gee, I should call the boss and let him know I have his daughter's best friend with me?'"

That gets Cornell all quiet and after a few seconds he starts kicking at the gravel on the asphalt and mumbling, "God dammit" over and over again. And this all puts me in an unfamiliar position: with the two girls going on and on about how they each had the same idea and how they didn't tell each other, and Cornell kicking the ground and mumbling to himself and God, I not only am the only quiet one, I musta looked like the only sane one. I decided to enjoy that feeling for a few moments. They don't come often and when they do, they need to be cherished, I figured.

After a while, Cornell either calms down or gets tired of kicking and mumbling and he comes up to me and says, "What're we gonna do now, Aggie?" I think about that for a bit because if I play this right, I know that I'm in the power position. *In the driver's seat,* I thought to myself and laughed. Cornell wants to know what I think is so fucking funny and I tell him I just remembered something that happened a few days ago. Then I say, "We keep driving to New York. We stick to the original schedule." Cornell does not agree and he has no problem telling me such. He goes on about how pissed Robert's gonna be that we knew where his daughter was and didn't say anything. I tell him he's probably right, Robert would be pissed if he knew that.

"But," I said, "Cook's gonna be pissed if we don't drop off this load of maple syrup and pick up the load in New York and get back by four o'clock Monday." I can tell Cornell is still not grasping this so I go on. "What if we just play dumb? We get to New York City and *then* we realize the girls had been hiding in the trucks the whole time. I mean, I was specifically instructed not to even look in the sleeper section. Let's say we discovered the girls once we got to the drop-off point and then we called Robert. He's gonna be pissed, there's no two ways about it. But, we got the syrup delivered and we got the girls and they're safe with us."

Cornell thinks on that and says, "You think he'll buy that?" I'm like, "Hey. We did what we were hired to do and then dealt with the unexpected. However pissed off Robert's gonna be, Cook's gonna calm him down because the job was done. At least half the job. Then we can ask Robert what he wants us to do from there."

"Whatta ya think he's gonna say to that?" Cornell asks me. I tell him I have no idea, and it's true I didn't. What do you say to the guy you were about to have killed and now that guy's driven stolen maple syrup for you *and* has your teenage daughter with him in New York City? I'm not sure what he's gonna say or do, but if I were in Robert's position I would not want to piss that guy off.

"So we keep going on like nothing's happened?" Cornell says. I tell him unless he's got another idea, yeah, that's exactly what we do. Well, no spoiler alert here: Cornell did not have a better idea. We go back to the girls to figure out how all this happened.

"I got mixed up," Missy tells us. "I thought I was supposed to meet Charlene at her place and we were gonna go into the city." By "the city" I knew that Missy meant St. Louis. How she got that idea, Charlene didn't have a clue 'cause she told us that she clearly told Missy that she told her folks she was staying at her place so she could go to *New York* City, not 'the city.'" I look over at Missy and she's got this look on her face that I've seen on two types of people: those who are in the wrong math class and those who I've just sold some real good stuff to. Let's just say if this girl was a knife, she couldn't cut through warm butter. Again, I'm thinking why would an apparently bright kid like Charlene involve this girl in her plans?

Missy goes on to say that when she got dropped off at Charlene's ranch, she saw the trucks and Charlene's dad, and a coupla guys she didn't know—she looked at Cornell when she said that part—and got scared, so she hid in the sleep area of one of the trucks. That's when she fell asleep. Next thing she knows, the truck's on the road and the driver is one of the guys she does not know. Now she's really scared and tries to call Charlene but she realizes that if she does, the driver's gonna hear her. That's when she does the one smart thing in this whole story of hers and shuts off her phone. She figures out at this point that she messed up and Charlene's gonna be calling her to find out what's up. If her phone goes off, the driver'll know she's back there and she's gonna get raped or some shit.

This is where Cornell jumps in and says, "I ain't no child raper." Then he goes on to say he wouldn't rape anyone, child or not. He looks at me to back him up, but I don't know this guy. For all I know he could be Jeffrey Dahmer's less behaved stepbrother. But, for the sake of getting on with it, I shake my head no and say absolutely not. Cornell seems somewhat grateful for my input.

It's at this point I think it finally hits Charlene she picked the wrong wagon to hitch her horse to, or whatever that expression is. But, like I said, this is a sharp kid and she says, "Here's what's gonna happen." And she goes on to have the exact same idea I just discussed with Cornell, but I don't tell her that. I let her think it's her idea because that gives her a sense of control I feel she needs at this point. I do add that she's gonna have to tell her dad, if and when he finds out—I leave out the part where Cornell and I have already agreed with each other that we *are* calling her dad when we get to New York—that Cornell and I had no idea what was going on. She agrees to that and the four of us stand around trying to think of anything else to say. None of us do, so Cornell says, "Let's hit the road."

Both girls start walking to Cornell's truck and he says, "No way. You two came in separate trucks, we're gonna keep going in separate trucks." He looks at me and adds, "That way we're sharing the responsibility if one of us gets pulled over." I'd be lying if I said I wouldn't've liked them both to be with Cornell, but the man had a point. *Even Steven*, my mom woulda said.

We're back on the road for a while and just about out of Illinois when Charlene asks me, "You'll make sure that Missy gets home all right, right?" Absolutely, I tell her. I see by the signs that we're just about to enter Indiana and getting close to Terre Haute. I know I'm not saying that right because that's one of those city names I don't know how to pronounce. I think it's French but how do you say it? Is it "Terry Hot" or "Terror Haught?" Anyway, it sounds snobby to me but I have no idea 'cause I've never been there. Maybe the people there are real nice, they just happen to live in a city that has an uppity-sounding name. Not their fault.

My walkie-talkie goes off and it's Cornell telling me that Missy wants to talk to Charlene. Charlene grabs the walkie from me and crawls back into the sleeper area so she can have a girl-to-girl chat with Missy. Good, I think. Maybe she'll fall asleep back there and I can drive in peace for a bit. I feel myself getting tired, so I decide to try one of those pills Cook gave me. I wash it down with some of the warm leftover Diet Coke I got from Mickey D's and it tastes like medicine,

124

which, I suppose, is because it is. I shake my head to help me stay awake until the pill kicks in. I also turn up the radio a bit because Charlene's conversation with Missy is getting on my nerves. It's all about what Charlene's gonna do when she hooks up with Moe, and what Missy wants to do while she's in New York, and maybe Moe has a friend for her and wouldn't it be great if they could all live together and I'm about to throw up listening to all this. Then this song comes on with some girls singing about what a cruel summer it is and I can't agree more. I wonder what they'd say if they had to listen to these two on the radio while trying desperately to stay awake. That's about as cruel as it gets, if you ask me.

After about fifteen minutes, three songs, and about a million "OMGs" coming from the sleeper area, the pill starts to kick in. At first it feels like I had too much coffee, then it feels like I had too much coffee and someone's trying to jumpstart my heart with one of them machines you see on those doctor shows where someone yells, "Clear!" I try to control my breathing but it's hard. Whatever this shit Cook gave me is, it's not something I've had before and definitely not something in my stock and trade. I look up ahead and Cornell's taillights are practically on my dashboard. I look down and realize I'm doing almost ninety miles per hour. Which, it occurs to me, is what it feels like my heart is doing. I take my foot off the accelerator and get the rig down to seventy-five.

It's at this point that I'm figuring I probably shoulda taken just half that pill 'cause not only is my heart trying to come out of my chest, but the music's getting to me. I'm starting to see lights like I'm in a nightclub or some shit. Only it ain't a nightclub, obviously, it's a cop car behind me with its bubble gum machine going. I'm like, *SHIT*, y'know? He's got me speeding and he's got me *speeding*. I start to slow down and tell Charlene to tell Missy to tell Cornell I'm getting pulled over. Then I tell her to shut the walkie off and keep quiet. I pull over to the side of the highway and take as many deep breaths as I can before the trooper comes up to my window and knocks on it. I reach for the window button and miss it the first time. I don't think the cop noticed, because when I do get the window rolled down all he says is, "License and registration, please."

I slowly take the redge off the sun visor and pull my license out of my wallet. I hand both of them to the officer and he says, "I'm not even gonna ask you if you know why I pulled you over, sir." I nod and say, "I know." And he says if I wanna drive that fast I should be at Daytona. I realize through my speed-induced haze that he's making a joke so I laugh.

He takes a minute to go over my documentation and I'm expecting him to tell me to wait while he goes back to his car. That's what they do, right? They go back and run the license and registration through the computer and see if I got any outstanding wants or warrants and make sure the registration and inspection's all up to date. But he doesn't do that. What he does do is say, "My brother-in-law's a big rigger. I sure hope he doesn't drive as fast as you 'cause I'd hate to see him make my sister a widow." I'm about to say how sorry I am and how much I agree with him when he asks, "Whatcha hauling?"

"Custom made furniture," I say. I don't know why but it's the first thing that pops into my head. I know I got the paperwork that says I'm carrying maple syrup, but knowing it's stolen maple syrup makes me not wanna say it's maple syrup. Now all I need is for him to ask to see the contents of the back and me having to explain how I got maple syrup mixed up with custom-made furniture. So my mind starts going; I can say I'm real tired from all this driving and I got confused between maple wood furniture maple syrup. That's when the trooper says, "Going to New York City then, huh?" I ask him how he knew that and he says that's where his brother-in-law mostly drives to and also that New Yorkers sure do love their custom-made furniture. "Like they're too good for IKEA or

Walmart," he adds. Again, I agree with him. Then he wants to know who I drive for and I tell him "Cook's Woodworking and Carpentry." Again, it just came to me. Now how hard would it be to explain the maple syrup? *"Oh, the boss decided to branch out."* Jeez.

He thinks on that a bit and asks if I have a card on me. I tell him I don't, but he can check out our website which I tell him is *Cooks woodworking dot com.* I can see him making a mental note of that and now I'm expecting him to excuse himself so he can go back to his car and write me a ticket. Instead, he hands me back my license and the registration and says, "You keep it to no more than five above the limit there, partner." He musta seen the surprised look on my face 'cause he adds, "I know how some bosses take the tickets out of your pay—and I know how much that sucks for my brother-in-law—so I'm letting you off with a warning this time." I tell him how much I appreciate that and he says he'll check out that website I gave him and maybe he can get a discount on some furniture. I tell him sure just mention my name—and I'm about to give him a fake one when I realize he's read my license—and he says, "Just like the guy who used to be on the Cardinals?" I say, "Yeah. I get that all the time." He slaps my door and says it'll be an easy name to remember, then he laughs and says that I'll get a kick out of this: his name is Trooper Gary Carter—like the guy who used to be on the Mets. He tells me to take care and drive safe and I tell him the same and add in to give my regards to his brother-in-law.

I sit there quietly for a while, hoping he doesn't come back with a change of heart. I watch in my rearview as he pulls away and gives me a double-honk. I give him one back and then let out a breath I didn't know I'd been holding in. From the back, I hear, "That was close, Aggie. Nicely done." Great, now I'm getting praise from an almost-sixteen-year-old girl. She wants to know if she can turn the walkie back on and I go, "Yeah, but give it to me first." She does and I radio Cornell to see where he is. He doesn't tell me where he is, but he makes no bones about *what* he is, and that's *pissed*. Royally. He saw me getting pulled over and wants to know why the hell was I driving so fast. I try to tell him about the pill I took, but he doesn't wanna hear it. He just tells me to get my ass back on the road. He says he's slowed down to the speed limit so I can catch up in about fifteen minutes if I stick to five miles above. I'm about to tell him that's just what Trooper Gary Carter just told me but I decide to keep my mouth shut about that. I just get back on the road and, sure enough, less than twenty minutes later I see Cornell's truck up ahead and flash my lights at him.

We keep on driving like everything's normal and before I know it, a coupla hours—and about a hundred and fifty miles—have gone by and I'm thinking maybe this schedule thing ain't so bad after all. Which reminds me that I gotta call in to check with Robert. I do and keep my voice nice and calm as if I don't have his missing teenage daughter sitting right next to me. Charlene says something to Missy over the walkie and Robert goes, "What was that?" I look over at Charlene and give her my best shut-the-fuck-up face and say, "What was what?" Robert's quiet for a bit and tells me never mind, he's tired and he's got a lotta stuff on his mind. Then he hangs up without saying goodbye. Charlene then she tells me she's going in the back to get some sleep. Within a minute I can hear her doing that half snoring/half breathing thing. Damn teenagers can fall asleep on a dime. It's the way they're hard-wired, I read. They're more nocturnal than—what's that word—diurnal. They work better at night than during the day, which goes a lot to show why I did so crappy in my morning classes in high school, I figure. Now that sucks for me. Even though the girl's annoying and yammering away on the radio, having someone else awake while I'm driving helps keep me awake. All I need is to hear her breathing away in the sleeper section, reminding me I haven't slept for days, right?

So I turn up the radio and John Mellencamp's singing about some boy who could grow up to be president. The song's implying that there's less than a fat chance of that but when you look who we got in the Big House now, I'm thinking, shit, these days even I can be president.

I can get right in front of all those TV cameras and big-ass crowds and get on Twitter and Facebook and announce my candidacy and say it's based on government-subsidized pot for everyone—grown and picked right here in the U.S. of A. by real Americans making a living wage—and fuck the rich guys, and I bet I'd come in no worse than second. But first, I remind myself, I gotta get this truck to New York by seven o'clock tonight, and just about now I'm seeing those tell-tale signs of the sun coming up. It's midway between five and six in the morning and I look at my gas gauge and I know it's gonna be time for another fill-up in an hour or so. I'm more concerned now about keeping the gas tanks full than I am my stomach 'cause that not-so-happy meal is still sitting there. I can almost picture it, poking up at my large intestine and all that stomach acid being released. I feel a big burp coming on, but for some reason I think that'd be rude with a guest in the back. Then I feel a butt burp starting to form so I figure the lesser of two evils, right, so I let out a burp that would attract twenty bullfrogs. A few seconds later, I hear Goldilocks in the back mumble something in her sleep and then roll over. Man, if she could sleep through what just came outta my mouth, she can sleep through damn near anything. Kids.

Anyway, Cornell tells me we're gonna fuel up at the next stop and that's when I realize we've gone completely through Indiana and now we're in Ohio. The gas station we pull off into is in Columbus, Ohio, and I remember I got a friend from there who ended up moving to New York City after high school to be some sort of artist. A painter, I think. Last I heard he was bartending on the Lower East Side and still doing his art. It's funny, every time I hear a Buddy Holly song I think of him. He was the only kid in my high school—besides me—who even knew who Buddy Holly was. There was a guy who got the shit end of the stick, huh? Big time rock-and-roll star, probably got more money and girls than he ever thought he'd get—'cause if you've ever seen a picture of Mr. Holly, he wasn't much in the looks department—and then BAM! Plane crash kills him. Along with that Big Whopper guy and the Mexican dude who sang "La Bamba." I guess there's worse ways to go, but, still...

Anyway, we pull off and get some gas and some food. We pick up some for the girls—they're both still asleep—and then we're back on the road with a plan to stop and refuel when we hit one-eighth of a tank. I mention that we're going through gas pretty quick and Cornell says that's because we're hauling such a heavy load. Makes sense to me. I call Robert again and Cook picks up. Seems they're taking shifts and watching us through GPS. Cook knew we were in Columbus and said we should get outta there as soon as possible before we start gaining weight and losing I.Q. points. He says he's only joking.

That's another thing I hate: when someone makes an obvious joke and then has to point out that they're only joking. That tells me he thinks I'm either too slow to get the joke and/or he may or may not be actually joking. Just make the joke and get on with it.

It feels okay to eat again and the large coffee's doing its job so well I start thinking maybe I won't hafta take one of them pills for a while. Charlene crawls outta the sleeper and says, "Hey. You got breakfast." "I did," I tell her and hand her hers. She wolfs it down in the same amount of time it takes me to get halfway through mine. That's another thing about kids: they crave carbs and can eat and eat without putting on a pound. Until they hit their mid-twenties and then all of a sudden they look down and wonder why their high school jeans don't fit like they used to. *Enjoy it now,* I'm thinking.

Everything changes when you get into your twenties: your metabolism, your tolerance for alcohol, your responsibilities. I figure a rich kid like Charlene'll be going to college so she probably won't have many responsibilities until she graduates—she doesn't strike me as a summer job kinda girl—but just wait until she starts eating and drinking like a college kid and discovers those freshman fifteen that seem to show up mid-semester. That is, unless, of course, she and Moe decide that college is not for them and they can live on love and minimum-wage jobs.

The upshot of all this is that now Charlene's wide awake and she can't get Missy on the walkie-talkie—Cornell comes back that the girl is still asleep in the back—so she starts talking to me again. More like interviewing me, if ya wanna know the truth. She wants to know where I went to high school. Turns out I went to the same place she goes now but most of the teachers I had were either retired or dead now. The big exception is my old keyboarding teacher—the one I did the crosswords with—but now she's teaching computer programming. Charlene tells me she's getting ready to retire and I think how weird that is and how old that makes me feel. The woman who used to give me nearly daily woodies is old enough to retire. Jeez.

Then Charlene wants to know where I went to college, why I didn't go to college, what did I do instead of going to college, and what's it like being a dad. I tell her and she says, "That's pretty cool." I say, "What's pretty cool?" and she says, "Being a pot dealer for a living. I just thought that was something people do until they get a real job. But for you, selling pot is like a real job. It's like some kids I know at school who are really good at art and they know they ain't gonna be artists for a living when they get older, but what if one of them does become a professional artist? That would be really cool." I agree with her, mostly because I like to think the way I go about my business—selling pot and the occasional harder stuff—is an art. I gotta know who to sell to, when to buy my product, how much to sell it for, and the personalities of my customers—all of which, I tell you, change on a day-to-day basis. So, yeah. I think I can honestly say I am somewhat of an artist. And not just the bullshit kind. Although that does come in handy and is the main reason I'm driving this truck at that moment and not acting as breakfast for the turkey vultures.

So she's pounding me with questions and as annoying as it is, it keeps me awake and helps pass the time. I see a sign that tells me we're in Pennsylvania now. A lot of people don't know this about Pennsylvania, but it is one long-ass state. Look at a map sometime. From west to east, it goes on for miles. The good thing about it is that when you've driven through Pennsylvania, you're practically in New York. Ya gotta spend a little time in New Jersey, though. That frienda mine, the one who lives in New York City now, calls me once in a while and makes fun of the folks from Jersey. I asked him once why he did that and he said, "Think Kansas," and I go, yeah, I get it. If ya ask me, though, New Yorkers always seem to be thinking they're better off than the rest of us. There was that writer guy they made us read in my last year of high school—John Updike, I think his name was—who said that anyone not living in New York City was only kidding themselves. I remember thinking anybody with the last name of Updike oughta think twice before making fun a someone else, know what I'm saying?

After an hour or so of these questions, Charlene says to me, "So, Aggie. Don'tcha wanna know anything about me?" And I'm thinking I know about all I wanna know about this particular young lady. I know her dad's my boss and he'd kill me if he knew I had his daughter with me and didn't say anything. I also know she's got the ovaries to stowaway in one of her daddy's trucks and try to make it all the way to New York City to meet the true love of her life who she hasn't even met yet. So maybe I do have a few questions for her, after all, but before I can ask any of them, her phone goes off.

She looks at it and gets all excited, and she doesn't have to tell me who it is—I can tell by the look on her face—but she does anyway. This girl doesn't seem to have a thought she doesn't feel the need to verbalize. "It's Moe," she tells me, and I give her a fake surprise look, which I can tell is completely lost on her. She presses the button and says, "Hey, Sweetie. Where are you?" She listens for a moment and a little bit of the joy that was on her face turns to confusion. "Virginia?" she says and then looks at me and asks, "How far's Virginia from New York City?" I shrug and say, "It depends on where in Virginia he is." So she asks him and like the Sunshine State boy that he is, he's got no clue where in Virginia he is. I tell her to tell him to check the map app on his phone; that should give him a pretty exact location. She does and he apparently tells her his phone doesn't have that app. I shake my head 'cause I thought all phones could do that. I hear her say, "Well ask someone, Sweetie." She listens for a bit and says, "Yeah, that makes sense." She looks over at me and says he doesn't wanna ask anyone as that might draw attention to him and since he's a minor traveling alone he doesn't want any attention. *Boy has a point there,* I think.

The good news is the train's moving again and he's heading in the right direction and will eventually get to Penn Station in New York. She tells him she can't wait to see him and then says to me, "Can you drop me at Penn Station?" I tell her absolutely not. I don't know exactly where that is but I know it's in the same place as Madison Square Garden and that's in the middle of Manhattan. Her dad's got me on GPS and I have no time to be playing Uber with her and her boyfriend. He wants to meet up with her in New York City, he can meet us over on the west side of Manhattan by where the cruise ships come in. He can ask when he gets into the city, I tell her. Probably a short cab ride away.

I can tell she wants to keep him on the phone for a while,

but I guess he said something along those lines 'cause next thing I know she's saying, "I love you, too, and I can't wait to see you." She hangs up and tells me Moe's phone was running low and he doesn't want it to die before he gets to New York. I'm thinking he left home without a charger? What teenager does that? I know they got electrical outlets on those Amtraks 'cause I took one to St. Louis one time and was able to plug my iPad into one. Kid probably ran outta his house so quick, he remembered his phone but not his charger.

After a while of much-needed silence, I find myself getting tired again. I figure I'd put it off long enough, but it's time to pop another pill. I do and start feeling the effects in about ten minutes. Maybe it's the placebo effect or psycho whatever, but I'm more awake now and it's pretty good that I am because I mighta missed Cornell signaling for me to get off I-70 and onto I-76. I slow the rig down a bit as we switch Interstates. My tank's reading just below half, so I figure we'll be driving for a bit before gassing up again.

And now we start hitting some real traffic. Not too much, mind you, but enough where I find myself paying a lot more attention to the road and my speed than I did before. I figure it's gonna be like this for the rest of the trip. Jersey and New York are busy states when it comes to highways and Interstates and drivers.

Charlene's looking out the window, taking it all in, and then says to me, "You got any pot on you now, Aggie?" I don't, but even if I did, I wouldn't give her any. That's exactly what I need, right? An underage girl *and* the smell of marijuana in my cab. She gives me a look like she doesn't believe me, but I don't give a shit. She can smoke all the pot she wants with Moe and Missy when she gets to New York City.

"I'm hungry," she says. And I'm thinking, *Already?* But then I look at the clock on the dash and it is after noon. "We'll be stopping soon," I tell her. And I remind her that I gotta follow her dad's directions, which are basically to do whatever Cornell does. She mumbles something that sounds like, "Fudge Hormel," but I ignore it. This is when the walkie comes back to life, and it's Missy, and isn't this just the best trip ever? Charlene is all, "I know, girl. This is the furthest I been from home—ever." Part of me wants to correct her. She shoulda said "farthest" because she was talking about actual distance. My ex-mother-in-law taught me that. That and the difference between *less* and *fewer*. That woman was with words like my father-in-law was with numbers. Between the two of them, I was constantly being corrected.

I half-listen to Charlene and Missy chatting away, and again, it's annoying as a mosquito on crack, but it helps pass the time and before I know it, Cornell gets on the walkie. "Let's fuel up before we get into Jersey," he says. "It'll be less crowded and we won't need to worry about running close to empty when we're in the city." I tell him I think that's a good idea, but he doesn't respond to that. I follow him into the next gas station, we get fueled up, all four of us hit the heads, we grab some food, and we're back on the road within fifteen minutes. Not for nothing, but if I had to do this for a living, I think I'd be pretty good at it. I mean do it for a living *legally*. I wouldn't wanna have to worry every time I got on the road that I was gonna get pulled over or some shit. Just driving back and forth, listening to the radio, maybe some books on tape. I could get behind that, I think.

So, long story short—I'm just kidding, I know it's way too late for that—we're at the George Washington Bridge and we gotta stop to pay a toll. That takes about a half hour, I kid you not. Soon as we get across the Hudson—that's the river that separates Jersey from New York—I follow Cornell onto the highway that allows trucks.

Now comes the hardest part of the trip for me. I gotta drive this big rig through the streets of Manhattan. And it's rush hour. We got in an hour before schedule—don't ask me how—and we're in the middle of everybody else who's trying to get home to New Jersey and Long Island and the Bronx and Westchester. I know all that 'cause while we were stuck at the tollbooth, I gotta chance to pull up the map on the phone Robert gave me and see why this city has so many bridges and tunnels. Why the hell would anyone drive in this city if they didn't have to? I mean, I understand trucks and people who maybe gotta be all over the place, but with all the cabs, busses, subways—why the hell drive?

Anyway, by the time we get to where we're supposed to unload and load up, *it is* almost seven o'clock, so we're not as early as I thought. It's a weird kinda place we're at, I remember thinking. It's like an outdoor parking garage with no cars. There's a coupla garbage trucks down a ways and some plows are over to the side—I guess they put them on the trucks when it snows—but that's about it. I thought real estate in this city was at a premium but here's a place that's being seriously underused. It almost looks like you could fit a football field down here. Somebody could make a pretty piece of change by fixing this up and renting out parking spots.

I call up Robert and tell him we're here and he says, "Great," and then hangs up on me. Now I wasn't expecting him to ask how the drive went or how the weather is, but a little, "Nice job," wouldn'ta hurt him. But then I remember he doesn't know where his daughter's at, so…

Which then reminds me I still don't know what the hell Cornell and I're supposed to do with these two. Do we just leave 'em to their own devices? Let them loose in the big city? Whatever we do, I can't see how it's not gonna blow back on us. And Charlene's phone rings again. It's Moe and he's just pulled into Penn Station and wants to know where we're at. I look around and all I know is that we're under the same overpass I think we got off of a while ago. It's not like I got a street number or something. I tell her I think we're in the fifties. I look over at Cornell's rig—he's parked in fronta me—and I see Missy come running out the passenger side. My first thought is Cornell did something he shouldn'ta, but then she starts yelling, "Charlene, Charlene. We're screwed." Charlene gets out and I do the same. She tells Moe to hold on a minute and asks Missy what she means by we're screwed. Missy then says that her mother and father finally remembered they *do* have the GPS on her phone and she just got a text—turns out she wasn't taking their calls—from them asking what the hell did she think she was doing, running away to New York City. "Did you tell them I was with you?" Charlene asked. Missy says she didn't tell them anything yet, she wanted to check with Charlene first.

I leave them to figure out that shit—even though the final decision's gonna be up to me and Cornell—and head over to Cornell, who's on his phone. He shows me his index finger, telling me to wait a minute. I hadda finger I wanted to show him, but I controlled myself. When he's done, he tells me the other trucks are about two minutes away. I'm thinking to myself: Is that two *real world* minutes or two *New York* minutes? I don't say that, though. What I do say is, "What the hell are we supposed to do with these two? Missy's folks know where she is." And before he can ask how'd they know that, I say, "Her phone's got GPS." I pause and then say, "Girl Pretty Stupid." And that's the first time I see Cornell laugh. He looks at me and goes, "That's a good one. Maybe you're not the complete fuck-up Robert thinks you are." A left-handed compliment, my mom woulda called that.

He points out to me that it's not gonna take long for Missy's folks to call Robert, and Robert's gonna figure out that if Missy's in New York, so's Charlene, and it's just a quick leap to figuring out how they both got here, and we may end up in some shit. My brain starts working on that, and it can't get around that logic. But my granddad used to tell me, when things seem outta your control, control whatcha can. And right now it was the drop-off of the maple syrup and the pick-up of…whatever it was we were picking up. I express that to Cornell and he nods on it, and just like that, two trucks, about the same size as the ones we're driving, pull up—clearly with drivers more skilled in city driving than Cornell and me. Both drivers get out and head over to us. They're both dressed identically: black T-shirts, blue jeans and brown work boots. The only difference is one's wearing a Yankees cap and the other's wearing a Mets cap. We shake hands—none of us offers our name—and get down to business. That's when it occurs to me, How the hell are we gonna make the transfer of goods here? Our trucks are full, their trucks, I assume, are full, and we're not exactly in a loading dock here.

Yankee goes over to his truck—did I mention that the trucks are facing back-to-back—and pulls up the door. And I'll be damned if he doesn't have a forklift back there. Nice, right? The other driver—Mister Met, who's obviously done this before—explains how this is gonna work. We unload one of their trucks, stack the goods off to the side, then take the barrels offa one of our trucks and put them right into the empty one. Then we take those boxes and put them on the truck we just emptied. It's a great plan, but it's gonna take a while. I ask about how private this is all gonna be.

"Nobody comes down this way this time of night," Yankee tells me. "The whole thing should take no more than four or five hours." That's what Robert told me back before we left, I remember. I take a look in the back of the truck where Mister Met is lowering the forklift and I see what must be hundreds of boxes. I take a chance and ask what's in them.

Yankee smiles and says, "Jelly." He musta seen the look on my face, 'cause he says, "Maple jams, mostly. And some maple jelly, some maple candies, maple spreads, maple leafs on a stick, all that maple shit." And I'm thinking this is beautiful. We bring the syrup and they bring the products made from the syrup. If ya think about it, it's kinda like laundering money, except with maple syrup instead of cash. And by the way, what's the difference between jam and jelly? Never did know that. It's kinda like the difference between flammable and inflammable. Don't they both mean the same thing?

Anyway, they tell us they're gonna unload one of our trucks first with the forklift and while the Mister Met does that, the rest of us start unloading the boxes from the other truck. Even with the sun almost down, there's some lights on so we can see what we're doing. The three of us make kinda like a fire bucket line, y'know? We stack the boxes next to the truck being unloaded. It's a lot of work and I can see why it was gonna take so much time, but I gotta say, after driving for all that time, it felt good to do some manual labor. We took turns with who was in the truck and who was on the ground, and considering the number of boxes, we made pretty quick work of it. The boxes weren't all that heavy to tell ya the truth, and it got me to thinking of a word problem, which I do sometimes to pass the time. It had to do with the volume of the trucks being the same, but the density being different. Meaning the amount of space the barrels took up was equal to that of the boxes, but the mass was more with the barrels, meaning that we would use less gas per mile on the way back than we did on the way here. Ya get that?

Anyway, as we're doing all this manual labor, I realize I don't see the girls anywhere. I mention this to Cornell and he says he'll take a look. Like I don't know the real reason is he's getting tired and "take a look" is another way of saying he's taking a break. I don't mind, though. We got one of the trucks with boxes unloaded and the guy unloading the barrels—Mister Met—is almost done. It's a good time for a break, anyway, and I'm kinda worried about the girls. About five minutes later, Cornell comes back with the girls, both of them on their phones, and he says, "They went over to see the river and watch the sunset." Well, goody for them, I think. And then I start to wonder where the hell this Moe guy is because as soon as he gets here, we hafta have an idea what the hell we're gonna do.

The last barrel was being taken out of the first truck and that's when my phone rings. I let it ring a few times 'cause I'm ninety-nine-percent sure it's Robert, not Cook, and he's gonna wanna know what I know about Charlene being in New York City. I answer the phone and right after I say "Hello" the first words outta Robert's mouth are, "What the fuck, Aggie?" I take a deep breath and tell him we're almost halfway through with the loading and unloading of the trucks. His voice gets louder now and he screams, "You know what the fuck I'm talking about, you shit-eatin' redneck bastard! What the hell are you doing with my daughter?" I'm about to plead dumb when he says, "I spoke with Missy's mother and father, and she told them that she and Charlene are with you and Cornell, so don't try to sell me a pile of horseshit, boy."

I wave to Cornell and he jogs over to me. I mouth that it's Robert on the phone and Cornell's face goes blank. We look at each other for a few seconds, both trying to do some quick thinking, when Robert screams again. "Well, fucknuts! Answer me, god damn it!" I say the first thing that comes to my mind. The first thing I think I'd wanna hear if it were my daughter. I say, "She's here with me and Cornell, sir. She's safe."

"She ain't safe you asshole. She's in New York City with two strange men. How the hell did you let this happen?" I'm about to tell him she's actually with *four* strange men but I didn't think he was in the mood to be corrected right at that moment. I then decide to resort to something I'm not used to in these situations: I go with the truth.

I tell him the whole story: how I was driving along, following his instructions *to the T,* when Charlene popped her head outta the sleeper section, scaring the bejesus outta me, how she tells me she's hitching a ride to New York to meet up with the guy Moe from Florida, and if I say anything to anybody she's gonna scream kidnapping and rape and human sex trafficking, so I figured—me *and his man* Cornell, I point out—

that it would only make a bad situation worse if we stopped and turned around, what with all the product we had with us. Then I add that we *did* make it to New York safely—and on time—and we're doing what we set out to do.

You know that phrase "The silence was deafening?" I never truly understood it until that moment. I can only imagine what's going on inside his head and ain't none of it good. He's processing all this and I'm not sure which brain he's using: his business brain, his tough guy cigarette/maple syrup smuggler brain, or his daddy brain. Probably all three, I figure. But those two minutes of silence were some of the longest hundred-and-twenty seconds of my life.

Finally, he says, "God damn it, Aggie. You got a kid, right? Little girl?" I'm not comfortable that he knows that, but I tell him I do. "It don't get easier, son," he says. "Can ya put her on the phone?" I can do that, I tell him, and walk over to where Charlene's gabbing away with Missy, and hand her my phone. She gives me a look like she ain't got enough money to buy a clue, and I say, "It's your dad." She looks at me, then looks at the phone and says, defiantly, I might add, "I don't wanna talk to him." Well the phone is close enough to her mouth that Robert hears this. "You get on the phone right now, young lady!" You could hear him screaming all the way from Missouri. "Right. This. Second." I see tears start to well up in Charlene's eyes, but I gotta tell ya, at this point they are wasted on me. She shoulda thought this whole thing out better, including what her daddy's reaction was gonna be when he found out she's hitched a ride to New York City.

After about fifteen seconds, she takes the phone, and says, "Yes?" *Yes?* Like she didn't know what her father wanted to talk to her about. I'm telling you, kids these days. I'm hoping real hard that wherever my ex is with my daughter, she don't let her grow up talking like this. Then I get all misty-eyed thinking I may never get a chance to talk with Brooklyn again. I don't know how old ya gotta be before you age out of the witness protection program, but I gotta feeling it's gonna be right about the time to pay for college.

Anyway, Charlene's talking to her dad and I see Missy's got this worried look on her face, and I say, "You speak to your folks?" "We texted," she says to me. Well, that ain't the same as *talking* to them, I tell her. And she goes on to let me know that's the way they communicate mostly with one another 'cause both parents work—her dad outta town mostly—and they don't see all that much of one another. Now that's kinda sad, I think. As much as I can complain about how my folks brought me up, and the stuff I didn't get from them, we almost always had dinner together and my dad and I bonded over fishing and watching baseball games on TV. I tell Missy to *call* her folks, not text 'em. I tell her they're gonna wanna hear her voice and not just read a twenty-word text. They may be pissed as all getout, I say, but really, they're just worried. She gives me a look like she just doesn't get it—this girl does not get a lot of things—and I say, in my firm daddy voice, "Do it." And she does.

Cornell and I take this time to make sure the boxes we're bringing back are all stacked neatly and we start trying to figure out what Robert's gonna wanna do here. We both decide that his main concern is gonna be getting Charlene back home. As tough a businessman as he may be, he's a father and that's gotta trump all, right? How that's gonna happen, we don't know. *Yet.* But we're both sure Robert's gonna come up with a plan. As far as Missy goes, maybe we'll just stick her dumb ass on an Amtrak to Chicago and her folks can pick her up there. It's only about a five-hour drive from St. Louis.

Mister Met comes up to us and says they're ready to start on the next two trucks. He wants to know what's up with the girls and I give him the Reader's Digest version and tell him we're in the process of figuring that all out at the moment. I'm glad when we get back to the loading and unloading, as that keeps my mind busy.

In a little over an hour, we get about half the boxes off the second truck—we're getting good at this—when I see a guy about thirty or so with a big thick beard walk up to the girls. I have no idea who this guy is, of course, but I'm gonna find out. The three other guys keep working, I head over to where the girls are, and they're talking to this guy like they know him. When I get over to the three of them, he turns around, looks at me, and in a tone that can be called nothing but condescending, says to me, "Can I help you?" Well, I scratch my head and do my best James Dean and say, "Funny. I was just about to ask you the same question." As I'm looking at this guy, I can't shake the feeling that I've seen his face before. Like on TV or in the papers, some shit like that. But I can't quite place it. I ask him why he's talking to the girls and I point out they're like half his age.

That's when Charlene says, "Aggie, this is Moe." And that's when it hits me. He's the guy in the picture that Charlene showed me about a thousand miles ago. Only this guy ain't no teenager—you shoulda seen the beard on this guy—and that photo Charlene has of him, at best, musta been taken about ten years ago.

"You're Moe?" I say and he nods his head and says, "Yep." Then he says, like he's reading my mind, "I know I look older than my age. It's the beard." And I'm thinking, *bullshit it's the beard*. It's not the beard; it's the year you were born, motherfucker. I keep that thought to myself for the moment and say to Charlene, "Didn't your dad wanna talk to me again?" She tells me he's gonna call back soon, after he figures things out. That doesn't sound right, but I let it go for the moment and ask Missy the same question. "The call went to voicemail," she says. Now that's sad. Your kid's just run away from home, you know she's got her cell phone with her, and when she finally calls, you're too busy to pick up the goddamned phone? I can see that Missy's level of intelligence runs in the family. *They fell off the stupid tree and hit every branch on the way down,* Granddad woulda said.

I turn my attention back to Moe, because I may not know a lot about what's gonna happen, but I do know one thing. "You gotta get outta here, Moe," I tell him. "Charlene's already in enough trouble with her old man, and knowing her daddy like I do, you don't wanna be a part of making that worse." Well, Moe gives me a big ol' grin like he's heard this all before. Without saying a word to me, he pulls a phone outta his pocket, punches a button, and says, "We're here." Two words and he hangs up. Not much for small talk, this *teenager.*

Then Moe turns back to me, and when he's sure he's got my attention, he lifts his shirt and shows me he's gotta gun tucked in his belt. "I think you're the one that's going to want to make himself scarce, Aggie." Charlene sees the gun at the same time I do and she's all like, "What the fuck, Moe? You didn't say nothing about a gun." He looks at her, realizes she's a bit slow on the pickup and says, "The city's a dangerous place, Sweetie. I'm just looking out for you."

Charlene looks to me, to Missy, then back to Moe and says, "I don't know what that means, Moe." And he says he'll explain it all when they're in the car. "What car?" Missy asks. The first smart thing I've heard her say since we met, by the way. "Didn't you come up from Florida by train?" Now that immediately negates the smart thing she just said. At that point, a big black SUV pulls into the lot and parks about fifty feet away. Moe turns to me and says, "The smart thing here, country boy, is for y'all to let the girls and me walk over to the car and drive away. You take care of your business and I'll take care of mine."

I'm thinking on that for a few seconds and before I can answer, Charlene says, "Business? What the fuck you mean by business, Moe? I'm not anybody's *business.*" That makes Moe crack up and I get the picture way before Charlene does. Moe's what they call an "Internet Predator." You seen 'em on that TV show where the guy comes into a house carrying a six-pack of wine spritzers and a pocketful of condoms, and instead of the sixteen-year-old hottie he's expectin', he's met with a guy in a suit with a microphone and a cameraman. Charlene's phone rings and she's about to answer it when Moe grabs it from her, breaks it in two and tosses the pieces over his shoulder. "Not going to happen, darling," he says. He looks at me and says, "Let's go, girls."

Behind me, I hear a voice say, "They ain't going anywheres, asswipe." I turn and it's Cornell. And I have never been happier to see a guy I met for the first time less than twenty-four hours ago. And he's got a gun pointed right at Moe. Whatever he's been in the past, I'm guessing at one point Cornell was a Boy Scout 'cause he sure as shit came prepared. Moe puts his hands up in the air and that exposes the gun he's got under his shirt. "Why don't you go ahead and relieve him of that," Cornell says to me, and I do, and I'm thinking this is the umpteenth time over the past few days that I've been holding a gun. My parole officer would call this *a bunch* of bad life decisions. I stick the gun in my belt, but in my back, not the front. I know a guy who once tucked a gun in the front of his belt and damn near blew his pecker off. He's only working with one ball these days, and that seems to be a turn-on with some of the girls he's been with. According to him, anyways. Whenever we tease him about it, he gets all upset, and one of us is bound to say, "Now don't get all testy on us." Funny shit.

It's right after I tuck the gun away that Charlene says to Moe, "You sonuvabitch. You lied to me." Moe smiles at that, but the smile stays on his face a bit too long for my liking and that makes me think he's smiling at something else. That's when I remember the SUV that pulled up a few minutes ago. I turn to see it heading very slowly toward us. I point it out to Cornell, and he takes a few steps over to Moe, pushes the gun right into his back, and says, "If those boys're yours, ya better tell 'em to back off." I look at Moe's face and he ain't smilin' anymore. He slowly raises one hand like a traffic cop and the SUV stops about twenty feet from us.

All of a sudden I hear someone yell, "Hey, what the fuck?" It's Mister Met, and he and Yankee are over by the trucks. From this distance they look totally lost as to what's transpiring over in this part of the parking lot. They start to make their way over to us at the same point at which both doors to the SUV open and out come two of the biggest guys I've ever seen. I didn't know they made a vehicle that could hold that much man. They are both dressed in dark sweatshirts and jeans with bright white sneakers, and by the way, they also have guns. I take the gun I just acquired from my back and keep it at my side along my thigh. Right at this point, I'm thinking it's two guns against two guns unless Mister Met and Yankee came strapped. If they did, they hadn't pulled their pieces yet.

"What's going on here?" Mister Met asks, taking in the situation. Cornell musta stuck his gun deeper into Moe's back 'cause I hear Moe grunt a bit before Cornell says, "Seems there's more to this story than the girls knew. These gentlemen," and he gestures with his chin at the two bulls that just exited the SUV, "seem to wanna take Charlene and Missy for a ride." He pauses for a bit, then adds, "Me and Aggie disagree."

Moe grunts again and says, "You guys don't know whose business you're interfering with." He's about to say more, when Yankee interrupts him and says, "We can say the same about you, man. Now my partner and I are trying to complete a transaction with these two fellows from out of town. We'd hate to see them go back to their boss and say that we New Yorkers were inhospitable to them." I don't know who Yankee and Mister Met are, but they speak real smooth. I don't always know when to shut up, but I do know this is one of them times.

This is when the big guy who came out of the driver's side of the SUV decides to talk. "What about us?" he says in an accent that I think is Russian, but I can't swear to it. He could be from Germany or New Jersey for all I know. "We are supposed to go back to our boss and tell him we do not have what we came for?"

Boss? I think. *Shit.* These guys ain't like the ones on that TV show. These guys're human traffickers. I read about this on the Internet. There are these guys that lure unsuspecting girls—*hello?*—out of town and make them into sex slaves or use them to make underage porn. Now, not that you asked, but I'll tell you anyway, I am not a big fan of the death penalty. I think it's used randomly and usually against poor, non-white people who can't afford good lawyers. But with guys like this—evil motherfuckers—I might be persuaded to change my point of view.

There's silence for a bit, and then I say, "Considering what you came for is my boss' daughter and her best friend, yeah. Ya gotta go back to the office and tell him the deal didn't go through." He tells me his boss is not going to like that, and I tell him how much I care about what his boss likes or doesn't like. I'm concerned for my own health and well-being, and if that gets in the way of his, I'm gonna have to learn to live with that. Cornell gives me a look like he's impressed with me again. I could get used to that kinda respectful look. Maybe I've been selling myself short. I can play with these guys. The gun in my hand don't feel right—it's getting damned heavy at this point, if ya wanna know the truth—but what the hell really separates me from the big guys? Confidence. And financial backing. Confidence and financial backing. Maybe connections. I figure if I get outta this mess and back home with Robert's daughter safe and sound, I'm gonna have a little more of each. At least that's the way I'm seeing it at this point.

Then Cornell says, "You want your boy here back? Get back inside that tank of yours and drive away. We'll let him off at the exit ramp when we're ready to head home." Now that sounds like a plan to me and I can see the two bulls mulling that over. They put their heads together and whisper. When they're done, they smile at us and nod. "That sounds good," says the driver. Five seconds of silence later, the passenger raises his gun and shoots Moe right between the eyes. Now we're under the overpass and most times when you shoot a gun outside, it don't make all that much noise. Not like on TV. It's more like a "Pop!" But under the overpass, the sound is louder and the echo goes on for about fifteen seconds. The echo fades and then Moe drops to the ground. Driver says, "Except he is not our boy. Those, however," he points to the girls, "are our girls."

That gets Charlene and Missy screaming and that's when Yankee and Mister Met pull their pieces—finally, right?—and point them at the bulls. Yankee looks over at me and Cornell, and we do the same. So we got four guns pointed at them, they got two pointed at us, but...we got two screaming girls on our side, so I'm thinking it's all kinda Even Steven again.

All this started because of a bunch of shit people put on their pancakes and waffles? *Shit.*

Charlene falls to the ground and puts Moe's head in her lap. She's crying, and saying, "Why, why, why," over and over again. She's also getting a lot of blood on her shorts but doesn't seem to care. She's acting like the love of her life has just been taken from her and forgetting that her precious "Moe" was only here to take her off to God-knows-where to do God-knows-what.

Maybe she's crying, I think, *not because Moe's dead, but because her dream of a life with him also died.*

She looks over to where the two bulls are pointing their guns at us, and screams, "You bastards!" The two bulls laugh like they've seen this all before and I start to wonder how many other girls have been coerced by Moe and these guys to run away from home, thinkin' they're gonna meet a secret lover and live happily ever after. That's the thing about the Internet, man. Ya never know if what you're seeing and reading is true or what. Anybody can pretend to be anybody, say anything, and present it as the truth. I know a guy who once answered an ad that said you could buy grass through the mail. He was like, "Great," thinking it was a great way to get pot without dealing with anyone face-to-face. You can see where this is going, right? He orders the grass and two weeks later that's what he gets—grass. The stuff in your front yard. Cost him eighty bucks plus shipping and handling, but he learned his lesson.

So, back to the standoff. Never having been in one before...no that's not true, now. I was in one a coupla days ago when we were dropping off the cigarettes. So, this is like my second standoff in three days. Shit. At this rate, I was gonna be in about...two-hundred-and-seventy standoffs this year. They call them Mexican standoffs but that's probably not politically correct these days, so let's just say we're in an "undocumented alien" standoff. No need to bring the Mexicans into it. Unless, of course, that Mexican guy back home was holding one of the guns, but, he ain't, so let's not.

Anyway, we're all looking at one another and I know we're all thinking the same thing: how the hell do we walk outta here alive doing the job we came here to do? The answer is—we don't. We can't all get what we want here. Cornell and me wanna get back on the road with our product and the girls. Mister Met and Yankee wanna leave with the barrels of syrup, and the two bulls from the SUV need to take the two girls with them to complete their task. This, my high school English teacher. Mr. Thornton, would say, is conflict at its highest form.

Meanwhile, the silence goes on. Except, of course, for Charlene, who's still crying over Moe, but at least she's no longer calling anybody any names, making the situation worse. I'm still not sure if she's crying because she's never seen anyone shot before or because the whole thing with Moe was a lie. One thing I do know for sure is that the longer this standoff lasts, the worse the outcome for those involved. Somebody's gotta come up with an idea quick and we all gotta be getting on our way. Before that happens, my phone rings. I let it ring three times and then ask the two bulls if it's okay to answer it. "It's my boss," I explain. They both nod, but keep their guns pointed at us. I answer the phone.

"Hello," I say. Robert says to me, "What's the situation now, Aggie?" And I tell him all about Moe and the two bulls and how Moe's no longer amongst the living and how we've all got our guns pointed at each other. Robert's quiet for a second, he tells me to hang on, then I hear him talking to someone on his end. When he's done with that conversation, he says to me, "Who do these guys work for?" I tell him I have absolutely no idea, and he tells me to ask them. So I do. "Who's your boss?" I yell over to them. And Driver goes, "Who wants to know?" I tell him my boss wants to know. "Why does he want to know my boss's name, huh? Why do you not tell me the name of your boss?" he says. I ask Robert if I can do that, and he says it's okay with him. That's when I realize I have no idea what Robert's last name is. I don't want him to know that, so I cover the phone and ask Charlene, who's still cradling Moe's head like he's gonna come back to life with all this affection. She looks up and whispers, "Bee." I nod and tell that to Driver, and he says, "Now what?" *Good question.* I ask Robert and he tells me to hold on again, and I hear him talking to someone again, and then he says to me, "Have...what's-his-name tell you the name of his boss now." I ask again and Driver tells me. I relay that info to Robert, and he says, "Have your new friend call his boss and tell him it's me, and have him call me." I'm standing there holding the phone like an idiot and say to Robert, "You know this guy?" Robert tells me it's none of my business but he knows people who know this guy and maybe we can work it all out without anyone getting hurt. Sounds like an idea to me, and I tell that to Driver. He gets a quizzical look on his face and I shrug my shoulders in a "I don't get it either"-type of way, and I'll be damned if Driver doesn't pull out his phone and make a call.

He and Passenger keep their guns on us the whole time, as we do on them. Driver starts talking, but I tell Robert I can't hear exactly what he's saying. I can make out a few words like "trucks," "had to shoot him," and "fucking tourists." After maybe two minutes, Driver hangs up and says, "Tell your boss to call my boss." He gives me the number, which I repeat to Robert, and then he says he'll call me right back and hangs up. I hold the phone away from my ear, signaling that the call's over. Then I say, "Ya think we can all put our guns down for the moment?" Nobody seems to hear me—I know they do, though, they're just ignoring me—so the guns all stay pointed at everyone while we wait for our bosses to have a conversation.

It occurs to me at that point, that if Charlene hadn't hitched a ride with me, we not only wouldn't be in this situation, we'd probably have both trucks loaded and unloaded, and we'd all be on our ways home. Or wherever Yankee and Mister Met were going with all that maple syrup. And for some reason, my mind flashes back to a high school baseball game I was pitching before I blew my arm out trying to show off how fast I could throw. There was this guy from the other high school in town—the Catholic one, so they had better uniforms than we did—who I feel like I musta faced a hundred times in ballgames during high school and Little League. And, here I am, under the overpass on the west side of Manhattan with guns pointed all around, and I'm thinking of the last time I faced this guy. I can see his eyes, man, you know what I mean? Most people who've never pitched or played baseball before don't get that. There's so much of the game that has to do with the eyes, but no part more than with a pitcher and a batter.

I'm looking at this guy's eyes and I'm throwing him my best shit. I got the count to three-two—a full count—and I'm figuring I'll bust him inside. Jam him, right? Maybe that's why it came to mind right there under the overpass. We got a bunch of jam that needs to be hauled back west. Anyway, I'm throwing my best stuff; they're not strikes, but they're too close to take, he's gotta swing at them. And he just keeps fouling them off. I musta thrown a dozen of them at him and he fouls 'em all off, outta play. I'm trying to get him to pop up to the infield and end the inning, but he just keeps hacking away and fouling 'em back. His coach over at third base keeps clapping and yelling, "Way to stay alive, Stevie! Make him throw strikes." *Stevie*. I can't believe I remember that name.

So, I've thrown him at this point about twenty pitches, the longest at bat of my life. And we're in a standoff, kinda like the one I'm in now, except the one in high school didn't involve guns. I'm thinking I gotta end this, so instead of jamming him, I throw the next pitch low and outside, and he swings at it and misses. At bat over. I win and run off the mound, my coach and everybody patting me on the back. I look over at the other dugout and I catch Stevie's eyes. We give each other a look that says, "Nice job and we'll do it again sometime." Except *sometime* never comes 'cause the season's just about over and we're not facing these guys again.

That's how I'm feeling under the overpass. Everybody's doing a nice job—except, of course, for Moe, who's dead—even though we're all in the same jam. Nobody's losing their cool, not one gun is shaking. We're just waiting for the phone call that tells us the game is over and we can all go home. Easy peasy, mac and cheesy.

That's when another shot rings out and because of the traffic above us and the echo, it's hard to tell where it came from, but it's a lot less noisy than the shot that took down Moe. I look over at Mister Met, Yankee, and Cornell, and I know it didn't come from them 'cause they have the same confused look on their faces that I must have on mine. Then I look over at Driver and Passenger, and I see Passenger is holding his belly and there's red shit coming out between his fingers. Well, he just collapses to his knees like so many potatoes in a sack. Someone behind me says, "Fuck, yeah." I turn around and it's

Missy, and she's got a gun in her hand and it's pointed toward the SUV.

Now the gun in her hand is nothing like the ones the rest of us are holding. It's like something outta a Clint Eastwood. And she's holding it with a lot more confidence than I'm holding mine. Like she's a pro or some shit, like she's done this before. I give her a look that says, "What the fuck, Missy?" and she gives me a small smile. I can tell she's pleased with her shot, but I can also tell by the look on her face that she ain't never shot a person before.

"I'm a mounted shooter," she tells us, slowly moving the gun so it's pointed more directly at Driver. "*Competitive* mounted shooter." And I'm like, shit, I've seen that at the county fair. These guys and gals get on their horses and race through barrels shooting at stationary targets. "She's nationally ranked," Charlene says, and I can't tell if she's bragging on her friend or trying to threaten Driver, who at this point can't decide whether to look at us or his friend, who's kneeling at his feet and bleeding out through his gut. Then, Driver's phone goes off. He looks at me and asks, "I can take this?" And I say, "Yeah, yeah, take it, take it." He answers the phone and mostly listens. That's when my phone goes off. I say hello and Robert tells me he's spoken to the other guys' boss and they've agreed to let things go. "They'll leave with Moe's body and you guys go back to loading the trucks. It'll be like it never happened." He's silent for a bit, like he's waiting for me to confirm his instructions, and all I can think to say is, "There's been a new development." He wants to know what the hell that means, and I tell him. Again, there's silence and he lets out a huge laugh. Yeah, I think, from a thousand miles away this must sound like a real hoot. *Hee Haw Goes to New York.* Then he says, "Fuck, Aggie. You didn't know Missy had a gun on her?" Like how the hell'm I supposed to know that? "It didn't come up in conversation," I say to him.

I can tell he doesn't like the tone of my voice because he

says, "I don't like the tone of your voice, boy." He waits a few beats and asks, "What's the scene like there now?" I look over at Driver. "The other guy's on his phone," I say. "Talking to his boss." I tell him I can't hear the actual conversation, but from where I am, Driver doesn't appear to be all that pleased. "I imagine not," Robert says. Then he adds, "Lemme call ya back," and he hangs up. I guess Driver's boss did the same thing because now Driver's holding the phone and still pointing the gun at me.

Mister Met decides it's now time for him to chime in, and says to Driver, "There's a hospital about two blocks from here." Driver shakes his head and says it's too late for a hospital. Mister Met says, "How do you know that?" And without even looking down, Driver shoots his partner in the head and says, "I just know these things." *Fuck*. That was about the coldest thing I'd ever seen.

The four of us maple guys are now standing pretty close to one another, and Yankee whispers, "I think we gotta take this guy out right now, get back to business and get the hell out of here." I tell him that Robert just told me to hang on. I'm guessing Robert *now* knows this other guy's boss and that guy's just lost two of his guys, so Robert's got some smooth talking to do. "I don't wanna do anything until he tells us to." Mister Met shakes his head. "Robert isn't here," he says. "I say we take him out." Cornell agrees with me that we should wait to hear back from Robert. If we don't hear anything in five minutes, he says, then we'll take him out. "It's five against one," Mister Met says. "We got this." Yeah, I think, but Driver just showed he's willing to shoot his own guy and that guy also shot one of their guys. If Driver starts shooting again, he's bound to take one or two of us with him. With the way my luck's been playing out these past few days, I'm guessing I might be one of them.

Speaking of luck, I start thinking how come we ain't seen anyone down here under the overpass. I know it's outta the way and all, and it's now pushing ten o'clock at night, but it is New York City. *The city that never sleeps.* You'd think we'da come across a stray biker or some couple looking for a little privacy. Maybe even some of them tourist busses that drop people off at the theater or whatnot and need a place to park for a few hours. I guess Robert knows what he's doing and that's why he chose this place to load and unload. But, damn, I can't help worrying that a cop car's gonna come around pretty soon. Not that anyone heard the shots with all that traffic above us, but this seems like a pretty decent place for a cop to park for a few and take a cigarette or a piss break. Hell, we ain't even seen a homeless guy yet.

Well, four or so minutes go by and I can see that Yankee and Mister Met are getting antsy. I tell them—and Driver—let me call Robert again. Before I can do that, another big SUV pulls into the lot and parks next to the other one. Driver looks over at us and says, "I'll be back." Just like Arnold, I swear to God. I see Mister Met raise his gun to point at Driver, and I tell him, "Stop! We don't know who—or how many—are in that car. You just might get us all killed, man." He gives me a look like he doesn't like it, but he does what I say. I guess 'cause I'm the last one who spoke to Robert, I was kinda in charge. I liked it.

So we watch as Driver goes over to the other SUV and the passenger side window rolls down. Driver's talking for a minute and the door opens. Out comes a miniature version of Driver—I mean they are dressed exactly alike, down to the white sneakers—and he walks over to where we can get a better look at him. He's got his palms facing us, up to his shoulders, and gives us a quick spin, showing us that he's unarmed. He really does look like someone put Driver in the dryer and he shrunk. He looks at our group: me, Cornell, Mister Met, Yankee, and the two girls and Moe. "Can I have Moe, please?" he asks. And I'm like, "His name's really Moe?" The guy shrugs and says, "That is the name he goes by, yes." We all look at one another and come to a silent agreement. "Yeah," I say. Driver starts to come over and I say, "*Without* the gun, please." He stops, thinks about it, and looks at his little twin, who nods, and Driver hands him the gun and his phone. Then he walks over to us, picks Moe off the ground—and off the still-sobbing Charlene's lap—and walks back the other way. Charlene makes a sound as if he'd ripped her arm off or something. The way he carries Moe reminds me of the end of that movie where Richard Gere picks up that chick and they walk off into the sunset.

He takes Moe back to the SUV he drove in with, opens the back passenger door, and puts Moe inside. Then he picks up Passenger, brings him around to the other SUV and does the same thing. I used to drive a cab, I tell you that? Well, those back seats are going to be a bitch to clean, I know that.

By this point, Mister Met is apparently getting impatient. He says something to Yankee and Yankee nods. I ask them what's up, and Mister Met says to me, "We're going to finish unloading the other truck. You," he points to Cornell, "you come with us. You two," he looks at me and Missy, who's still got her pistol aimed at the SUVs, "can keep playing cowboy until Robert calls." I ask him if he thinks that's a good idea and he says, "If they're going shoot at us, they're going to shoot at us. Just make sure you two shoot better than they do." Then the three of them go off and start unloading the barrels from our truck with the forklift. Mini-Driver watches them go, but never moves his gun in their direction. Business is business, right?

Driver comes back over and takes the gun back from his boss. I'm not sure how long this whole thing is going on, but I do know it's gonna put us off our schedule. But, the trucks are being loaded and unloaded, and, at least at this point, the girls are safe. All in all, given the unforeseen circumstances, things could be a whole lot worse.

And that's when another SUV pulls into our area. This

one, though, is white, and it kinda reminds me of the one that OJ tried to escape in. Anyway, it drives slowly over to us and I'm thinking we're screwed. When it stops, we all look over as the passenger side door opens and out steps...wait for it... Robert! I know, right? We were just talking on the phone and here he is. Charlene sees him and runs up to him screaming, "Daddy! Daddy!" He pulls her into a big hug and takes in the situation around him. After he scopes out the competition, he sets his eyes on me and gives me a look like somehow all this is my fault. *Again.*

He's still holding Charlene when he looks over at Driver and Mini-Driver—Ha! I just realized how funny that sounds because there's an actress with that name—and says, "Mr. Thompson?" Mini-Driver nods and says, "Mr. Bee?" Robert nods as well. Then Robert looks at me and says, because he knows what I'm thinking, "I was on my way to meet an associate in Boston. I was already in the air when you called and told me what was transpiring. I had the pilot land at Teterboro." He points over at where I know New Jersey is. His speech pattern sounds a lot more New York at this point than it does Midwest. "Then we drove over here. Fuckin' traffic."

A couple of guys get out of Robert's white SUV, and then a couple more get out of the black SUV and stand next to Driver and Mini—Mr. Thompson. And I'm thinking the situation just got worse. More guys equal more guns and more of a chance of this whole thing going south when I thought we were finally heading in a northerly direction. Shows you what I know, right?

"So," Mr. Thompson says. "What are we going to do here, Mr. Bee?" Robert breaks the hug with his daughter, but still holds on to her hand. "I think you all should leave and let us finish up our business." Thompson smiles and says, "Is that what you think?" Robert says yeah, and Thompson replies, "What about my guys? I have got two dead guys here." I'm about to say that two out of the three bullets in his dead guys came from his guy, Driver, but Robert beats me to it. "That's on you and yours, Mr. Thompson. Not on me and mine. We came here to do our business and you, with all due respect, were not invited." Robert pauses for a bit and looks over to where Cornell, Yankee, and Mister Met are taking care of the syrup trucks. He seems pleased to me. "What is it exactly," he says to Thompson, "that you want?" Mr. Thompson looks over at me and Missy. We've both still got our guns pointed in his direction. He raises his hands again, shows his palms and says, "Can we agree to lower our weapons?" Robert thinks on that and then gives me a nod. I lower my gun, Missy does not follow suit. "Put it down, girl," I tell her. "I wanna go home without any holes in me." She takes five seconds—just like a teenager—and lets out a sigh, but lowers her gun. Driver does the same across the way.

"Now," Thompson says, "I want to say I would like what we came for, but since what we came for is your daughter—and now her friend there—I do not believe that is going to happen." Robert says, "You do not believe correctly." I'm not sure about the grammar of that sentence, but his point is made. Then Thompson says, "But I cannot leave here empty handed and down two men. That would be bad business. I am sure you understand that, Mr. Bee?" Robert nods and says, "I do, I do." After a few seconds' pause, he says, "How do you feel about maple syrup?" Thompson gives Robert a look like he has no idea what he's talking about. Then he looks at Driver and they both laugh. "I do not feel anything about maple syrup," he says to Robert. "A poor attempt at humor," Robert says. He then nods at one of his guys and that guy pulls an envelope out of his jacket. Driver's about to raise his gun again, but Thompson puts his hand on his arm. "What is this?" he wants to know. Robert says, "Our mutual friend—*your boss*—says you'll accept a small token to make up for your lost time. And the unfortunate loss of your men." Again, I'm thinking, that's two-thirds their fault, but I stay shut.

"How small of a token?" Thompson asks, and Robert's guy goes over and hands him the envelope. Thompson opens it up and counts the bills inside. "This," he says, "is a *small* token." Robert shakes his head and says, "Your monkeys joined my circus, not the other way around." If Driver takes offense at being called a monkey, he doesn't show it. Thompson says, "And if I refuse to accept this *small* token?" Robert tells him he should call his boss, and that's what Thompson does.

It's not a long phone call. All I can hear Thompson say is one "hello" and four "yesses," and then he hangs up. He slips the phone back into his sweatshirt and does not look happy. Then he says to Robert, "I am not happy about this." "I don't blame you, Mr. Thompson," Robert replies. "I would not be, either. But again, not my monkeys." They stare at each other for a bit. Robert breaks the stare-down first by turning to me, and saying, "Help with the trucks, Aggie. Missy, you come with me." I reach out my hand and help Missy up. We both walk over to Robert. Robert takes Missy's gun and Missy grabs onto Charlene—who's still crying—and I keep walking over to where Cornell and the other two guys are doing the loading and unloading, and I get back to work, which feels so much better than having a gun pointed at me or pointing a gun at someone else.

Some time later, I watch as the two black SUVs pull out of the lot. The way they were moving, I'd bet they left about a pound of rubber behind. That's the way people drive when they're pissed off. Robert comes over and calls to me and Cornell. Yankee and Mister Met keep working—we're almost done—and we huddle up with Robert. He tells the girls to wait in his vehicle. Robert says to us, "I'm about as unhappy with this shit as Mr. Thompson was. But—and I had a lot of time to think about this—I can hardly blame you boys for what happened here." I let out a big breath I didn't even know I was holding in. "Since we've fallen behind schedule," Robert says, "you two can take a little more time getting back, let's say by midnight tomorrow." At that point it was just after midnight so he's giving us twenty-four hours to get home. That's more than doable. "Last thing I need now," he adds, "is to lose one of these trucks to the state highway folks." He pauses and takes a deep breath of his own and says, "You boys done good what with the circumstances being what they were. I appreciate it." He shakes our hands, tells us to get back to work, and goes back to his SUV, which pulls away at a much slower speed than the other ones did.

Cornell looks at me and says, "You heard the man, Aggie. Let's get back to it and back on the road." It takes us another hour to complete the transfer of goods and then we say good-bye to Yankee and Mister Met, and I say that thing where if ya ever find yourself in…and they both laugh before I can finish. Like that's not gonna happen. We let them pull away first. We follow them out and get back on the highway, and in a few minutes we're back on the George Washington Bridge and I'm thinking there is one helluva lot of maple products on that bridge right now.

We get enough fuel to get us well into Pennsylvania, but I'm sure we're gonna pull off before that to get some fuel for ourselves. I'm dying for a cup of coffee and wouldn't mind one or two of them sticky buns they always have at truck stops. I'm even craving some pancakes with all this talk about maple syrup. I figure that'll wait until we're on the road for a few hours. Just as well. I was so juiced up from what went on under the overpass, I probably couldn't eat much now anyway.

That's when I get this real sick feeling in my stomach, almost like I wanna throw up. It takes me a while to figure it out, but I do. We were just gun-to-gun with people who don't smuggle smokes or maple syrup products. They smuggle real live human beings. They were gonna take Charlene and Missy and do whatever they wanted with them. What kinda evil fuck does that? I mean, I've come across some cold people in my life—the last three or four days especially—but to buy and sell human beings?

I get on the walkie and call Cornell and ask him how he's feeling. He says, "Okay. Why you wanna know?" So I tell him and he's quiet for a bit and then says, "Yeah, me, too. That's some sick shit, but what're ya gonna do, right?"

He's right. What are we gonna do? I think on that for a bit and then ask him if he's got any plans for after we drop off the jams and jellies and shit. He says, "No, why?"

And that's when I say, "Wanna come back to New York with me for a bit?"

THE MAYBRICK AFFAIR

CHARLES SALZBERG

For everyone I've ever known
who's believed in me as writer

1

If there's anything more boring, make that deadly boring, than a town council meeting I've yet to experience it. But when you're a young reporter for a small newspaper in a small state—Connecticut—and you're low man on the totem pole, you don't have much choice in what you cover. Thank goodness, I only have to do it once a month or in the unlikely event an emergency meeting is called.

It's not exactly what I had in mind when I broke into journalism after graduating from Yale a couple years ago. I can hardly budget my own meager salary much less understand the town's budget, and the idea of sitting through lengthy, mostly pointless discussions about traffic violations, Christmas festivals, parades and holiday decorations, well, let's just say I can think of at least a dozen better uses of my time.

The truth is, not much goes on up here, so you wind up praying for something big, like a multi-car pile-up, a domestic dispute, a burglary, or even a small fire. Nothing too serious, just anything to break the monotony.

But it's my job to be here, and so I make sure I pay attention and take good notes, which I'll have to decipher later, since my handwriting leaves much to be desired. My friends used to joke that with that scrawl I should have been a doctor. Not much chance of that, since I gag at the sight of blood.

The way I figure it, I'm just biding my time, paying my dues, impressing my boss with my work ethic in hopes he'll see he's wasting me on crap like this and gives me something more interesting. Something like the crime beat. Not that there's all that much crime up here, but every so often there is a break-in or a domestic squabble, or some two-bit white-collar crime that can possibly make it below the fold on the front page.

I am a fish out of water, living and working in a small town like New Milford. I'm a city kid, born and raised in New York City. Yorkville, to be precise, which is on the upper east side of Manhattan. I literally grew up on the wrong side of the tracks, the tracks of the elevator train, also known as the subway or just plain el. The wrong side of the tracks in this case being east of Park Avenue. My family isn't German, Czech or Hungarian, but that's who mostly inhabit my neighborhood and that heritage is reflected in the local restaurants and bakeries, places like the Bremen House, Geiger's, Schaller and Weber, and Kleiner Konditorei,

A small-town council meeting is a stretch for me, especially since the usual issues under discussion are so provincial and, for the most part, intrinsically uninteresting, at least to me.

At this moment the First Selectman, Martin Whitley, and two of his colleagues—it took me long enough to distinguish one from the other—are going at it with Whitley's political rival, John Tudor, while Jim Stowe, a carpenter and builder by trade and Whitley's right-hand man on the board, looks ready to jump in to defend his pal if needed.

The issue at hand: a motion to appropriate five hundred bucks from the General Fund to hire Towson Cabs for the 1941 Annual Christmas Festival, which is less than a month away.

"Do we have a second?" asks Whitley.

This is Stowe's cue to do what he does best: rubber stamp anything Whitley proposes. "I second," he says, raising his hand like he was a schoolboy asking permission to go to the john.

"Well done," says Whitley. "Any need for discussion?"

"Yes, very well done, Horace," John Tudor pipes up, sarcasm dripping from his voice.

I like John Tudor. He's a long-time selectman, local attorney and descendant of one of New Milford's founding families. It's no secret that he likes to spend an inordinate amount of time at the local tavern, which means he's likely had a couple drinks before he arrived at the meeting. But maybe he's on the right track. Maybe the only way to get through an evening like this is to have a few pops beforehand.

Tudor is in his early fifties and he can afford to lose a few pounds. He's the leader of the board's Democratic minority. The other member of the council is Horace Green. Thin, pale-faced, he is a teacher of English at the local high school. He's a man who takes his duties on the board very seriously, much too seriously, if you ask me. He's about to do what has become his sole honor and privilege to do at every Board of Selectman meeting: call an end to it. But before he can, Tudor, who is obviously enjoying his role as provocateur, says, "I might be mistaken, but isn't Harold Towson married to Eleanor Towson, formerly Eleanor Stowe, who just happens to be your niece, Jim?"

Bingo! Now things might get interesting and my mind, which might have been wandering a little before, snaps back to attention.

"Yeah, that's right," says Stowe. "So, what?"

"Well, I wonder if there isn't the slightest whiff of conflict of interest in giving this account to a relative of one of the selectmen on this board. Is five hundred dollars really the lowest bid?"

"John, I'm not sure what you're getting at but if it's what I think it is, then you're calling me a crook, and I gotta tell you, I'm very offended."

"It's just business," says Horace.

"You know as well as I do that Harry Towson is an upstanding member of the community, with a sterling reputation. But if it'll make you feel any better, John, I'll recuse myself," says Stowe, as he pops a lozenge into his mouth.

I should be taking notes, but I've got a pretty good memory for the spoken word and frankly, I'm hoping things will escalate to the point where maybe a punch or two is thrown. Now that would make this assignment almost worthwhile and give me something to write about other than budgets and horse buggies.

Horace looks at his watch, then at the large clock on the wall at the other end of the high school auditorium, where this meeting is taking place. The committee sits at a long table in the middle of the stage, near the edge, while spectators—and anyone is eligible to attend—sit in the audience. Tonight, it's just me. After all, who in the world would actually show up at one of these meetings on a Tuesday evening if they didn't have to be there? If I wasn't in attendance to report on the goings-on, they could just about pass any damn thing without the public knowing. I wouldn't put it past these jokers. And if you ask me, the town would deserve it. I guess it only goes to prove that you get the representation you deserve.

"The next item on the agenda is a two hundred dollar appropriation for hiring a horse, buggy and operator to give rides around the town green during the Christmas Festival. Do we have a motion?" says Whitley, trying to throw cold water on any brewing brushfire.

"I move that we extend the search for a lower bid for at least two weeks," says Tudor.

At first, there's silence, but that silence is soon filled by Horace Green, who scolds, "That's totally unrealistic, John, and you know it. It's already close to the end of November. Two weeks would take us well into December. We can't put off planning this thing till then. I move to vote on this here and now. Do I have a second?"

All eyes shift to Horace Green who seems to have nodded off. Can't say as I blame him. If I didn't have to file a story I'd be in dreamland, too. Whitley, who's sitting next to him, gives him a nudge and his eyes pop open, just like in the cartoons.

"Would you like to second the motion, Horace?"

Green looks a little confused, but not so confused as to not play along. So, he does by mumbling, "I second the motion."

Whitley bangs his gavel and then calls for an end to the proceedings. The selectmen stand and stretch which is my cue to get the hell out of there.

I'm at the water fountain just about to take a drink when John Tudor approaches. "Cutting things a little close there, weren't you?"

I assume he means that I got to the meeting a little late. It's hard not to be noticed when you're the only one in the audience.

"I don't think I missed much."

"You're probably right. But you never know. So, how is New Milford's newest fearless reporter?"

"Not bad. But not quite as good as you getting under Jim Stowe's sweaty collar. I admire your fervent defense of the democratic process and attempt to stifle even the hint of corruption"

He smiles and pats me on the shoulder.

"Well, I just can't stand to see Whitley and his lackeys get whatever they want."

"By lackeys I assume you mean Stowe."

He smiles and runs a finger across his lips, then tosses his hand back, obviously signifying that his "lips are sealed."

"I get it. But is a two hundred dollar appropriation for a horse and buggy really the proper battleground for your crusade."

"What's the matter, Jake, bored with these small-town matters? I bet you're just aching to expose some major scandal and get your name on the front page. But I don't think that's going to happen covering this town."

"You never know," I say, even though I do know that he's right.

"It's not a pretty sight seeing a young man like you so

down and lacking hope. Why don't you meet me at the Grill
in half an hour? I might have something interesting for you."

The Grill John is speaking of is the Tudor Grill. The name
is not a coincidence. Like so many other establishments in our
fair town, the Grill bears the Tudor name because it's owned
by his family. Other signs that this is a Tudor town are the
Tudor Floral Shop, the Tudor Funeral Home and then, of
course, there's Tudor Road which, as it happens, is where the
rooming house I inhabit is located.

"Sure thing," I say. I'm guessing Tudor will be springing
for the drinks and that's not something I'm in a position to
turn down.

When I walk in I immediately spy Tudor sitting at his regular well-placed table to the left of the entrance. It might as
well have had a reserved sign on it since everyone knows
that's John's table and only John's table. It is located in a spot
where he can see everyone who enters the establishment and
once they're in everyone can see him.

I pull up a chair and sit down.

"What'll you have, Jake? On me, of course."

"Beer is fine."

"Nothing stronger?"

"That's strong enough, John. I'm young. I haven't built up
the tolerance you have yet."

"Very funny," he says, puffing out his chest because he
knows it's true and on some level his capacity for alcohol is
something he's very proud of.

"Where's that cute girlfriend of yours tonight, Jake? She
waiting for you somewhere?"

"It's been a long day. I'll see her tomorrow."

John signals to the bartender with his hand, indicating two
beers.

"The bartender's my nephew, Peter's son, and so the service is superb."

"Is there no business in town that's not owned and operated

by a Tudor?"

"Son, there wouldn't be a town if it weren't for the Tudors. My great, great grandfather built the first church. There's been a Tudor on the Board of Selectmen since Connecticut was a colony. And whatever we've taken we've given back tenfold."

The waitress arrives with our drinks. She places John's scotch on the rocks in front of him and starts to pour my beer into a glass.

"So, John, the suspense is killing me. What have you got for me? Did the school drama club go over budget? Is the board considering a special tax for people who wear hats?" I ask, as I take a sip of beer. It's very cold and very satisfying.

"The name Philbin mean anything to you, Jake?"

"You mean as in the Philbin Brass Works, off Route 7?"

Tudor nods, then takes a swallow of scotch. "The very same. And you know about the so-called accident that happened about six months back, right?"

"What do you mean, 'so-called'?"

"A watchman falls out a window, breaks his neck. That doesn't seem strange to you?"

"Should it?"

"Don't you think it's a mite odd that in the middle of the night a watchman should be upstairs in a half-finished building, where he has no cause to be and then suddenly tumbles out a window?"

"You know, John, all this happened before I moved here, so I'm a little unclear as to what you're getting at. Are you saying this guy's death wasn't an accident?"

"I'm not saying anything, Jake. I'm just asking. You're the reporter. You're the one who's supposed to come up with the answers. All I know is the Brass Works might become a very important place, what with the War coming and all."

"You really think we're going to wind up in this thing?"

"I think it's inevitable. The Brits and the French have been pressing us to join their side and I don't know how much longer Roosevelt can hold out. Something will come along to tip the scales. You can bet on that."

"What does a watchman dying at the Brass Works have to do with all this?"

"Maybe he saw something he wasn't supposed to see. Or heard something he wasn't supposed to hear. It just strikes me as rather odd that someone so familiar with the place should suddenly take a wrong step and fall twenty, thirty feet."

"Maybe he'd been drinking?"

Tudor shakes his head. "I knew him. He didn't touch the stuff."

"You think I should look into it?"

"I'm not your editor, Jake. I'm just making idle conversation."

"I don't think it's so idle, John."

Tudor shrugs. "It's getting a little late. My wife's gonna start worrying if I don't get home soon. It's been fun, Jake. And the drink's on me. In fact, if you want to stick around a while, maybe get something to eat, that's on me, too."

He finishes his scotch, in two big swallows, leaving two ice cubes melting in the glass, pats me on the shoulder, then heads over to the bar where he says something to his nephew, the bartender. He looks back at me and smiles. It isn't the kind of smile in reaction to something funny. No, come to think of it, it's much more sinister than that.

2

The next morning, I find myself sitting in Dave Barrett's office. He's the *Litchfield County Gazette* editor-in-chief and to be honest, he scares me a little. Either he's got that gruff act down pat, or that's his real personality. It doesn't matter which because he's effective. I actually like him, despite all his bluster. Maybe that's because he reminds me of my dad, who was always tough to please. And yet, we never had any doubt that he loved my brother and me.

I'm not saying Barrett, who boasts having cut his journalistic teeth working for the *Herald Tribune*, loves me, but I do sometimes get the sense that he likes me. And that'll do for now.

The office is on the second floor of the building and its windows face the Village Green. Headlines commemorating major events of the past few decades are framed and hang on the wall. Prohibition's repeal in 1939, the stock market crash of '29, and Lindbergh's 1927 solo flight across the Atlantic.

Barrett is sitting at his desk, his feet up, his tie loosened, in rolled-up shirtsleeves. Barrett loves being the lord of the major and in many ways he thinks he's the big man in town. And maybe he is.

I'm not alone. Sitting next to me is George Doring, the newspaper's managing editor. Barrett, at fifty-six, is the elder statesman of the paper while Doring, thirty-six, is a little more than a decade older than I am. But he's well-respected by the staff because he knows the business and he's probably the best headline writer in the northeast corridor.

We're waiting for Barrett to start the meeting, but before he does a copy editor sticks his head into the office.

"Dave," he says, "when you get a chance we need you to check out the feature layout."

"I'll be there in a few minutes," Barrett replies, then he looks back at me. "So, Jake, what is it you think you've got from last night's meeting?"

"Not much. John Tudor put up a silly fight over a budget item to get an appropriation for the Christmas Festival. It was just to annoy Whitley, I'm sure."

"Did it work?" asks Doring.

"Oh, yeah. Stowe practically challenged him to a fight."

"Next time maybe we ought to send a photographer and hope for the best," says Doring.

"Our sports page can use some action shots," says Barrett. "As it is, we'll give it a couple inches and maybe put it on the comics page."

We both laugh. Barrett can be intimidating but he's also got a good sense of humor. He doesn't take himself or anything else in town too seriously. I'm still working on not taking myself too seriously, but it's an uphill climb.

"Anything else?" he asks.

"Maybe," I say. "John Tudor insisted on buying me a drink after the meeting. He said he had something for me. Now, I don't know how much faith..."

"Cut to the chase, kid," says Barrett, who I can see is fidgeting in his chair.

"Tudor says the accident over at the Philbin Brass Works last spring might not have been an accident at all."

Barrett sits up in his chair, looks at Doring then back at me. "Based on what?"

"He wouldn't say."

"You think we should put someone on it?" Doring asks.

"We're not quite out of the Depression, but this War over

in Europe is heating up and it's going to make a whole lot of people a whole lot of money and the Brass Works will be right in the middle of it. Maybe it's nothing but I think it is worth a look."

I raise my hand. I don't know why. Maybe it's a holdover from the classroom.

"You don't have to raise your hand to take a piss, kid," says Barrett. "Just get up and go and we'll figure out why.

He's embarrassed me a little, but I go along with the joke and laugh. There's no way I'm going to let them think I'm thin-skinned. If I did, that would be the end of me.

"Well, I wasn't with the paper then, but I'd like to look into it. Just in case..."

"I don't think so," says Barrett. "You've got other fish to fry." He looks at Doring. "Put Al on it. See if he comes up with anything."

"It's my story," I say with a sudden burst of courage. Both Barrett and Doring intimidate me, not that they know it. Or maybe they do.

"We need someone a little more experienced than you, Jake. If this is anything we have to get the facts and get them quick. Al's the only one I'd trust on a story like that. Besides, I have something else I need you to work on."

"Let me guess. The church holiday bake sale."

"Hey, kid, stop pouting. It's unprofessional," says Doring. "Al's worked the New Milford beat for ten years. He knows everyone and everything. He can put this to bed in half a day."

"I got a call from the fire chief up in Gaylordsville," says Barrett. "Some woman named Elizabeth Chandler, who lived in a small house on Old Stone Road died yesterday. The head-master at South Kent School reported it after some students who were delivering her groceries found her. It turns out the woman had something like twenty, thirty cats. Folks love those kinds of human interest stories. Especially, if there are cats involved. Me, I'm a dog man, so I don't understand the attraction. I want you to go up there and check it out."

"Yeah, I'm sure it'll be fascinating." I mean to say this in my head but it actually comes out of my mouth.

"Listen, kid, you want to be a journalist these are the kinds of stories you have to do. You don't have to like 'em, you just have to do what you're told. Capiche?"

"But Tudor handed this to me. Shouldn't I be the one to follow it up?"

Neither Barrett nor Doring answer. They don't have to. They are the generals, I am the private. My dad always said life isn't fair, and I'm finding out he's right.

As soon as I step out of the office to get started on my assignment I spot Maggie Hine walking toward me. She's coming from her parent's bakery shop on the other side of the Village Green. She's wearing an apron under a windbreaker and she's carrying a fresh muffin wrapped in a napkin. She smiles and waves at me. We've been seeing each other for the past couple months. I met her when I went into the bakery to buy some muffins and I walked out with her phone number. Maggie grew up in town and her brother, Wally, is on the police force.

"Hey, stranger, where have you been keeping yourself?" she says, with a big smile. To me, she looks like a movie star, though she doesn't use much makeup at all. She's a brunette with shoulder-length air, a perfect little nose, and is five-foot-two with eyes of blue. She reminds me a little of the English actress Vivien Leigh. When I told her that she just laughed and said, "I wish." With two simple words, she won me over completely.

I am still kind of pissed at the injustice of losing a potentially hot story that I brought in and am busy struggling a little fixing my knapsack onto the back of my motor bike.

"Need some help there?" she asks.

"No, thanks. I'm fine."

"I thought you might be hungry." She hands me the muffin.

Suddenly, my mood shifts. It's such a sweet thing to do, how can I be brusque and so self-involved?

"What's wrong?" she asks.

"Does it show?"

"Sure does."

"It's just work, Maggie. I'm pretty sick of being low man on the totem pole, getting all these crappy assignments. Like last night. The board meeting, and you can spell that b-o-r-e-d."

She laughs. I love her laugh. It's not one of those tee-hee, girly kind of laughs. It's full-throated and she throws her head back so there's no doubt that she's actually amused. She has this sunny outlook on life I wish I had. But I don't. I always see the dark cloud while she sees the silver lining. But maybe that's why we're together, so both of us can learn something from the other.

"You've only been working here six months. What do you expect?"

"I expect to work on stories that actually mean something. I don't want to spend the rest of my life working on a small town paper, you know."

"Excuse me?"

"You know what I mean, Maggie. They've got me working on a damn cat woman story, for God's sake."

"I guess that's called paying your dues. So, are we still going to that movie tonight or are you planning to be in a bad mood till then? Because if you are…"

"You're much too cute to sustain any bad moods, Maggie. I'm pretty sure my mood will improve by then."

I lean over and kiss her on the lips, making sure I don't hold it too long. It is a small-town, after all, and who knows who might be watching.

I hop on my motor bike that's parked a couple doors down from the bakery, gun the motor, and head north, toward Gaylordsville. It is late November and there is a definite chill in

179

the air, so I'm wearing a sweater under my brown leather jacket, a heavy, wool scarf is wound tight around my neck, and my Boston Red Sox baseball cap is fixed firmly on my head.

The leaves have long since turned but despite the fact that most of the trees are bare, it's still a pretty drive up Route 7, along the Housatonic River. New England is beautiful, no matter what time of year, but sometimes, I think, that beauty camouflages ugliness. That's one of the reason I've chosen to be a journalist. I want to reveal that ugliness so folks can concentrate on the beauty.

My mind wanders as I close in on Gaylordsville. I think about many things. Like how I wound up working for a small New England newspaper. I made a list of all the papers within three hours of New York City and, one by one, I visited them asking for work. The *Gazette* was the only paper that had a position. They offered it to me and I took it. I think about Maggie and how lucky I was to meet her. I think about my future. Nineteen-forty-one is nearing an end and war is in the air. If we are dragged into it my life and the life of so many others will be changed. As for me, I hope to be sent overseas as a war correspondent. Unless, of course, I'm drafted.

I think of many things, but getting a cat lady story is definitely not one of those things.

Eventually, the road narrows and I come to a cluster of three buildings, set close together. One of them is a post office, another a general store, and the third a firehouse. This is Gaylordsville and I have arrived.

I park my bike out front of the firehouse and knock on the rolling door behind which, I assume, is the local fire truck. There's no answer. That's not surprising. Small towns like this have volunteer firemen and there's no reason anyone would be in the firehouse unless there was some kind of inspection, or work being done on a piece of apparatus.

I take a few steps over and enter the post office, which is pretty much empty except for one woman addressing an envelope at the long table in one corner of the room, and another reading notices tacked to a bulletin board. It looks like so many others throughout rural America. There's a wall covered with postal boxes, and next to that there's the bulletin board with all kinds of local announcements. There are two service windows, one of which is closed. I head to the one next to it, where I find a middle-aged woman reading a magazine. I rap on the cage and she looks up. She puts down the magazine, smiles, and asks, "May I help you, kiddo?"

Do I really look that young, I wonder?

"I hope so. My name's Jake Harper and I work for the *Litchfield County Gazette*. I'm looking for the fire chief, but there's no answer when I knocked on the door."

"That's 'cause he isn't there. Hardly ever is. You're looking for George Buckbee and you'll most likely find him over at the general store. He owns the place."

The general store, or Buckbee's Emporium as it's called, is packed with every item imaginable, proof that it is, indeed, a "general" store. Standing at the counter is a tall, heavy-set man. He's shooting the breeze with an elderly fellow dressed in overalls and a heavy, corduroy jacket. I approach, but he pays no attention to me. I don't wish to be rude, so I stand there, waiting for him to finish. But that doesn't seem to be happening and so, too impatient to wait for something that may never come, I interrupt.

"Excuse me."

He looks over at me. "What can I do for you, young fella?"

"I'm looking for Mr. Buckbee, the fire chief."

"You're not looking for him, pally, you're looking at him. You need a fire put out?" He laughs at his own joke. "Sox fan, huh? Your boy Williams had some kind of year, didn't he?"

"Four-oh-six with thirty-seven round-trippers. I'd say that qualifies as a pretty good year."

"I'm a Yankee fan myself, but you gotta give credit where credit is due."

"We'll see what happens next year, with Williams in his prime."

"If there is a next year. What with the way things are going in the world you can't be sure. A fella like you better be careful. I was in the last one and it weren't no picnic. So, what can I do you for?"

I take my pad and pen out of my knapsack.

"My name's Jake Harper and I'm a reporter for the *Litchfield County Gazette*. I was sent up here to do a human-interest story on that cat lady who died recently. Know much about it?"

"Not much to tell. Got a call from the headmaster from over at the South Kent School. Some kids who usually bring her groceries were worried 'cause no one answered the door when they stopped by."

"Why were they worried?"

"She rarely left her house and when she did she didn't go far."

"What did you find when you got over there?"

"Found a whole buncha hungry cats, that's what I found. Upstairs, I found her lying in her bed, just like she was sleeping. Only she was stone, cold dead. Probably been lying there that way a couple days."

"What did she die of?" I ask, hoping it wasn't natural causes. Anything to liven this story up.

"Far as I know, old age. Heart just stopped pumping. It happens that way sometimes, ya know. No real point in doing an autopsy. She was an old woman and, far as I know, there were no relatives."

"Could you tell me how old she was. How long she'd lived there. Where she was from. Anything at all I can use?"

"Slow down, pally. All's I know is that her name was Elizabeth Chandler, and that they called her 'the cat lady.' Not much other than that. Can't even say I seen her more than two or three times in all the years she lived here. Strange woman maybe, but harmless, far as I could tell."

"Where is it? Her house, I mean."

"On the Old Stone Road."

"Where's that?"

"About three quarters of a mile up from here. It winds from South Kent Road to Bull's Bridge Road. The road's unpaved and it's narrow. And you gotta be careful, 'cause it's pretty thickly wooded and you'll find an area where it's sloped and there are the remains of a stone wall, which is where the name comes from. House is on the left, set back about fifty, seventy-five feet from the road. I'm guessing she lived there at least twenty-five years, maybe more. The only people who ever really saw her were the kids from over at South Kent School."

"Do you know anything about her past," I ask, as I scribble down notes. "You know, like where she came from?"

"Beats me, son. Maybe those folks over at South Kent know something. You know, they buried her up in the school cemetery, right alongside the school's founders."

"Do you think it would be all right if I went up to the house?"

"I don't see why not. I'm guessing since she didn't seem to have any relatives, and we didn't find any kind of will or anything, the town will just take over the property. You let me know if you need anything else from me, won't you? And you got the spelling of my name right, I hope? That's two Es at the end and no Y."

"Sure thing. Copied it right off the sign in front. "

3

I get directions to the South Kent School from Buckbee, then grab a quick lunch at a local diner, not far from town.

The school is about a mile northwest of town, amidst rolling, snow-covered hills. When I reach South Kent Road about a quarter of a mile in front of me I see a cluster of several buildings. As I get closer, I see one of them is a field house, another a two-story residential dorm, another a small chapel, another a library, another the school itself. Set apart from these buildings, up a small hill, there's another one with a sign in front that reads "Administrative Building."

I enter the Administrative Building and ask directions of an elderly woman who's seated at a desk to the right of the entrance. She directs me to the office of the Headmaster, Carrington Raymond. He's an elderly gentleman, bald except for a fringe of white above his ears. He has a round, red face with a receding chin, and he sports a pair of wire-rim spectacles. He's wearing a maroon tie and a blue blazer with what I assume is the school crest on the breast pocket.

He motions me to sit in the chair in front of his desk and for a brief moment I am a kid back in public high school, sitting outside the principal's office awaiting a dressing down for one infraction or another.

At first, Raymond is rather crisp and formal, but as soon I introduce myself and explain why I'm there, he seems to warm a little, even flashing an occasional smile.

"It's so sad, to end your life alone like that." He shakes his head. "The poor woman. No family, no friends. Of course, she did have her cats."

"Did you ever meet her?"

"No, I'm afraid I didn't. I believe the only ones who had anything to do with her over the years were a number of boys who performed errands for her. Frankly, I'm not sure any of them ever got inside her house. But I'm not really the proper person to talk to about her. Mr. Tallamy, one of our English teachers, would be a better..." He stops for a moment, searching for a word. "Source. That's what you call it, isn't it?"

"Yes," I say, trying to suppress a smile.

"Mr. Tallamy was a student here twenty years ago, since his family moved into the area. I believe he was one of the first of our boys to give her a helping hand. His room, 222, is down the hall." Raymond glances at the large clock on the wall opposite his desk. "Fourth period is just about over and I believe he has fifth period free, so I'm sure you'll find him in his room, Mr. Harper."

I thank Raymond, shake his hand, then head toward the building that houses the classroom. When I get to room 222, I peer through the glass panes on the door. There are fifteen boys, all wearing the same jacket and tie as Raymond, sitting at their desks, books open in front of them. Mr. Tallamy, wearing a tweed jacket and bowtie, is at the blackboard writing something in chalk. He doesn't look much older than me. Maybe in his mid-thirties.

A bell rings, the boys close their books and the room fills with chatter as they head for the exit. I nearly get run over as the stream of boys brush past me and empty out into the hall. Several of them bump into me, but it doesn't seem to slow them down.

I wait a moment or two until the room clears, and then I enter the room just as Tallamy is removing his jacket and hanging it on the back of his chair.

"Excuse me, Mr. Tallamy." He looks up. "My name's Jake

Harper and I'm with the *Litchfield County Gazette*. I'm doing a story on Elizabeth Chandler and I understand from Mr. Raymond that you might be able to help me."

"I'll do what I can," he says as he motions for me to sit down at one of the student desks. "I'm afraid I haven't got a whole lot of time, Mr. Harper. I've got a pile of papers to correct, and my next class is in forty-five minutes. But I'm happy to give you a few of those minutes, not that I have much to say on the subject of Elizabeth Chandler that could be particularly newsworthy."

"Thank you, sir. I promise I won't take up too much of your time." I pull out my pad and pen. "I understand you knew her when you were a student here."

"I wouldn't say I knew her. In fact, I suspect no one really knew her. She was a nice enough old woman, but a real recluse. I was new in town and used to pass by her house on the way to school and then back home. It was a short cut for me. Sometimes, I'd see her in the yard working on her garden. One day, out of the blue, she came to the edge of her lawn and asked me if I'd help her carry a bag of fertilizer out from the garage. She tried to pay me for doing it, but I wouldn't take anything. That must have been fifteen, no, make that twenty years ago."

"What was she like?"

"She was a very sweet woman, but there seemed to be an unexplained sadness about her. Maybe it came from the fact that she was alone. Or maybe it was something that happened to her earlier in life. But living alone like that, and being elderly, she got a reputation from a lot of the neighborhood kids. You know, a witchy kind of thing. But she wasn't like that, at all. She wouldn't hurt a fly and I think she actually liked kids. I came back a few times to help her with odd jobs around the house, and occasionally I'd bring a friend with me. Pretty soon it became something of a tradition for the students here to help her out every so often. Get things like groceries, mow the lawn. Carry in wood for the fireplace. Things like that."

"Did you talk to her much?"

"Not really. In fact, we rarely saw her. Every week, it was always on a Thursday, there'd be a list of what she needed and some money in a box on the porch. When I'd return with the groceries, I'd knock on the door, she'd answer it, and I'd offer to bring the packages in. Usually, she'd just thank me and tell me to leave everything on the porch, outside the front door. Once, she did ask me in for 'a little refreshment,' she called it. As I recall, she served tea and cucumber sandwiches. I told her they reminded me of a scene in Oscar Wilde's *The Importance of Being Earnest*, which we'd just finished reading. She laughed and told me she'd lived in England a long, long time ago, and it was there she developed a fondness for afternoon tea."

"Is that where she was from?" I ask, while furiously taking notes.

"Honestly, I don't know. She never talked about herself. She'd ask about me and seemed to get a kick out of hearing about my life. But I do know where she ended up." He points toward the window and in the distance, I can make out what appears to be a small, fenced-in graveyard with a number of small gravestones sticking out from the earth. I can even make out a small mound of dirt, and what appears to be a freshly dug grave. "Apparently, she expressed a desire to be buried here, on the school grounds."

"And she never spoke about her past?"

He shakes his head no and shrugs. "Wait. You know what, I suddenly remember the oddest thing. It was that time she invited me in for tea. As I recall, she kept referring to me by a funny name."

"What was it?"

"I'm trying to remember. Something like, Bubby? Bobby? No, it was Bobo. That's what it was."

"Did she ever say why?"

"When I asked her who Bobo was, she got kind of quiet

and then said it was the name of a boy she once knew and that I reminded her of him."

"Did she say anything else about him?"

"Not that I can remember. But it was a long time ago and a lot has happened to me since then. And remember, I was a teenager, so not much of what any adult said was of much consequence to me."

"Can you remember anything else about her that I might be able to use for my story?"

He shakes his head. "I wish I could, Jake, but as I said, she just wasn't the chatty type."

"I suppose I should visit her house. Could you give me directions?"

"Of course." He jots them down on a piece of stationary with the school insignia on it and hands it to me.

I memorize the directions, but before I hop on my motorcycle and head toward the old lady's house, I decide to take a look at her grave.

The school graveyard is on a small hill overlooking the chapel. The freshly dug grave is marked with a wooden cross bearing the initials F.E.C.M. etched in Gothic style, and under that are the dates, 1862-1941. I get what the E.C. stands for, but I'm not sure what the F.M. stand for. I make a note to find out who made the arrangements for her internment and ask about the F.E.C.M.

I take the main road until I find a sign for Old Stone Road, which isn't really much of one. As I was warned, it's unpaved and it looks like it leads to nowhere. After about half a mile I see a thick canopy of trees, which is one of the landmarks that's supposed to alert me that I'm close. That's where I lean my bike up against a tree and walk the rest of the way to the house, which is a small, white cottage.

The sagging porch creaks as I make my way toward the front door. It's locked. I walk around to the back of the house and there's another door, but it's also locked. I step back and see that to my right there's a just-above-the-ground storm door which probably leads to a cellar. There's a lock on it, but it's all rusted out. I find a rock as large as my fist and bang it against the lock. It busts open.

I lift up the storm door and go down the steps. It's dark and dank and smells of mildew. I pull a pack of matches out of my pocket and light one. Holding it up, I see the small basement is filled with a lot of junk: a few pieces of beat-up furniture, yard tools, a hose, and old newspapers. To my right, there's a set of stairs, leading up into the house. I climb them and emerge in the kitchen. On the floor there are several bowls, a few of them still hold the remnants of cat food, a couple look as if they held water. Otherwise, the room is remarkably neat, everything in its place. I open the cupboards and find nothing unusual. The refrigerator is empty except for half a bottle of milk, a stick of butter, half a dozen eggs, and a couple apples. I maneuver around the empty cat dishes and walk into the living room, which is furnished simply with Victorian-era furniture, giving the room a decided English flavor.

Above the fireplace, on the mantle, there are several framed photographs. One is of a young boy, another of a young girl, and a third of a young woman, possibly in her late teens, holding hands with an older woman. Both are wearing period clothing and there's a ship in the background. I assume the older woman is Elizabeth Chandler's mother and the teenager is Chandler herself. I pick up the framed photo and turn it over, hoping there might be something written on the back to identify it. There's not. I put it back in its place and wander through the rest of the house.

Upstairs is the one bedroom, which has a low, sloping ceiling. There's a four-poster bed, with an old trunk at the foot of it. There's also a small night table with a lamp and a box of tissues on it, and a mahogany dresser. On the wall, there are a few etchings of horses. I open the closet door and find clothing hanging. There's really nothing of interest, so I move on to the dresser and night table. I open the drawers. Nothing of particular interest there, either.

I feel a little creepy, going through a dead woman's things. It feels like some kind of violation, but I remind myself that I'm only doing my job as a reporter.

I open the trunk and find linens stacked one on top of another. I'm about to move on when I decide to pick up the linens to see if there's anything beneath them. There is. It's what looks like an old photo album. I take it and sit on the bed, which has been stripped bare down to the mattress. I open up what I assume is an album of family photographs but instead it's more like a scrapbook. I thumb through it and find that it's filled with yellowed newspaper articles with headlines like "Murderess Sentenced to Death," and "Maybrick Proclaims Innocence." The clippings are from *The London Times*. I turn the pages. "Maybrick's Sentence Commuted." "Former Murderess Speaks on Prison Reform." As I riffle through the pages of the album, what looks like a business card falls out. It reads "Herbert Findlay, Esq." There's a New Haven address. I tuck the card in my pocket and, with the album resting in my lap, I sit there staring at the wall, wondering what in God's name all this has to do with an old woman living in the boondocks of Connecticut, surrounded by cats.

It's getting dark and it looks like it might start to snow, so rather than read the tarry—driving my motorcycle in the dark on slippery streets is not a good idea—I decide to take the album with me. It's not really stealing, I tell myself, because I have every intention of bringing it back. I stuff it in my knapsack, leave the house the same way I came in, hop on my motor bike and head back to New Milford. I don't want to be late for my date with Maggie for dinner and a movie.

I arrive back in New Milford just in time, or at least what I consider close to on time, because I'm only a few minutes late. When I go inside I see Maggie's already sitting at a table. She's all dolled up and I look down at myself I realize I'm filthy and wet from my time on the road. I expect I'll hear about it but Maggie surprises me by not bringing it up. I lean over and kiss her.

"I'm sorry," I say.

"What for? You're only ten minutes late. For you, I count this as being on time."

"I do, too, but I'm a mess. I should have stopped by my place first to shower and change my clothes."

"Then you really would have been late."

"But is this worse?" I ask.

"No," she says, smiling. "I kinda like you like this. It's very...manly. So, how'd it go?"

"Let's order first and then I'll tell you all about it."

Maggie orders the chicken. I order steak. We both have a beer. I like that about Maggie. She's not one of those prissy girls who insist on umbrellas in their drinks. She even prefers drinking it out of the bottle.

Once we settle in, she asks again about my day.

"Turns out, I may have stumbled onto a good story. But I'm not sure yet."

"What do you mean? The cat lady's a good story?"

"I think there's more to it than just some old woman who keeps cats dying."

I look around to make sure no one's listening. I don't know why. It's not like anyone cares, but I don't like the idea of anyone knowing my business. Seems to me, flying under the radar is always a good idea, especially for a reporter.

"This is between us, Maggie."

"Oh, aren't we the dramatic one?"

"Maybe. But this is my story and I don't want anyone else horning in on it."

She raises her left hand and puts her right hand on the menu which is still on the table.

"I swear on..."

I grab her hand and pull it toward me. "Okay, okay. I get

191

it. I'm ridiculous."

"No. You're not. You just take your job very seriously, that's all. And it's one of the things I like about you. You're not...superficial."

"I hope not."

"So, what's the story?"

"It's about this Elizabeth Chandler woman, but it doesn't have to do with her cats. That's just how the locals referred to her. She did have a couple dozen cats, but I guess after she died they found homes for them. At least I hope they did. Anyway, no one seems to know much about her, so I had to dig around. I talked to a few people and then I wound up getting into her house..."

"Got into?"

"Yeah, well, I kinda broke in. Well, not really broke in, because I just used the storm cellar to get into the house."

"But you didn't have permission, right?"

"Haven't I warned you about how dangerous I am? How the law means nothing to me?"

"Very funny. But it doesn't matter. In case you didn't notice, I have a soft spot for bad boys."

She leans over and kisses me quick on the lips. I like Maggie. I really do. And this is probably one of the reasons why.

"Who's going to give me permission? She's dead...no living relatives so far as I know. The state will probably take over the house."

"Were you scared?"

"Not really. Actually, it was kind of exciting."

I tell her what I found out about the cat lady, including all about the murder clippings in the album involving a British murderess named Maybrick.

"You stole the album?"

"More like I borrowed it." I pat my knapsack. "It's right here."

"Good thing my brother, Wally, wasn't around. I don't

think he'd go along with your concept of the word 'borrowed.' He'd be all too happy to arrest you. But don't worry, if he does I promise I'll bring you at least one hot meal a day."

Her brother, Wally, is one of the town cops. I've only met him once, but he seems to be an okay guy. A little stiff, maybe, not the kind of guy I'd pal around with, and maybe he's a little over-protective of his little sister. But I can understand that.

"So, what's in the articles?"

"I haven't read through all of them yet. And some of them are just headlines and captions. But then there's this." I take out the business card and hand it to her.

"What's this?"

"It dropped out of the album."

She reads the card. "Who is this Findlay guy?"

I shrug. "I don't know, but I'm hoping he was Elizabeth Chandler's lawyer and he can tell me something about her past."

I look up to see the waitress is standing over us.

"Excuse me," she says.

"Yes," I respond.

"Mr. Tudor asked me to tell you that your meal is on him." She gestures toward the left of the entrance and I see John Tudor, sitting alone at his regular table. He smiles at us and raises a glass. I do the same and then tell the waitress, "Please tell Mr. Tudor that I appreciate his offer, but I'm afraid I can't accept it."

"Why not?" asks Maggie.

I smile. "Because nobody owns me."

"Owns you? What are you talking about, Jake? The man just wants to buy us dinner," says Maggie.

"I'm a reporter, Maggie. I can't take favors from anyone. What if I have to write a not very flattering story about him?"

"And you think you'd be beholden to him for the price of a meal?"

"No. But I wouldn't want anyone to think I might be. You

get it, right?"

"I suppose I do." She takes my hand and squeezes.

On the way out, I ask Maggie to meet me by the front door of the restaurant while I make a detour to Tudor's table.

"Thanks for the offer, John."

"My feelings are hurt that you turned me down."

"You understand why, don't you?"

"Not really."

"I can't be taking free meals from people I might have to write about someday."

"I would have thought it would take more than a free meal to go easy on me."

I laugh.

"I guess it would, but I can't control what other people might think. It just doesn't look good."

"I stopped worrying about what things look like years ago, Jake. One day you'll feel the same way. Have you looked into that matter I mentioned the other day?"

"Not yet. They've got me on another story. But I haven't forgotten about it."

"I'm only trying to help you out. No skin off my nose if you don't follow up."

That's what he says, but I don't think he really means it or he wouldn't be bringing it up now. This only makes me more certain there's some kind of story there, that John knows much more than he's letting on, even if he won't tell me what it is.

We go to the local movie house and see a Humphrey Bogart movie called *The Maltese Falcon*, which was made from a Dashiell Hammett book. It's pretty good. I love Bogart. He's got that swagger and self-assured air about him that I hope I can duplicate someday. As I walk Maggie home, I perform my best Bogie impression.

But somehow, Maggie isn't very impressed.

I guess I'll have to work on it a little more.

4

The next morning, I head over to the local garage where I purchased my trusty motor bike. I'm looking for a favor from Randy, the guy who runs it. I don't feel like making the long trip over to New Haven in this kind of icy weather on my bike, so I need a car and I'm hoping to convince Randy to lend me one for the day. I find him under the hood of an automobile he's repairing. I tell him what I want but he's not buying it.

"Jake, I can't just go lending out people cars."

"Why not? It's only for the day. I'll have it back to you no later than five. I promise."

"You think I'm running a car dealership?"

"It's a favor, Randy. You know I can't afford to rent a car. Not on what I make."

"First the cycle, now this?"

"I bought the cycle, Randy."

"Buying implies that money changes hands, Jake."

"I gave you a down payment, right?"

"Twenty-five bucks? You call that a down payment? And what about the weekly payments you were supposed to make?"

"So, I'm a little behind."

"Two weeks, if I'm not mistaken. And I'm not."

"They only pay me every two weeks and my last check went for rent."

"That's supposed to be my problem?"

"No. But I promise next check I'll catch up."

"What makes you think I've got a car to lend you, anyway?"

I gesture toward the area behind the garage where he's got at least half a dozen cars parked.

"They're here to be fixed, Jake. And besides, they're not mine to lend out."

"You don't have one car that's ready to go?"

"The only car I've got running is old man Lillis's and he's supposed to be picking it up around four, four-thirty."

"Then I'll have it back by then."

"What am I supposed to tell him if he comes by earlier?"

"Tell him one of your associates is test driving it, just to make sure it works. It'll make you look good."

"Jesus, Jake."

"Come on, Randy. I'll owe you one."

"One what? What could you possibly do for me?"

"How about one year's free subscription to the newspaper?"

"You know I don't read that rag."

"Then how about a free ad?"

"You could do that?"

"I've got connections," I lie. The truth is the paper believes in the separation of church and state, just like the country does. There's no way I could get them to hand out free ads, but Randy doesn't know that. To pay off, I'll have to purchase the ad myself. But maybe I can wangle a discount for myself.

Randy scratches his head. "Well, I guess that might be worth my taking the chance."

"You wouldn't be taking a chance at all, Randy. I promise. I'll have it back by four. Three-thirty, in fact. How about it?"

"Jeez, you don't give up, do you?"

"Nope."

"Okay. Throw in a beer and next Saturday you come by and help me clean up the place and you've got yourself a deal."

"You drive a hard bargain, Randy."

"But if you don't have that car back here by three-thirty, Jake, you'll be writing your own obit."

"What makes you think I haven't already done that?"

* * *

A couple hours later I pull into New Haven, where I haven't been since I graduated Yale a couple years ago. I was an English major but all I ever wanted to be was a novelist, like Hemingway or Fitzgerald or Faulkner. When I graduated I realized no one was going to pay me to write the Great American Novel, and so, with no discernible skills other than being able to string a few sentences together, and a healthy curiosity—some might call it nosiness (my dad always did)—I figured journalism was as good a place as any to try to make a living. I had worked for a semester for the school paper and that was fun. So, why not make a profession out of it? Turned out I liked it. It was the closest thing I could find to working for myself.

Findlay's office turns out to be in a six-story stone office building in the middle of downtown New Haven. It's a little too early for lunch, so the sidewalks are pretty deserted and I'm lucky enough to find a parking spot only a block away from my destination.

Findlay's office is on the second floor. Rather than barging in, I knock on the door which has Herbert J. Findlay, Attorney-at-Law stenciled on it. At first, there's no answer, so I knock again. A female voice rings out, "Come on in!"

The voice belongs to a middle-age woman sitting at a desk in a reception area.

"May I help you?" she asks.

"I'd like to see Mr. Findlay, please."

"I don't believe you have an appointment."

"I'm afraid not."

"He's quite busy, you know. I'm not sure he can see you."

"I can wait."

She hesitates a moment. I'm guessing she doesn't like the idea of someone like me sitting in her reception area all day. "I can see if he's available."

"Please. I'd really appreciate that."

"May I tell him what your name is and what business you have with him?"

"Jake Harper and I'm a reporter with the *Litchfield County Gazette*."

"And what is this in reference to?"

"Mrs. Elizabeth Chandler."

I note a glimmer of recognition. She knows who Chandler is. It's a sign I'm on the right track.

She disappears behind the office door behind her. I hear voices and then a moment later she reappears with a smile on her face.

"Mr. Findlay will see you now."

"Thanks so much."

Findlay, who gets up from behind his desk and steps toward me, is in his mid-fifties, I guess, with graying hair and a thin mustache. He's very distinguished-looking, slim, well-groomed, wearing a dark, pin-striped suit, rep tie, starched collar and glasses. He projects just the right image for a lawyer: steady and responsible.

He offers his hand. "Pleased to meet you, Mr. Harper."

I don't think of myself as a mister, but there's something about the respect the word carries that makes me feel almost equal to this man who has probably studied and practiced the law for more years than I've been on this earth.

"Pleased to meet you, Mr. Findlay."

"Won't you have a seat," he says, pointing to a chair in front of his desk.

I sit and he takes his place back behind his desk.

"So," he says, "what brings you to New Haven and to my office?"

"I'm working on a story about a woman I think you know. Elizabeth Chandler."

His poker face does not change expression. I'm guessing he's very good at what he does.

"What makes you think I know this woman, Mr. Harper?"

"She passed away the other day and while going through her possessions I came across your business card."

He looks surprised.

"Elizabeth has passed away?"

"Yes, I'm afraid she has. Did you represent her?"

"Over the years I have handled a few, uh, affairs for her."

"What kind of affairs, if you don't mind my asking?"

"I'm afraid that falls under attorney-client privilege, Mr. Harper."

"Does that privilege continue after the death of your client, Mr. Findlay?"

He doesn't answer. I take that as a sign that although he's hesitant to talk about the woman, he'd really like to. So, I press on.

"As far as I know there are no heirs…unless you know differently—so I can't imagine who might be hurt by your providing me with a little information for my story."

"What story is that, Mr. Harper?"

"A woman surrounded by dozens of cats, a woman who no one seems to know anything about, dies suddenly, people are interested. They want to know who she was. How she got here. We call it a human-interest story, Mr. Findlay. I certainly don't think there's anything nefarious going on." I give it a hopeful beat. "Or is there?"

He laughs. "No, no, nothing nefarious. The truth is I was entrusted to make sure she received a very small stipend every six months. That's all."

"A stipend? From who?"

He smiles. "I'm afraid I can't divulge that information. That remains very much privileged information."

"Why?"

"Because the source of that stipend is still very much alive and I'm obligated by law, not to mention the canon of ethics, to keep that confidential."

"Is it a family member?"

Findlay doesn't respond.

"Because if it is, I'd just like to track him or her down so I can learn more about Miss Chandler."

He shakes his head. "I'm afraid I really can't say anymore, Mr. Harper. Even if I wanted to. I was simply hired to perform a service and that's what I did."

"Well, perhaps you can tell me what interest she might have had in a murder trial that took place in England almost fifty years ago."

"Why would you ask a question like that?"

I note a hint of irritation in his voice. I've hit a nerve.

"Because among her belongings, I found a scrap book with newspaper articles about the murder trial of a woman named Florence Maybrick."

Findlay removes his glasses, rubs the bridge of his nose, and stares out the window.

"If I tell you something, will you promise to keep it off the record?"

"Of course."

"This is a woman who had a very rough life and all she wanted was to live out the rest of it alone...and in peace."

"Are you telling me that Elizabeth Chandler was Florence Maybrick?"

"Well, you can write that, son, if you want to, but you didn't hear it from me. It would be a wild and unsubstantiated conclusion. I only knew her as Elizabeth Chandler."

This is something I hadn't considered. Elizabeth Chandler wasn't really Elizabeth Chandler.

I ask a few more questions but get no more answers. I realize I'm going to have to do more digging to find out if it's true.

I thank Mr. Findlay and, looking at my watch, I realize I have to get going or I'll never make it back to Randy's by three-thirty.

I'm so excited I can hardly keep my eyes on the road. My mind wanders all the way to a front-page story in the *Gazette* and then perhaps even national papers like the *New York Times* and the *Herald Tribune,* about a murderess living amongst us for all these years without anyone being the wiser.

I make most of the trip traveling at least ten miles above the speed limit and consider myself lucky I'm not stopped for speeding. If I were, there'd be no way I could afford the ticket and no way I could explain it to my bosses at the paper without giving away what could be the most important story of my life. And I am pretty sure that's exactly what they'd do: give the story to someone more senior on the paper. I'm not about to let that happen. Not after all the work I've put into it.

Could a silly cat-woman story turn out to be a story that changes my life? I certainly hoped so.

I make it back to Finch's garage with fifteen minutes to spare, surprising both me and Randy.

5

The next day is Saturday, my day off. Perfect timing. It will give me the opportunity to find out as much information as I can about Florence Maybrick and her murder trial and see if somehow I can find proof connecting her to Elizabeth Chandler. I've promised the day to Maggie, and so I convince her to go down to New York City with me, where I'll do some library research.

"It'll be fun, Maggie. I promise."

"Fun for who? You'll be working."

"Not the whole day. How about this? While I'm at the library you can do some window-shopping on Fifth Avenue, and then we'll have dinner and take in a movie or maybe even a show."

"You can afford all that?"

"Of course not. But I'll find a way to pay for it. It'll be great. And I'll make sure we make the last train back up here. What do you say?"

What can she say, other than yes? It even sounded pretty good to me while I was making it all up.

Early Saturday morning, we hop the train down to the City. Maggie is all decked out for our little outing, wearing what looks to me like a new hat pinned to her long, black hair, which is piled atop her head. She's also wearing what I think is probably a new dress, or at least it's one I've never seen her wear before. When I compliment her on it she blushes, which means I've done the right thing.

Me? Well, I'm a little more casual, wearing slacks, a blue blazer under my overcoat, and a black fedora on my head. The hat is a last-minute touch giving me, I hope, a devil-may-care look.

While Maggie stares out the window at the passing scenery, I read a copy of the *Gazette*. When we reach Greenwich, I'm interrupted by the conductor taking tickets. I take out ours and hand them to him.

"How long before we get to Grand Central?" I ask.

"Forty minutes, give or take," he answers.

I turn to Maggie. "Having fun yet?"

"Loads," she says, squeezing my arm.

"I'm glad your father gave you the day off from the bakery."

"My brother's off-duty today, so he offered to go in and help out."

"I owe him one."

Maggie goes back to the book she is reading while I return to one of the newspaper articles in the paper about the war in Europe. It seems to me it's only a matter of time before we're dragged into it. Churchill is doing all he can to convince Roosevelt it's the right thing to do, but best he will do is the Lend Lease Act, which was just enacted this past spring.

When I finish reading the paper, Maggie asks me what I already know about Florence Maybrick. I've read the articles from the scrapbook, but several of them were just headlines and others were much too faded from age to get any real information from.

"Not much, which is why we're taking this trip down to the city. But here's what I gleaned from these articles in Elizabeth Chandler's scrapbook. Florence Maybrick's maiden name was Chandler and she was born here, in Mobile, Alabama. On some ocean liner trip to England with her mother, she meets this guy named James Maybrick. He's quite a bit older than she is—she was nineteen and he was forty-two..."

"Forty-two! He was old enough to be her father," says

Maggie, her mouth wide open.

"It happens, Maggie."

"Not in New Milford, it doesn't. Go on."

"Anyway, they get married and eight years later he dies. Supposedly, he was poisoned and they think Florence is the one who poisoned him. She's tried and convicted and sentenced to death."

"When was this?"

"In 1889.

"Over fifty years ago, Jake."

"That's right."

"Go on."

"There is no going on. That's all I can get from the articles. Just the bare bones facts. That's why I need to go to the main library to see if I can find any other information."

"What do you think this has to do with your cat lady?"

"I can't be sure. There are all kinds of possibilities. Maybe she was related to either Florence or James. Or maybe, and this is a long shot, maybe she was Florence Maybrick. That's what I hope to find out today."

She grabs my arm and squeezes.

"This is so exciting, Jake. It's a real-life mystery. Wouldn't it be something if she really was this famous murderess? And you broke the story!"

"It sure would be," I say, trying to tamp down my excitement. But the truth is, that's exactly what I'm hoping. "And I'm going to follow it for as long as I can. I smell a story here, Maggie. Possibly a big one."

We pull into the city a little before ten and as I head over to the 42nd Street branch of the New York Public Library, Maggie heads up Fifth Avenue, in the direction of the big department stores. We arrange to meet around one at a Chock Full of Nuts in Times Square.

The library gives me pretty much all the background I need and by noon I have pretty much the whole story about Florence Maybrick and her husband, James.

As we eat our nutted cheese sandwiches—cream cheese and chopped nuts on dark raisin bread, a Chock Full of Nuts specialty—I fill Maggie in on what I've learned, reading from the notes I've jotted down.

"In 1880, when Florence, known as Florie, was eighteen, she took a trans-Atlantic voyage aboard the S.S. Baltic with her mother, Baroness Caroline von Roques, whose name and title were courtesy of her third husband, a Prussian cavalry officer. Florie's real father, a Southern aristocrat named William G. Chandler, passed away in his thirties. The baroness was suspected of murdering him with poison, though nothing ever came of the accusation.

"James Maybrick, forty-one, was on the ship and took a liking to Florie. They were married a year later at St. James's Church, in London. After returning and living in the States for a couple years, they settled down with their two children, James, whose nickname was BoBo—which, by the way, is the name on the back of one of the photographs—and Gladys, in Battlecrease House, in a suburb of Liverpool. Florie fit in immediately and evidently was a real hit on the social scene. They seemed to be a very happy, successful couple. But Maybrick turned out to be a hypochondriac, and as a result of treating himself he became a regular user of arsenic and patent medicines, some of which contained poisonous chemicals. He was also unfaithful to Florence. He had a number of mistresses, one of whom actually bore him five children."

"You're kidding!"

"It's true. And while her husband was dallying, so was she. She was even suspected of having an affair with one of her brothers-in-law. One of her affairs was with a local businessman named Alfred Brierley, and when her husband found out about it they fought. Maybrick assaulted her and announced he wanted a divorce."

"Is that why she killed him?"

"Well, it's a little more complicated than that, Maggie. The facts are that in 1889 Florence purchased flypaper containing arsenic from a local chemist's shop and soaked it in a bowl of water. She claimed this allowed her to extract the arsenic for cosmetic use, but soon after James was taken ill after self-administering a double dose of strychnine. His doctors treated him for acute dyspepsia, but his condition got worse. A few weeks later, Florence wrote a compromising letter to her lover, Brierley, which was intercepted by the nanny, who passed it on to James's brother, Michael, who was apparently the head of the family. On Michael's orders, Florence was immediately deposed as mistress of her house and held under house arrest."

"They could do something like that just for adultery? And what about her husband? He was an adulterer, too."

"Double-standard, Maggie. A few days after that blow-up a nurse reported that Florence surreptitiously tampered with a *Valentine's Meat Juice* bottle which was later found to contain a half-grain of arsenic. She claimed her husband begged her to administer it as a pick-me-up, but it turned out he never even drank it."

"Sounds pretty suspicious to me."

"Especially so, after James died in his home on May 11, 1989. His brothers, who were suspicious as to the cause of death, had his body examined and it was found to contain slight traces of arsenic, but not enough to be fatal. And it wasn't certain whether this arsenic was taken by Maybrick himself—remember, he was something of a hypochondriac and into self-medicating—or administered by someone else. They had an inquest and Florence was charged with murder. She stood trial in Liverpool, and she was convicted and sentenced to death."

"What a story," Maggie says, shaking her head.

"There's more. After a public outcry the Home Secretary

and some Lord concluded the evidence clearly established that Florence administered poison to her husband and intended to murder him, but that there was ground for reasonable doubt whether the arsenic that was administered did actually cause his death. And so, the death sentence was commuted to life imprisonment as punishment for a crime with which she was never charged."

"It gets juicier and juicier, doesn't it, Jake?"

"It didn't stop there. The case became a *cause celebre* both in Great Britain and here—remember, she was an American—and it was argued that back then some men considered arsenic an aphrodisiac and that James was known to have taken it regularly. In fact, a city chemist confirmed he had supplied James with quantities of the poison for a long time and when they searched his home they turned up enough of it to kill at least fifty people. And the truth was, Florence didn't really have a motive to kill her husband. The financial provision Maybrick had made for her and their children in his will was tiny and she might have been far better off with him alive but legally separated from her. Others believe she poisoned him because he was about to divorce her which, in Victorian society, would have ruined her. And she might have even lost custody of her kids."

"What happened to her after she was convicted?"

"She was sent to prison and spent her first nine months in solitary confinement. She suffered from insomnia and ill health. After she got out of solitary she was sentenced to hard labor, and was permitted to leave her cell during the day to assist in carrying meals from the kitchen. She scrubbed tables and furniture, washed dishes, and scrubbed floors. After seven years, she was transferred to another prison and in 1904, after spending fourteen years in prison, she was finally released. By this time, she'd lost her American citizenship, but she still returned here in 1920."

"And then what?"

"The trail gets ice cold. I can't find out anything else about her."

"What about their children?"

"They both died while she was in prison. And remember I mentioned that the inscription on her grave marker was F.E.C.M.?"

"Yes."

"F for Florence. E for Elizabeth. C for Chandler. M. for Maybrick. All this pretty much cinches for me that Elizabeth Chandler was Florence Maybrick."

"Do you think she did it?"

"I have no idea. But it seems like everyone in England thought so. James's brother, Michael, did. By the way, it turns out Michael Maybrick was a pretty famous songwriter and a friend of the Royal Court."

"It's an amazing story, Jake. Are you ready to write it yet?"

"Not yet. I think there's more out there and I need more proof than just the clippings and the photos. But I'll get it."

After lunch, I take Maggie to a double-feature both starring Humphrey Bogart—*The Maltese Falcon* and *High Sierra*—in a Times Square movie theater and before we hop back on the train up to Connecticut we have a quick dinner at Toffenetti's, an enormous restaurant that opened the year before. It's known as "the busiest restaurant on the world's busiest corner" and I remember reading about the opening in the newspaper when Mayor Fiorello LaGuardia's secretary cut the ceremonial ribbon because the mayor had to back out at the last minute. The restaurant is open twenty-four hours a day and has room for one thousand diners. The prices are remarkably reasonable, even I can afford it on my paltry salary. I have the Roast Sugar Cured Ham and Maggie has the Spaghetti A la Toffenetti with fresh meat sauce, and for dessert we split a huge plate of Old Fashioned Strawberry Shortcake, which has an avalanche of whipped cream spread over two huge homemade biscuits, smothered in fresh strawberries and strawberry sauce.

"Jake," Maggie says, as we walk back to Grand Central, "I don't think I'll ever eat again."

"Me, neither," I say, patting my bulging stomach.

Maggie takes my arm in hers and leans in against me. "I had a wonderful time. Thank you so much for letting me tag along."

"Are you kidding, Maggie. You made this whole thing fun."

We arrive back in New Milford around eight-thirty and walk from the station into town.

"I don't want this day to end," Maggie says.

"It doesn't have to. We can go back to my room and listen to some music, if you like."

She smiles. "It's a little late, don't you think?"

"It's not even nine o'clock yet and tomorrow's Sunday. You don't have to be at work, remember?"

"Okay. But only for another hour. I'm exhausted and my father will stay up until I get home. I told him I'd be back by ten and so..."

"Don't worry. I'll get you home by then. Believe me, I don't want to get on his bad side. Your brother's either."

We climb the stairs to my room. I open the door and flip on the light and when I turn to take Maggie's hand to lead her inside she gasps.

"What's wrong, Maggie? You look like you just saw a ghost. Or worse."

"Oh, my god, Jake. Look at your room. You didn't leave it like this, did you?"

I turn around to see that the room is in shambles. My belongings are strewn all over the floor. The cushions from my couch, which doubles as my bed, are on the floor. The closet door is open, every drawer in my dresser is pulled out and the contents scattered all over the floor.

"No. Of course not." It hits me what's happened. "Oh, my God, someone must have broken in while we were in the city."

Maggie pushes me aside and begins to walk into the room,

but I stop her.

"Maggie," I whisper. "We don't know if there's still any-one here."

"Jake, you have one room. Where could he be?"

She is right, of course, but I've never been in this situation before, only seen it in the movies. To save face and not seem ridiculous, I say, "What about the bathroom?"

She laughs. "I don't think so, Jake. Let's look around and see if anything's been taken. And then we can call my brother." She shakes her head. "Nothing like this *ever* happens up here. It's actually a little exciting, if you want to know the truth."

I wander through the room, half in a daze. It feels like it's happening to someone else...or at least should be.

"Is anything missing, Jake?" asks Maggie, rousing me from wherever else my mind is going.

"I don't know. I don't really have anything worth stealing." Suddenly, something occurs to me. "Maybe my typewriter."

I go to the closet, but there it is, sitting on the floor, just where I left it. "No, it's here."

"It's seems so odd. Why would someone break in and then not take anything?"

Suddenly, something occurs to me. I go to my bed and lift up the mattress, feeling under it.

"It's gone!"

"What's gone?"

"Elizabeth Chandler's scrapbook."

"Are you sure, Jake? Maybe you put it somewhere else."

"No. That's exactly where I put it."

"Why would you bother hiding it?"

I sit down on the edge of my bed.

"Because I stole it, Maggie. Remember, it's not mine and I had no right to remove it from her house. If someone came in here and saw it, I'd be in big trouble. For one thing, I'd prob-ably get fired."

"Who would take it, Jake?"

210

"I don't have the foggiest idea. It's not like it has any value."

"Well, you've already read everything in it, right?"

"Yes, but that's not what I'm worried about."

"What is?"

"Someone knows I have it and someone thinks it's valuable enough to steal it from me. That's what bothers me, Maggie."

"What are you going to do now?" she asks, sitting down beside me.

I look around and shake my head. "Clean this place up."

6

Maggie wants me to report the break-in to her brother and I agree to do it in the morning, but after a restless night's sleep I think better of it. What, I wonder, would that accomplish? Nothing was taken except for the album and that's something I'm not supposed to have in my possession. Besides, if I do report it I'll also have to report it to Barrett. And then, since we have so little crime of note in New Milford, it will become a story. A story someone else will write.

No. I'm much better off keeping this to myself, at least until I can put all the pieces together and figure out what's going on.

Maggie was worried about me staying in my room that night and offered me a spot on the family couch, but I turned her down. I'd feel strange sleeping in her house, with her parents there. Besides, I don't want to appear to be worried.

Nevertheless, I am. The lock on my door is busted, so in order to feel safe I prop a chair up against the door knob. I have no idea if that'll keep anyone out, but if someone does try to break in, I'll certainly hear them before they get inside.

I don't sleep particularly well that night. I jump at every sound, whether it be from outside or the creaking noises made by an old building. I can't help thinking about the break-in. I'm confused as to why anyone would want to steal that album. Who could possibly be interested in Elizabeth Chandler or this Florence Maybrick woman?

The next morning, Sunday, while most people in town are either in church or sleeping in, too restless to stay home I decide to take a morning stroll. As I'm walking the deserted streets, I see John Tudor coming toward me. Usually, he's smiling, but not this morning. Instead, he seems lost in thought. I consider just walking across the street, so he can't see me, but it's too late when he looks in my direction.

"Hey, John," I say. "How are you this morning?"

"Not so good, Jake."

"What's wrong?"

"Something strange happened to me last night."

"What's that?"

"Am I talking to Jake Harper reporter or Jake Harper private citizen?"

I take a chance that the right answer is "I haven't punched in yet, John, so it's Jake Harper private citizen."

"Good. Got a few minutes?"

I check my watch. I'm due at work in five minutes but no one punches a clock at the *Gazette* and I'm curious enough to chance being late and getting reamed out by my boss.

"Sure," I say. I hear urgency in John's voice. I think he's got something important to tell me. Maybe it's about that night watchman thing. Whatever it is, it might lead to another story.

"It's getting cold out here. What say we duck into the Grill for a few minutes? I'll treat you to a cup of Joe and maybe a plate of bacon and eggs."

"Sounds good. But you know I'll have to pay for my own, John."

Tudor laughs. "You really are incorruptible, Jake. I'm gonna have to stop trying."

A few minutes later we're sitting in a booth toward the back, facing each other over two cups of steaming java and plates of food.

"So, what's the problem, John?" I ask.

"I'm not sure there is one, but last night something strange happened and it's got me a little worried."

"What was it?"

"Remember, Jake, this is strictly between the two of us."

"Of course, John. Jake Harper, private citizen. Remember?"

"It was a little after eleven and I was just leaving the Grill. I got to my car and since I'd had a little too much to drink, I decided to wait a few minutes until I was sure I had all my senses. So, I'm sitting there in the front seat and I noticed this car parked about fifty feet behind me. There was someone sitting in the driver's seat, but it was dark and I couldn't see who it was. I didn't think too much of it. After a few minutes, I started up the engine and pulled out but as soon as I did I checked my rearview mirror and noticed the headlights went on in the car parked behind me and it pulled out and started following me."

"You're sure, John? After all, you did say you had a few."

"I'm sure. I don't see things that aren't there, no matter how buzzed I am, Jake. Anyway, I got on the road I always take home and the car was still behind me. As I picked up speed so did it. I slowed down, and so did it. We did this for a few minutes more and finally, just as I reached the turnoff to my house, the car sped up and roared past me. I couldn't make out the driver. As soon as I made the turn onto my road, it kept going. I actually thought about turning around and following it, but I thought better of it. It was late and like I said, I was a little tipsy. But it spooked me."

"What do you think that was all about, John?"

"I haven't the vaguest notion. But I know I didn't imagine it and I can't shake this feeling that something was going on."

"Are you going to report it?"

"To who?"

"The police."

He shook his head.

"There's nothing to report. It's just a feeling I have. I have no proof."

"Why tell me?"

"You're the Fourth Estate, Jake. If anything happens to me

I want it on the record."

"Why should something happen to you? You don't think it's about that matter you mentioned to me the other day, do you?"

He shrugged.

"The only thing I can say, John, is to keep your eyes open. And if you need any help from me, just let me know."

"Thanks, Jake. I appreciate that. Just getting it off my chest helps a little."

All the way back to my office, I keep thinking about what John just told me. Suddenly, some very strange shit was happening in New Milford. My room being broken into and something is stolen, and now someone seems to be following John Tudor. I can't imagine what the connection might be, but something tells me there is one.

7

The next day, as soon as I get in I head straight for Barrett's office for our usual Monday morning meeting. He's on the phone and he seems agitated. When he spots me standing in the doorway he gestures for me to come in, then waves me toward a seat to the left of his desk.

"I don't care how long it takes, Al. You stay there until you get something. Understand? This is a big story, pal, and I want you right on top of it."

Barrett hangs up the phone, goes to the door, sticks his head out and yells, "Doring. I want you in here. Right away."

Barrett returns to his seat.

"What's up, Chief?" asks Doring as he takes the chair to my right.

"I just got some disturbing news," Barrett says. He removes his eyeglasses and places them on the desk. "You're friends with John Tudor, aren't you, Harper?"

"I wouldn't exactly call us friends. More like friendly. Why do you ask?"

"I've got some bad news, kid. He died last night."

"What? You're kidding..." I sputter, though I know he's not. "What happened?"

"Evidently, he'd had a little too much to drink. Got home late. Tried to take a shower. Fell in the bathtub. Hit his head. Died instantly."

Doring, shakes his head. "I guess they're right about accidents in the home. We did a story on that a couple years back, remember, Dave?"

Barrett nods.

"Who found him?" asks Doring.

"His wife was away. She kept calling and couldn't get an answer, so she asked one of the neighbors to check up on him. She found him in the bathtub, with the water still running."

"Something doesn't sound right," I say. I can't help but think of what Tudor told me yesterday.

"What do you mean?" asks Barrett.

"I mean, why would someone be taking a shower in the middle of the night. Especially if he was drunk?"

"Maybe he wanted to sober up," says Doring.

Barrett shakes his head.

"It doesn't matter why, Jake. The fact is, he's dead. And that's a damn big story around here. He was only fifty-two."

"Don't you think it might be suspicious, especially with the tip he gave me the other day on that Philbin thing last week."

I don't mention what Tudor told me yesterday, about his being followed. Right now, since they're convinced it's an accident, I figure I'll hold back on that for a while.

"Al couldn't come up with anything," says Doring. "I think it was just a case of John having a little fun with you, Jake. You being the new kid and all."

"He wouldn't do that, Al. I think there's more to this than it appears."

"It was an accident, Jake," says Barrett. "Accidents happen. Lots of them in bathrooms."

"Why don't you let me look into it, Mr. Barrett? There's been some weird stuff going on lately."

"What's that supposed to mean?" asks Doring.

"The other night my room was broken into. And now this. Maybe it's a coincidence, but maybe not."

"I don't believe in coincidences, kid," says Barrett. "What'd they take? I can't imagine it was much since we don't pay you enough here for you to actually have anything worth stealing."

I consider whether or not I should mention the album and decide against it. It would mean revealing so much else that I'm not ready to reveal yet. Besides, if I'm honest with myself I'm afraid they'd take both stories away from me. I don't want that to happen and so if I come back with more ammunition about both of them, I figure they can't take the stories from me.

"Nothing I can see, but I'm still cleaning up."

Doring pipes up. "Might be some kids playing a prank. Happens here near the holidays, when they have nothing better to do."

"What's happening with that cat lady story, Jake?" asks Barrett. "What's taking so long?"

"I'm working on it. It's a little more complicated than I thought."

"Complicated how?" asks Doring.

I shrug, hoping they'll drop the subject. "There's just a little more there than meets the eye."

"Like?" asks Barrett.

"She was a recluse, but I've started tracking down some leads about her past. I just need a little more time."

"We'll need some art for the piece, if it's going to be anything more than just a simple obit," says Doring.

"There were some photos back at her place. I'm sure I could borrow a couple of them."

"You got into her house?" says Doring.

Shit. I've probably said too much. Now the only way out of this is to tell a little white lie.

"Yeah. The town fire marshal had a key and he let me in."

"Why don't you take a camera with you when you go back. Might be nice to have some photos of the house—especially if any of those cats are still around," says Barrett.

"The cats are gone, but I can take some shots."

"Okay, see what you can get. And Jake, I want that story no later than next Monday. That'll give you the long weekend to write it up. And I want you to stay away from this Tudor-Philbin thing. Understand?"

I nod yes, but I don't really understand and there's no chance I'm going to obey the order. This isn't the army and they can't tell me what to do on my own time.

"Maybe we can put Al back on it for a day," Doring says.

It's *my* story, but I know I can't go down that road with these guys, so I keep my mouth shut. If Al comes up with something, fine. But I don't think he will. Especially if they all think Tudor's death really was an accident.

"Okay," says Barrett. "We have to run something about John, a feature, so put Al on that."

I suppress a smile. They've just handed me the gift of more time.

After I finish with Barrett and Doring, I head over to the police station. The desk sergeant tells me Wally Hines, Maggie's brother, is next door, picking up coffee at Ledbetter's for the rest of the guys.

Wally is sitting at the counter talking to the waitress as she's filling his order. He's wearing his police uniform, which always makes him appear to be a little bigger than he actually is. Not that he's small. He's about five-eleven, but solidly built and that coupled with his Marine buzz cut makes him look like someone you shouldn't tangle with.

I sit down next to him.

"Hey, Jake, what's up? Haven't seen you in a while."

"They've got me working on a story that's taken me out of town."

"You're gonna own that paper one day."

"I doubt it. Besides, I've got bigger fish to fry."

"Like what?"

"Like working on a big city paper, while writing novels."

"Maybe one day I'll read one."

He laughs and I laugh with him.

"So, what can I do you for, 'cause I know this isn't just a coincidence."

"That's why you're such a good cop, Wally. You've got that cop's instinct."

"Yeah, yeah. So?"

"Were you over at John Tudor's place this morning?"

"Sure was. Poor guy."

"Notice anything suspicious?"

"Guy slips in his bathtub, hits his head. What's suspicious about that? Maybe you want me to arrest the soap?"

"Very funny, Wally, but I'm not kidding around. Last week John told me I ought to look into that so-called accident over at Philbin's Brass Works seven, eight months ago. He intimated it wasn't an accident."

The waitress sets a cup of joe in front of Wally and says, "The rest of your order will be out in a minute, hon. Anything for you, hon?" she asks me.

"I'm good," I say.

Once she's gone, I whisper, "So, my room was broken into last night."

"You're kidding? We haven't had a burglary here in, hell, I don't know how long. You report it?"

I shake my head. "I'm not even sure this counts as a burglary because they didn't take anything of value. That's why I'm thinking maybe this has something to do with John. Maybe someone knows he talked to me about the Philbin thing and was afraid I'd come up with some information."

"Did you?"

"I mentioned it to Barrett and Doring, but they wouldn't let me investigate it. They put Al on it and he hasn't come up with anything. But I'm not sure he's put much effort into it."

"I don't know how you get from that to John's death, Jake."

"I bumped into John yesterday. He told me this weird story

about him being followed home the night before after he left the Grill. He was worried. Maybe whoever followed him came back the next night and murdered him and made it look like an accident."

"Jeez, Jake, when did you get your Junior G-Man's badge?"

"I'm serious, Wally. I think you ought to look into it. It might even give your career a boost."

"What makes you think my career needs a boost? Molly tells me you're the one chasing after cat ladies."

"Yeah, and you're the one pounding a beat. What would it hurt for you to go back there and nose around a little?"

"Nose around for what?"

"I don't know. Signs of forced entry, maybe. You're the one with the badge and the training, Wally. Why don't you tell me?"

He just shakes his head. I'm not going to fight him on it. Here I am giving him an opportunity to distinguish himself and he gets all by the book on me. I'm just hoping I put enough of a bug in his ear that he'll go back out to Tudor's and nose around.

Meanwhile, I've got two mysteries to solve. Was John Tudor murdered and, if so, why? And, why is someone so interested in my pursuing the Elizabeth Chandler-Florence Maybrick connection?

To answer the latter, I need to go back to the Chandler house and nose around again. As an excuse, I'll use the need to get photos.

As soon as I leave Wally, I head up to the Chandler house. I park my bike in the same spot it was a few days earlier and rather use the storm cellar entrance, I try the front door again. Before I get a chance to try, I notice that the door is slightly ajar. Either someone's been inside the house since I've been there or they're in there now.

I listen for telltale sounds. Nothing. I circle the house to see if there are any vehicles parked out back. None. I return to the front porch and check the lock on the front door. It's been jimmied. Whoever's been here didn't use a key which means they didn't have permission to enter.

I open the door, stick my head in and call out, "Anyone here?"

No answer.

I venture into the house. It doesn't look anything the way it did the other day. Everything is in disarray, not unlike what my room looked like after it was tossed. The furniture has been pushed around, toward the center of the room. Pillows from the sofa and chairs are strewn on the floor. A hutch has been emptied. A small bookcase is bare, its contents on the floor. The kitchen is in pretty much the same condition: cabinet doors flung open, refrigerator door wide open.

Upstairs, the bedroom is also in disarray. Linens from the trunk are scattered over the bed and the floor. The closet door is open and clothing lying in a pile in front of it.

Maybe, I think, it's the work of a bunch of kids, hoping to find something they can sell or use. But I don't really believe that. More likely it's someone looking for something like Elizabeth Chandler's scrapbook. And if that's the case, the house was probably searched before they searched my room and wound up finding what they were looking for. I ask myself, why is that scrapbook so important and to who?

I hope on my bike and head back to New Milford. I park in front of Maggie's bakery. I can see her through the window. Her hair is pinned back and she's wearing an apron, as she puts trays of pastries into the glass counter.

When I enter the store my arrival is announced by a bell.

"Jake, what are you doing here?"

"I need to talk to you."

"I'm here alone and as you can see, I'm a little busy. Can't it wait?"

"I've need to talk to you now." I reach out and grab her arm. "Come with me."

She resists.

"I can't just leave, Jake. I'm the only one here. It's almost lunch time and people will be coming in."

"There's no one here now and this'll only take a couple minutes."

She gives me an exasperated look. "I sure hope my dad doesn't find out about this." She wipes her hands on her apron and heads toward the front door. She takes the Open/Closed sign and flips it to Closed and pulls the shades down.

I follow her to the back of the store, through the kitchen, where the sweet aroma of fresh pastry fills the air. We step outside the back door to the alley. Standing in front of the fire escape stairs that climb up to the third floor of the building, she turns and says, "Okay, Jake. What's wrong?"

"There's something very strange going on, Maggie. I thought the break-in of my room might have something to do with John Tudor, but I'm not so sure anymore. I just got back from Florie's house and someone's broken in there, too. That's much too much of a coincidence for me."

"Was something taken?"

"I'm not sure. But it doesn't matter. What matters is some-one's taking a serious interest in me and what I'm working on. It means I must be getting closer to something important."

"What are you going to do now?"

"More sniffing around."

"Be careful, Jake," she says, giving me a quick hug. It feels good that she worries about me, but I know what I have to do, even if it might be dangerous.

As soon as I leave Maggie, I go back to the office and call the South Kent School and ask to speak to Mr. Tallamy. I'm told he's with a class but that he should be free in about an hour.

On my way to my motor bike a fellow literally bumps into me. He's heavy-set, over six feet tall, and wearing an over-coat. He's got a bulbous nose, his hair is slicked back and it looks as if he hasn't shaved in a few days.

"Sorry, mister," he says.

"That's okay," I say. "No harm done."

Before I can move on he pulls a pack of cigarettes out of his pocket and asks, "You wouldn't happen to have a match, would you?"

"Sorry, I don't smoke," I say, and start to brush past him. But before I get far I feel a hand on my shoulder.

"Say, don't I know you?" he asks.

"I don't think so."

"Sure, I do. You're that reporter, Jake Harper, aren't you? I've heard good things about you. You're a real go-getter, ain't you?"

He gets real close to me. Close enough to smell his sour breath, like he's been drinking too much coffee.

"You're real nosy, aren't you? But I guess that's part of the job, ain't it?"

"I've got to be somewhere," I say, pulling away.

"Sure, you do. You got stories to check out, right? But I'm wondering, isn't your line of work kinda dangerous? I mean, can't you get into trouble investigating things that ain't your business?"

"Look, pal..."

He grins, baring a set of yellow, uneven teeth. "I ain't your pal, Jake. We just met, right? But I'm gonna give you some free advice. Things can get dangerous, you sticking your nose where it don't belong. You could get it cut off, right? I mean, I know it goes with the territory, you being a reporter and all, but I'm thinking sometimes you gotta watch what you're doing."

He stares into my eyes for a moment, a scary moment. He brushes against me and I feel something hard in his midsection. A gun? When he knows I've felt it, he smiles.

"Well, Jake, I surely don't want to keep you from wherever you're going. A guy like me doesn't get much chance to meet a guy like you. I mean, it ain't like you and me got much in common, right?"

He pats my shoulder.

"It's been a real pleasure, but for your sake, I hope I don't see you around."

He turns and starts to walk away. He stops, turns to face me, pulls a package of cigarettes out of his pocket, removes a pack of matches from another pocket, and lights up. He looks back at me, smiles and waves.

He creeps me out, but the only thing he's accomplished is to let me know I'm onto something, something important. He's right about one thing, though. I'll have to be more careful from now on.

I find Tallamy in his classroom. He's sitting at his desk grading papers. I stick my head in the door.

"Mr. Tallamy, Jake Harper. Remember me?"

"Sure do," he says, waving me in. "And why don't you just call me Peter?"

"Sure thing, Peter," I say, as I pull up a chair and sit in front of his desk.

"So, what can I do for you today, Jake Harper?" he asks, putting his red pencil down and leaning back in his chair.

"I've been doing some research since I last saw you and it appears that Elizabeth Chandler had a far more interesting life than you may have known."

"What do you mean?"

"I'm on deadline and I don't have a lot of time to explain how I know this but I have reason to believe Elizabeth Chandler might have been someone else."

"Like who?"

"A woman named Florence Maybrick."

"Should I know who that is?"

"There's no reason you would. She was a woman who

spent time in prison in England for murdering her husband fifty years ago. It was quite the scandal at the time."

Shaking his head, Tallamy says, "I can't believe it. That sweet, old woman, a murderess. And living right here in Connecticut? Are you sure about this, Jake?"

"I don't have all the proof yet, but I'm pretty sure. And evidently I'm digging into areas some people might prefer I left alone. My room was broken into the other day and a scrapbook she kept was taken. And then, when I went back and visited her home the other day to get some photos of her to use in my story for the paper, I found it had been broken into and ransacked. I'm pretty sure both break-ins are connected. Someone's looking for something and whoever it is must think I have it."

"Are you sure you're not letting your imagination run away from you?"

"I'm sure. I thought you might be able to help me figure things out."

"I'll try to help, Jake, but I don't know how what I can add to what you already know. My time with her was so limited and I was a kid. The only real time I spent with her was one day when she invited me in for tea." He stops and rubs the back of his head, as if he's trying to dislodge some old, faint memory.

"Tell me everything you remember about that day."

"It was a day when she asked me to dig a hole near her garden. She told me she had to bury one of her cats."

"And you did it?"

"Sure."

"Didn't it strike you as odd?"

He smiles. "Everything about that woman was odd, Jake, and digging a cat's grave ranked toward the bottom."

"Tell me more."

"She handed me a metal box with the dead cat inside. Then, she had me fill the small hole and plant some bulbs on top. I couldn't tell you what the bulbs were, though."

"Did you see the dead cat?"

He laughs again. "The last thing I wanted to see was a dead cat. Besides, I don't think I would have had the nerve to ask her to open the box. Why would I doubt her? To a teenager, she was kind of scary."

"Anything else?"

"Not that I can think of."

"Do you happen to know who arranged for her to be buried here?"

"I believe it was the idea of some lawyer."

"Did he arrange for the grave marker, with the initials on it?"

"I believe he did."

"It's more proof that she was Elizabeth and Florie."

"How do you mean?"

"Think about those letters."

"The letters? Yes! You're right. The two names."

I tear a piece of paper from my notebook, write down my phone number at the paper, and hand it to Tallamy. "In case something else comes to mind, this is where you can reach me."

"I hope you'll let me know what you find out, Jake."

I don't answer him. Suddenly, everyone is suspect, everyone a possible enemy. I trust no one. Is this, I wonder, the downside of journalism?

After I leave Tallamy, I head back to Elizabeth Chandler's house to see if I can find whatever Tallamy helped her bury. I realize the chances of it still being there after all these years are slim, but even slimmer are the chances of it holding anything meaningful. After all, it is possible it's just what Chandler claimed it was: a dead cat.

About fifteen or twenty yards behind the Chandler cottage, I find an area that looks like it might have been a garden. I can tell because it's obvious that at one time the area was cleared. Left untended for so long, weeds have grown around what looks to me to be a rosebush.

I look back toward the house and see that the sight-line to the road is obscured, giving me plenty of privacy. I go back to the cellar and bring back a small shovel.

The wind, coming in from the northeast, has picked up, bringing a sharper chill. The sky has filled with menacing grey clouds and there's a feel of snow in the air. I've forgotten to wear a sweater under my leather jacket, so I feel the growing chill. I pull my watch cap out from my jacket pocket and put it on.

Despite the growing cold, I work up a sweat. I dig up one hole after another, each one no more than six or so inches deep. I move on when I hit roots or large rocks.

After about twenty minutes of digging, when I'm close to giving up, I jam the shovel into the ground and hit something hard and I hear the sound of metal against metal. I shovel quicker. I uncover the top of something that looks like a rectangular metal box, about twelve inches by six inches. I toss the shovel to the side, get down on my knees, and work the box out of the earth.

My heart is beating so fast I think it'll leap from my chest.

The box is locked.

Suddenly, I get a feeling I'm being watched. Is there someone inside the house watching me? Tucking the box under my arm, I scan the area. I don't see anything or hear anything out of the ordinary. I look back to the house, which sits there like a menacing, silent witness. On the second floor, I see that a curtain I was sure was covering one of the windows isn't covering it anymore. Am I mistaken, or is there someone up there spying on me?

I won't wait around to find out, and I'm not foolish enough to go into the house to see if anyone's there. Heroics are for someone else. I stuff the box into my knapsack and walk quickly back to my motor bike. I hop on and get out the hell out of there as quick as I can. I don't look back until I pull up in front of the *Gazette* office.

Only when I'm back at my desk at the paper do I pull the metal box out from my knapsack. I place it on my desk in front of me and stare at it a moment. It's rusted and there are still clumps of dirt clinging to the sides of it. The lock doesn't look like much of a challenge. I open my desk drawer and remove a letter opener. I jam it into the lock and twist it around until I hear a click. I look around to make sure no one is watching me before I open the box.

There's no dead cat. What is there is an old, tattered, leather-bound book that looks like a diary, a diary Elizabeth obviously didn't want anyone to see.

Carefully, I open the book. The pages are faded from time. I begin thumbing through it, careful not to tear one of the fragile, aged pages. The entries, all of them dated, are written in green ink, the letters and words so close together it's hard to tell them apart, which makes it difficult to decipher.

Randomly, I stop at a page near the end of the book. It's dated 1888, and under that is the word Battlecrease. I begin to read.

"B and G look at me with increasing fear in their small eyes. I cannot blame them. They should be frightened. I am as unfamiliar with myself as they seem to be. I answer a sinister calling. I see F's face in every Whitechapel harlot I take. Mary comes and goes in the dark of the night. He kisses the whores and gives them a fright. With a ring on my finger and a knife in my hand, I spread mayhem throughout this land…"

B and G, that fits Florie's children, one of whom was known as Bobo. And F, could that stand for Florence. But what about this "Whitechapel harlot?" What does this mean, "Mary comes and goes in the dark of night. He kisses the whores and gives them a fright?"

Suddenly, it occurs to me that this isn't Florence's diary.

Much more likely, it's the diary of her husband, James.

I flip ahead a couple pages where I find an old photo tucked between the pages. At first I can't make out what it is, but after staring at it a few moments it becomes clear. It's a photo of what appears to be a nineteenth-century crime scene. The bloody, mangled body of a woman lies on a bed. Just above the body on the wall the letters F.M. are clear.

I shut the book quickly, as if reading anymore will unleash some kind of vile, evil spirit. What, in God's name, have I found? And what am I going to do with it?

8

Still shaken, I realize Findlay knew more than he let on. He certainly knew, for instance, who Elizabeth Chandler really was. I phone his office and get his secretary. I ask to speak to Findlay and she says she'll see if he's available. A few moments pass before she comes back on the line.

"I'm afraid Mr. Findlay is in the middle of an important conference and can't come to the phone."

"Tell him it's important. Tell him I've found what he's been looking for."

"As I said…"

"I know what you said, but this is urgent and I'm sure Mr. Findlay would rather I speak to him before I go to the authorities." An empty threat, but she doesn't know that.

A moment passes then Findlay comes on the line.

"Mr. Harper, you've caught me at a very inopportune time. What is so urgent that you've pulled me from a very important meeting?"

"For starters, you can tell whoever's following me to cut it out."

"I'm afraid I don't know what you're talking about."

"I think you do."

"You're quite mistaken, Mr. Harper. I'm completely in the dark…"

There was something in his tone, way too cool and calculated, that not only pissed me off but made me certain I was on the right track.

"I'm not making a mistake, Mr. Findlay. And I suggest you speak to your client or clients and make my position very clear. I'll be filing my story tomorrow morning and so if you'd like to make a statement, now's the time. Oh, and you can tell your client that I do have what they're looking for, but it's safely hidden."

There is a moment of silence. I can practically hear the wheels in his head spinning. I've spoken to enough lawyers in my time to know they're very careful about what they say. Findlay was no different.

"I have no idea what you're talking about, Mr. Harper. But perhaps the only way we can straighten this out is face to face. I'm sure we can clear the air."

"I have no problem with that. But it'll have to be no later than tomorrow afternoon. I can only postpone my deadline one day."

"Tomorrow will be fine. There's an outdoor ice skating rink in New Haven. Are you familiar with it?"

"I am."

"I have part of the afternoon free, so how about we meet there at three o'clock?"

"That's fine. I will see you tomorrow at three."

There is an unofficial wake for John Tudor at the Grill that evening. It's not something I would normally attend, but very little is normal of late and there's a chance I might pick up some information. I decide to take Maggie with me. She's familiar with the situation and two pairs of eyes are better than one. Also, it will make it appear I'm not there on business if I bring her.

John Tudor was a popular man and that's reflected in the attendance. The wake is called for seven-thirty and by eight the Grill is jammed with mourners, many of whom I don't recognize. The noise level is particularly high, and every so often it's punctuated by laughter. At first, that seems out of place at a wake, but when I think about it, knowing John, it seems far more appropriate than solemn silence.

As soon as I arrive I head toward the bar with Maggie in tow. Charlie, one of John's nephews, is on duty tonight. He smiles when he sees me and asks what I'll have. I hold up two fingers and point to the draft spigot.

When he sets them on the bar, I reach for my wallet, but Charlie stops me.

"Everything's on the house tonight, Jake. It's all on John. That's the way he wanted it."

Just like John, to make sure everyone is taken care of.

After we get our drinks, we move to a corner of the room, where Maggie identifies many of the people there.

"That's his widow over there," Maggie says, pointing to a woman dressed in black. She's standing at the back end of the bar, talking to several people.

"She seems so young," I say.

"Second wife," says Maggie.

"Is his first here?"

"Actually, she's back with John."

"You mean she passed away?"

"About six years ago. That's Kate. She was a waitress here. They were married about a year after Susan died."

"Really?"

Maggie smiles. "I know what you're thinking, Jake, but Kate only moved to town six months after Susan's death. So, no, there was no hanky-panky."

"How did you know that's what I was thinking?"

She smiles and raises one eyebrow.

There are several people Maggie doesn't know, but I figure they might be people John had business with, or relatives from out of town. Maggie informs me that he has one son, but he's in the army and won't make it back until the funeral, which is in a couple days.

"Will you hold onto this a minute, Jake. I have to visit the little girl's room."

"Sure thing," I say, taking her beer. "I'll do a little mingling while you're gone."

"You mean sleuthing."

I grin as Maggie gives me a quick kiss on the cheek and heads toward the bathroom at the back of the Grill. Slowly, I work my way through the crowd, which seems to be growing larger by the minute. Either John had an awful lot of friends or word has gone out the drinks are free.

As I near John's favorite booth, which is roped off in honor of John, I notice Maggie's brother, Wally, making a beeline toward me.

"Jake," he says, "I've got to talk to you."

"Sure thing. What's up?"

"Not here. Outside."

"I'm with Maggie. She just went to the bathroom and I'm holding this beer for her."

"She'll take forever. I only need a couple minutes."

"Okay."

I put the beers down on a table and follow Wally outside. It's begun to snow. We step off to the side, under an awning. Wally takes out a cigarette, pops it into his mouth then offers the pack to me.

"No, thanks," I say. "I've managed to resist the temptation so far."

"Suit yourself." Wally seems a little nervous. He lights the butt, turns his head away from me and exhales a puff of smoke.

"Shit, it's cold out here," I say, crossing my arms across my chest to try to keep warm.

"It's winter," says Wally. "It's supposed to be cold. Listen, Jake, I think you might have been right about what happened to Tudor."

"You found something?"

"Yeah. It seems someone broke into Tudor's house the

night he died."

"How do you know?"

"I checked out the back door and I'm pretty sure it was jimmied. There are scratches around the lock. No one looked for it when it happened, because it appeared to be an open and shut case of accidental death. But when you mentioned your suspicion I went back and took a look. Besides the jimmied lock, I found a couple cigarette butts on the ground, near the back door. And then I found a crumpled cigarette pack in the kitchen trash bin. Camels. As far as I know, John didn't smoke."

"I never saw him light up."

"My guess is someone broke in and was waiting for him to come home. When he did, he grabbed him, maybe hit him over the head, then dragged him up to the bathroom. He undressed him, filled the bathtub, then holds his head under water. Then he drains the tub, keeps the shower running, and makes it look like Tudor slipped in the shower."

"So, you guys are investigating this as a murder case?"

"It looks like we should."

"How about that so called accident at the Brass Works last spring? You know, the one…"

"I'm way ahead of you, Jake. I went back over the police report and the evidence and, sure enough, we found a cigarette package on the floor, near the window where he fell from. Camels. It's not conclusive, but it does make you wonder."

"I knew it."

"But Jake, you're not going to help us any by writing a story about this. We can't let anyone know we think these weren't accidents."

"I'm a newsman, Wally…"

"I don't care what you are. I'm not about to let you hinder an ongoing investigation. And don't get all up in my face about freedom of the press."

"Okay, but you make sure no one else gets this story when

you get ready to break it. Remember, you wouldn't even have a story if I didn't come to you. I get first shot."

"You've got my word on it. But I'm warning you, you have to stay out of our way. Understand?"

I nod but what I'm thinking is, staying out of the way is a vague order. It doesn't mean I can't stay on the story.

9

I borrow another car from Randy and head down to New Haven. In my knapsack is the diary I dug up from Elizabeth Chandler's garden.

As soon as I arrive in the city I head straight to my old haunt, the Yale campus. A wave of nostalgia hits me as I see students heading to and from classes. It wasn't so long ago that I was one of them.

I head for the Hall of Graduate Studies to speak to one of my old history professors, David Ogden. As I stand at the door of the professor's office I check my watch and see I'm a few minutes late. I smile, because some things never change: I was always a few minutes late for his class. It was the first one in the morning and since I sometimes worked late waiting tables at a local greasy spoon, I often had trouble getting up in the morning. I wonder if he'll remember.

I knock on the door and the professor's booming voice calls for me to come in.

He's sitting at his desk, his sport jacket off, sleeves rolled up, wearing his trademark black bow tie and red suspenders. His eyeglasses are atop his head, and his white hair seems a little whiter than I remember, and a little longer. His desk is cluttered, as usual. The professor has been at Yale for as long as anyone can remember, and he is still one of my heroes. I loved attending his class because he made history come alive. He is also one of the smartest men I've ever met. At least he seemed that way back when I was a student.

"*Plus ca change, plus c'est la meme chose,*" he says, greeting me.

"I guess I am a little late," I say sheepishly. I'm a little surprised at myself because even though I'm no longer a student, and the professor no longer holds my fate in his hands in terms of the grade he's going to give me, I still feel like a small child facing a stern parent.

"Long time no see, Jake."

"It hasn't been that long, has it?"

"When you see hundreds of students a year, it always seems more time has passed than it actually has. How long since you've been here?"

"A little over three years."

"That's practically a lifetime in academe. I was pleased to hear from you. I like to keep tabs on my favorite students."

"I was one of your favorites?"

"I always had a soft spot for you, Jake. I liked your spunk. I even liked that you seemed to have your head stuck firmly in the clouds. It means you've got imagination. And curiosity. Two essentials if you're going to make it in the world. What've you been doing with yourself since graduation?"

"I'm a reporter for the *The Litchfield County Gazette.*"

"Writing history down, are you?"

"Instead of making it, I guess."

"Interesting times to be in journalism. I don't think it's going to be too long before we're pulled into this war. Then you'll really be chasing stories. Have a seat and can tell me the reason for your visit."

I sit down, open up my knapsack, remove the diary, and place it in front of him.

"I'd like you to take a look at this and tell me what you think."

"What's this all about, Jake?"

I give him the abridged story. About Elizabeth Chandler. About Florie Maybrick. About finding the album with the newspaper clippings. About being pretty sure they are one in the same.

"And now this," I say, gesturing toward the diary. "I think it's very important but I'm not quite sure what the significance of it is. That's where I thought you might be able to help."

The professor picks up the diary, shifts his eyeglasses from atop his head to his nose and slowly and carefully turns the pages. Several minutes pass before he reaches a page I've marked with a photograph.

"I put that photograph there, professor."

"To mark this particular page?" he asks, as he removes it and puts it on the desk without looking at it.

"Yes."

He reads a little more, then looks up.

"Jake, exactly what do you know about this diary?"

"It was in the possession of Elizabeth Chandler or rather Florie Maybrick. I think this was her husband, James's, diary and I think there's some importance to it. But I'm not sure what it is. I'm not even sure it's genuine, which is why I wanted to show it to you."

"From the style of writing and the condition of the book itself, I believe it is authentic in terms of the period you're talking about." He looks down at the diary again and gingerly turns a few more pages.

"Do you have any idea what it appears you have here, Jake?"

"Not really, which is why I came to you. It sounds like I should know what it is, but I can't quite place it."

"You've heard of Jack the Ripper, I assume?"

"Of course."

"When Jack the Ripper killed those five prostitutes the newspapers called them the Whitechapel murders. These lines here, 'see F.'s face in every Whitechapel harlot I take. He comes and goes in the dark of the night. He kisses the whores and gives them a fright. With a ring on my finger and a knife in my hand. This May spread Mayhem out throughout this far land.'"

The professor looks up.

"The murderer left rhyming notes like this at the scenes of the crime. I can't be sure, Jake, but this might very well be the diary of the man who came to be known as Jack the Ripper and, if you say it was owned by James Maybrick, it would follow that he, in fact, was Jack the Ripper. Of course, this is mere speculation and that's what it will remain until the authenticity of this document can be proved."

He stops for a moment, flashes a triumphant smile, then continues reading from the diary.

"May comes and goes. This May spreads Mayhem..."

"May and Mayhem could be a play on words for Maybrick."

The professor picks up the photograph and looks at it. He flips it over.

"The initials here are F.M."

"Florence Maybrick."

"Yes. What if every time he killed one of those prostitutes he was really murdering his wife, Florence. It's possible you've made a very important discovery here, Jake. But as scholars, we have to take responsibility to be as thorough as possible. When did you say James Maybrick was murdered by his wife?"

"If she actually murdered him, you mean?"

"Yes."

"The spring of 1889."

"Then it's very possible Florence Maybrick, or someone else who knew who he was, actually murdered Jack the Ripper."

"The evidence I've read was incredibly flimsy in terms of her guilt. He supposedly died of arsenic poisoning, but he was addicted to arsenic. And there's even some doubt that that's what caused his death." I point to the photograph. "Take a look at the photograph, and the letters scrawled above the body. What if, and I'm just saying what if, there were others who knew James Maybrick was Jack the Ripper. Maybe they were behind his death and then framed the likeliest person for it? His wife."

"Who did you have in mind, Jake?"

"He had a brother named Michael, who was well-connected with the Royal Court..."

"I'm afraid you can't just jump to those conclusions without proof. First of all, I'd have to examine this material much closer before I accept the fact that it's authentic. I'd have to study the language, the references, the paper, the ink. I'd have to compare the dates."

"But if you do that, and it fits, then that might clear up everything!"

I'm so excited I actually jump up from my chair.

"Thanks so much for your time, professor."

I take back the diary and the photograph and start to head out of his office.

"Jake," he calls after me, "you've got to promise to bring that diary back to me so I can examine it more closely. If it's authentic, this is a very important historical discovery."

"I will, Professor. I promise."

10

Once again, I manage to return the car to Randy in plenty of time. Am I suddenly going to get a reputation for responsibility and reliability?

"Five minutes to spare, Jake. You're a lucky son of a bitch," says Randy.

"And you, sir, are a gentleman among men. How about that beer I promised? I was thinking we could head over to the Double R."

"You think I can just take off from work anytime I want?"

"Sure. You're the boss, aren't you? Come on, half an hour, tops."

"Okay. You talked me into it. Just let me close up shop and I'll meet you over there in fifteen minutes."

The Double R is the watering hole of choice for the town's blue-collar workers. It's a seedy bar, on Railroad Street, just a few blocks down from Finch's garage. I arrive there about an hour before quitting time, so there are only a few guys at the bar, smoking, drinking, passing the time yapping about sports and what's happening in Europe. The patrons are dressed mostly in dungarees or overalls, and flannel shirts and baseball caps, announcing the baseball team they favor, either the Red Sox or the Yankees.

I order a beer and take a seat at the corner of the bar closest to the entrance, so I can see Randy as soon as he arrives.

I look around and I spot a familiar face at a table near the back. It's Jim Stowe, and he's sitting between two guys I've never seen before. I think about going over and saying hello, but they seem to be talking about something important, so I stand my ground. Eventually, Stowe sees me, but makes no acknowledgment.

Curiosity finally gets the best of me, so I head over to Stowe's table. As soon as they see me they fall silent.

"Hey, Jim," I say, "it's me, Jake. How ya doin'?"

By the look on his face, Stowe is not happy to see me. But the politician in him wins out and after flashing one of those smiles you know is fake he says, "Hey, Jake, good to see you. Guys, this is Jake Harper, a reporter from the *Gazette*."

The way he says it comes out as not so much an introduction than as a warning. The two guys, their heads down, don't even bother to look up or acknowledge me. I wait for Stowe to introduce me, but he doesn't. This strikes me as odd, but I don't make a big deal out of it. There is something slightly familiar about one of them, but since I can't get a good look at him, I can't quite figure out why.

"I'd ask you to join us, Jake, but this is business."

"That's okay. I just had a couple questions I'd like to ask you"

"You see I'm busy here, Jake. Can't it wait?"

"Actually, no. But I promise, it'll just take a minute." I stare at the guys with him, but they still keep their heads down and turned away from me, as if they're trying to hide from me. "I promise, guys, I'll have him back to you before the next round comes."

Stowe hesitates a moment. He looks first at one guy then the other, but he sees he's between a rock and a hard place and that I'm not going to give in so easily.

"All right, kid. Boys, I'll be right back and the next round's on me."

Stowe follows me toward the back of the bar, which is empty. When we get there, I turn to face Stowe whose earlier phony smile has melted into a hard, mean look.

Before I can say anything, Stowe says, "What does your paper have against me, Jake?"

"I have no idea what you're talking about, Jim."

"I'll tell you exactly what I'm talking about. That item you ran after the last council meeting. You made me look like some kind of schoolyard bully."

"I'm sorry you feel that way, Jim. I didn't even plan on writing about the meeting at all, so little happened. But my editor insisted I write something."

"Yeah, just doing your job, right? Well, fuck that. You made it sound like I was gonna take Tudor outside and beat the shit out of him."

"Well, Jim, you have to admit, you sounded pretty combative. All I wrote was that you seemed to take offense at what Tudor was saying. He didn't come off looking any better, if that's what you're worried about."

"I don't worry about anything, Jake. I just think you guys can spend your time finding something a bit more serious to write about."

"I agree, Jim, and that's what I want to talk to you about?"

"What do you mean?"

"I wanted to ask you about that night watchman's accidental death at the Philbin Brass Works last spring."

"Yeah? What about it?"

"If I'm not mistaken, your construction company handled that project."

"So, what's your point?"

"I just wanted to know if you thought there was anything suspicious about that accident."

He leans into me. He's so close I can smell the alcohol on his breath.

"You know, kid, I'm not in the mood to talk nonsense with you. I think you're suffering from hallucinations. This ain't New York City and you don't work for the fucking *New York Times*. This is a nice, quiet town, so take my advice, stop bothering people with nonsense or you'll just get yourself into trouble."

Stowe turns to leave.

"Hey, Jim, I just…"

He turns back to me. His face has turned hard, mean even. "Kid, this interview is over."

He walks back to his table, leaving me standing there.

By the time Wally shows up, Stowe and his pals have left the bar. I'm tempted to talk to Wally about what just happened, but I think better of it and just keep my mouth shut.

Something's going on, and I plan to do my best to find out what it is.

11

The next day, I take the train down to New Haven and arrive a little before one. I find the area in the train station where I can rent a small cubby-hole locker. I pay for a key then take the diary out of my knapsack and put it into my cubby-hole.

With time to kill, I have lunch and walk around the city until two-fifteen when I find myself a block away from the outdoor skating rink. There are about half a dozen skaters, all bundled up against the cold. It has begun to snow lightly, and the wind has picked up considerably.

At one end of the skating rink there's a refreshment area, with several tables and chairs. Adjacent to this is an area where patrons can rent skates. There's a large clock above the booth and it reads two-thirty. I'll keep my eye on it so I know when to start looking for Findlay.

I haven't skated in years, but I decide that to pass the time I'll see how I do. I rent a pair of skates and sit on one of the benches, tying them on.

As soon as I finish, I look up and see a fellow with a top-coat and fedora approaching the rental booth. He's smoking a cigarette. He looks around, sees me, makes eye-contact for a split second, then looks away. He takes a couple puffs, then flicks the cigarette away. There's a certain familiarity to him, but I don't get a good enough look at him to figure out why. It seems odd to me that he's here, because he certainly doesn't look as if he's ready for an afternoon skate. Maybe, like me, he's just waiting for someone. Or passing the time.

I hadn't skated since I was a kid, when my mom took me to the Rockefeller Ice Skating Rink. But like riding a bicycle, ice skating comes back to me without even thinking about it. When I was a kid, I used to play ice hockey at a rink in Queens. I was a good skater, not great but good, and although I was only an average hockey player—I was much better at baseball—I was pretty quick on the ice. And, I have to admit looking back, a little reckless. Thinking about it, I recognize that that hasn't changed. I still sometimes act before thinking it out. I ought to work on that, I promise myself.

After a couple times around the rink, I look up and see the guy in the topcoat and fedora leaning against the railing of the rink. He seems to be watching me. He gives me the creeps, but I try to dismiss him from my mind. It's because you're such a good skater, Jake, I tell myself, though I don't really believe a word of it.

I make another loop around the rink and this time when I look for the topcoat-fedora guy I can't find him. I decide to make one more loop before I turn in my skates and start looking for Findlay. I'm halfway through when suddenly someone whizzes by me. It's the fellow in the topcoat and fedora. He looks back but his face is covered by a scarf. I have no doubt he's following me. But why? And now I realize why he seems familiar. I can't be sure, but I think he's one of the guys who was talking to Stowe yesterday.

I consider my options. Do I ignore him and just get off the ice? Or do I confront him? And, if I do, what do I say?

I make another loop around the rink while I consider both options. The man in the topcoat and fedora, his hands in his pockets, drops behind me. I look back beyond the railing and I see someone who also looks familiar, though at first I can't quite place him. He's wearing a bulky jacket and a ski cap pulled down over his face. He seems to be watching me and the man in the topcoat and fedora skating behind me. Only when I pass him do I realize that he's the same guy who asked me for a light, a couple days ago back in New Milford. Was he the second guy talking to Stowe yesterday? I can't help wondering if these two men know each other, whether maybe they're working together.

I check the clock on the wall. It's ten minutes to three. Findlay, if he's on time, should be here soon. I skate off the ice, hurry back to the skate rental area, remove my skates and turn them in. As soon as I do, I turn and see Findlay walking toward me. He's with someone I don't recognize. The stranger is dressed very formally, knee-length dark blue topcoat, bare-headed with a multi-colored scarf wrapped around his neck. His black shoes are so well-shined they practically sparkle.

I look for the man in the topcoat and fedora and the man in the bulky coat and ski mask, but they seem to have disappeared.

I walk toward Findlay and the stranger. We meet near a row of benches for spectators watching the skaters.

"Hello, Mr. Harper," says Findlay, extending his hand.

"Who's your friend?" I ask.

"Why don't we go someplace where we'll have some privacy and then I'll make the proper introductions?"

"It's not that I don't trust you, Mr. Findlay," I say, "but I think I'd prefer to stay in view of as many people as possible. But I am getting a little chilled just standing here. A cup of coffee would hit the spot, so what say we head over to the refreshment area?"

The look on Findlay's face lets me know this suggestion doesn't make him happy, but what else can he do other than agree?

We order three coffees and sit down at one of the tables which looks out onto the skating rink.

"Would you like to introduce your friend now?" I say.

"Certainly. This is the client who provided the stipend for Elizabeth Chandler."

"You mean Florence Maybrick, don't you?"

The look on Findlay's face betrays that he's surprised I know who Chandler really was.

"So, you know about that?"

"Yes." I turn to the stranger. "I didn't catch your name."

"That's not important right now," he says. He speaks with a clipped, upper-class English accent. The kind I'm used to hearing from British actors like James Mason.

"It is to me."

"I'm afraid you'll have to remain in the dark for now, Mr. Harper. This is a very sensitive matter."

"Are you the person who took care of the grave marker?"

"I am."

"And are you the person behind the break-ins?"

"I have no idea what you're talking about."

"My room was broken into and searched and something stolen from me. And then there was a break-in at Elizabeth Chandler's home. But I don't think they found what they were looking for."

"And what would that be?"

Should I play one of my cards, I wonder? Why not, I think?

"A diary."

"Once again, you have me at a disadvantage. Why would I be interested in anyone's diary?"

"I can't be sure, but I think it might have something to do with the Whitechapel murders. You are familiar with them, aren't you?"

"I am. But I don't know what they have to do with me. They occurred some fifty years ago."

"I don't know either, but maybe together we can find out."

"I think we should stop beating around the bush, Mr. Harper. I would like that diary. What would it take for you to hand it over?" the stranger asks.

"The whole story. I'd like to know why this diary is so important. I'd like to know more about Florence Maybrick's life here as Elizabeth Chandler. And I'd like to know why anyone's still interested in this poor woman."

"I'm afraid I can't discuss any of that without proper authorization. But I can take your proposition back to my people and see if they're interested. Do you have the diary with you?"

I smile. "No. It's in a safe place."

Both Findlay and the stranger seem disappointed, which tells me that they've planned on getting their hands on the diary, without or without my cooperation.

Findlay, who up to now has remained silent, speaks up. "Well, Mr. Harper, I guess that's all the business we have to conduct at this particular time. However, we will be back in touch with you no later than tomorrow. However, we must be assured that you are willing to hand over the diary."

"I don't think I can make promises like that until I know more about the situation, Mr. Findlay. I'm sure you can understand my position."

"Then I believe that concludes our business for today," says the stranger. He stands and reaches into his pocket, presumably for his wallet to that he can pay for the coffees. But I beat him to it.

"Please. Allow me. I'm on an expense account," I lie.

Findlay shrugs. "If you insist."

As the two make to leave, out of the corner of my eye I'm pretty sure I spy the man in the topcoat and fedora in the distance, off to the left of the refreshment area. But as soon as I spot him the figure retreats out of my sightline. I get up quickly, drop three singles on the table, and quickly follow Findlay and his client out the door. As they head toward the exit, I look around to see if the man in the topcoat and the man wearing the ski mask are around. I don't see either of the two mysterious men, though I'm pretty sure they aren't far off.

I find the restroom and go in. There is a man standing at the urinal at the far end, but all I can see is his back. There's another man standing at the sink, who passes a comb through the stream of water coming from the faucet then runs it through his hair, while admiring himself in the mirror. His coat is off, folded neatly and placed on the sink next to his. My first thought is to wonder if either of them is one of the men following me, but I can't be sure unless I get up close to them and I'm not about to do that.

Instead, I go into a stall and sit on the toilet. I can see partially through the opening at the bottom of the stall, and a little through the slit where the door opens and closes. I see the man's feet at the sink. I hear the water stop running and I see the feet disappear toward the exit door. I see a pair of legs move from the urinal to the sink. I hear water running. Then the feet also disappear toward the exit door. But before I hear the door close I hear mumbling voices. Are the two men talking to each other?

I flush the toilet and leave the stall. As I approach the sink the door opens and a man enters. He's dressed shabbily. He stands next to me at the sink.

"Hey, pardner, got any spare change?" he asks.

I dig into my pocket and come up with a quarter and a couple dimes, which I hand over to him.

"See anyone loitering outside the bathroom?" I ask.

He shakes his head.

"You're sure?"

"There was these two guys, but they walked away. Wouldn't give me nothin' but the stink eye."

"Okay. Thanks."

I check my watch. It's almost four-thirty. I can make a five-twenty back to New Milford, if I hurry. I leave the bathroom and walk to the train station. I walk quick, but every so often I check to see if there's anyone following me. If there is, they're either very good at it or keeping back a good distance.

When I get to the train station I find a bench with a good view of the front entrance. I sit there for several minutes watching to make sure I don't see any familiar faces. Once I'm fairly satisfied I haven't been followed, I head for the lockers. I find the one where I stashed the diary, take the key out of my pocket and open it. I remove the diary and stick it in my knapsack. Just as I do, I hear the track announcement.

"The five-twenty to New York City, Grand Central Terminal, making stops in Stamford, Bridgeport, Norwalk, Greenwich, and Grand Central Terminal will be leaving from track four. Change at Norwalk for connections to Westport, Ridgefield, Bethel, Danbury, and New Milford."

I turn around, ready to head for track four, when I see a man standing only a couple feet from me. It's the man in the ski mask, only this time he isn't wearing it. I recognize him as the same guy who accosted me back in New Milford. He walks toward me as he pulls a cigarette from a pack of Camels. When he gets a few feet from me he says, "Got a light, pal?"

"I think we established at our last meeting that I don't smoke," I say, my heart pumping like crazy.

I turn to get away but he grabs me by the shoulder, pulling me back. He pins me against the lockers.

"Where do you think you're going, Jake?"

"What the hell?" I stutter.

He clamps one hand over mine, jams his other hand into a pocket and removes a knife. He sticks the blade right in front of my eye and, still holding on to me, he looks around to make sure no one is watching.

"I warned you not to be so nosy, didn't I? Now unless you want this thing stuck nice and deep in your kidney, you'll just walk with me. Nice and easy. Like we're old pals. Got it, tough guy?"

With his hand on my shoulder and a knife sticking into my side, the man steers me toward a staircase leading to a boarding platform. When we get there, we start to walk down the stairs. At the bottom of the stairs, the platform is deserted. The man looks to the right of the platform, across the track, where there are a few small clusters of people waiting for the train to Grand Central. The man steers me down the platform, where he takes me behind the wall that encloses the stairway, so that I'm out of view of the waiting passengers across the track.

"You know, Jake, you're a pest and pests got to be exterminated. I've been told to take care of the problem. Once and for all."

"By who?"

"That's none of your damn business. I'll take that knapsack…"

As he grabs for it I stomp hard on his foot while at the same time giving an upward thrust with my knee into his crotch. Surprised, he drops his knife and buckles. I start to run back toward the stairs and just as I get there I run smack into the panhandler from the bathroom.

"Sorry," I mumble, as I brush past him and start up the stairs.

I look back and see the "exterminator" coming up on the panhandler, who is in his way. The "exterminator" guy tries to push past him, but the panhandler doesn't move. The "exterminator" grabs him and tries to push him out of the way. They scuffle. Punches are thrown by the "exterminator." The panhandler goes down. I make a split-second decision, probably not the best decision in my life, to go back and help him.

The "exterminator" guy is big and hard to stop. He's getting the best of me as the panhandler lies on the ground, moaning in pain. I spot an empty bottle lying near the foot of the steps. I grab it and hit the "exterminator" over the head with it. He seems dazed, but doesn't go down. I hit him again. A loud, ugly sound, like a wounded animal might make, comes from deep inside him. This time, I draw blood. He goes down and stays down.

The panhandler starts to get up. I look around to see if anyone has witnessed what just happened. I see no one.

I bend down and search the big guy and find his wallet. I take out his identification and find a scrap of paper with a phone number and the initials J.S. written on it. I also find a few five and ten dollar bills. I hand them over to the panhandler.

"You'd better get the hell out of here," I say, still trying to catch my breath. With my knapsack still strapped to my back, I run up the stairs and cross over to the track where my train is just pulling in. I look back over to the other track and can see the edge of the big man's body, still lying on the ground, motionless. I wonder if I've killed him. The panhandler is nowhere in sight.

Ten minutes later, I'm on the train back to New Milford, my heart still racing, knowing that I'm still in danger, but not having the foggiest notion of why.

12

That evening, back in my room, I try to make sense out of everything that's happened. It's obviously very important to someone that they get their hands on this diary that now sits on my desk in front of me. But why? What possible reason could anyone have to read about a series of murders that took place over fifty years ago and in another country? What possible relevance could it have?

And then there's the guy from Jim Stowe's table who followed me all the way up to New Haven. Why? Does Stowe have any connection to Florence Maybrick and the diary? And what about the death of John Tudor and the connection to the death of the night watchman at the Brass Works? Does that fit in? And, if so, how?

I pull out the scrap of paper I took from the big man who attacked me and look at it. J.S. and a phone number. I have a strong suspicion what the J.S. stands for, but as a reporter I have to make sure.

I go out in the hall where there's a phone for the use of the boarders and dial the number. A woman answers.

"Stowe residence."

No doubt any longer.

I'm ready to hang up the phone but then, just to make absolutely certain, I say, "That's Jim Stowe?"

"Yes, that's right. But I'm afraid he's not in right now. Who may I say is calling?"

"Just a friend. It's not important. I'll reach him another time."

I hang up the phone. The rest of the evening is spent trying to sort things out, trying to put together all the pieces of a puzzle. Some fit, but others don't. I know I'm on the trail of something big, I just don't know what it is. But I have a very strong feeling that things are about to come to a climax.

Finally, around 2 a.m., I manage to fall sleep.

The next morning I'm having breakfast at Ledbetter's Coffee Shop, sitting at a table near the back, when I'm approached by a man I've never seen before.

"Mr. Harper?" he asks.

"Yes.

"I don't mean to bother you," he says, in an English accent, very much like the accent Findlay's client has. "But I wonder if I might have a few minutes of your time."

"I've got to be at work in fifteen minutes."

"I promise you, it won't take long. And I believe it might be beneficial to you to hear me out."

"Okay," I say, "pull up a chair."

"Thank you."

He does.

"My name is Stephen Maybrick. I believe you might be familiar with the family name."

"Maybe," I say, as calmly as I can, though my insides are jumping up and down. Here, right in front of me, is an actual Maybrick. Now things are getting very interesting.

"As I understand it you've come into the possession of what we consider a family heirloom."

"I'm not sure what you're talking about, Mr. Maybrick."

"Of course you do, Mr. Harper, and this meeting would go ever so much quicker and smoother if we didn't play games. I am related to Florence Maybrick, though not by blood. My uncle James was married to her."

"Then I assume you must be the one who was providing

her with money each month."

"That would be a correct assumption. Family ties and all."

So where did that leave the Englishman who was with Findlay yesterday? Maybe I can find out.

"I met a gentleman yesterday, up in New Haven, who claimed to be behind the stipend for Miss Chandler or rather, Mrs. Maybrick."

"It's possible that was someone from the government office."

"The government? Whose?"

"Great Britain. But that's neither here nor there. I have no idea how he's involved but it's me you'll have to deal with. Michael Maybrick was my father and so, in actuality, the property you found rightfully belongs to me."

That's two government men in two days. Something big is going on and somehow, I'm right in the middle of it.

"What are you doing in America, if I might ask?"

"You might. I can only tell you that I'm a high official with the British government and I was posted here to deal with your government in terms of affairs having to do with the war against Germany."

"What kind of affairs?"

"I'm afraid that's something I can't get into at this juncture. But I can show you my credentials, in case you doubt my authenticity."

He takes out his wallet and shows me his ID. It looks official.

"Okay, so you're legitimate. So, what?"

"Rather than waste my time and yours, Mr. Harper, I'd appreciate it if you'd just turn over whatever you've found, since it certainly isn't your property. And if you do, it will end here and we won't prefer charges."

"Charges?"

"You took something that doesn't belong to you, Mr. Harper, and I believe that is still a crime in your country."

"I'm not turning over anything until I understand what's going on. Why are you so damned interested in what I've got?

Interested enough to have me followed, to have my room broken into, to threaten me…"

"I admit, Mr. Harper, we did have someone inspect your room and remove property that wasn't yours, that you illegally appropriated. But we've never had you followed, nor did we threaten you."

"Well, someone sure did. And I'm not turning over anything."

"You have no right to keep something you've stolen from private property. If I so desired, I could call the authorities and have you arrested and then get back my property that way."

"Where's the proof, Mr. Maybrick? The proof that I even have whatever you think I have."

His expression turns grim and he says nothing.

"It seems to me that right now I'm holding the highest cards in this game."

"Without conceding anything, Mr. Harper, it is very possible you may have found a way to delay satisfaction. But mark my words, this is not the last you'll hear from me."

"I don't doubt that but remember this, if someone other than Florence Maybrick murdered your uncle, and we both know who that might have been, and with whose cooperation, then I'm sitting on a bombshell of a story. I have very compelling evidence that your uncle, James Maybrick, was Jack the Ripper and, more importantly, that there's a very good chance that Florence Maybrick was framed for her husband's murder."

"You think you know something, but the truth of the matter is, I don't believe you can prove anything. Yes, it's possible my family might be embarrassed at the release of some untoward, unproven and untrue revelations and accusations, but unless you have undeniable proof you'll open yourself up to serious charges of libel and slander. And what's more, there's a good chance this will turn into an international incident. You should remember, Mr. Harper, that at this particular moment in history nothing could be more important than a close relationship between your government and mine. It's just a matter of time until America is dragged into this war, whether you want to be or not. The ramifications of your releasing that document, or even writing a story about it, would potentially be catastrophic to the relationship between your country and mine, especially at this delicate moment. We can't allow that to happen, Mr. Harper. We will not allow that to happen. Lives are at stake."

"That's ridiculous. All this happened over fifty years ago."

"Unfortunately, Mr. Harper, as good as a reporter as you think you are, you don't have a very good grasp of international politics. Revelations like the kind that might be contained in that diary could and would have dire consequences in terms of our governments. And at this time anything that might undermine the public's confidence would be catastrophic. I need that diary. And I need it as soon as possible."

As crazy as it sounds, Maybrick is actually starting to make sense. There are people inside our government and out who do not want to be drawn into the European conflict and it's possible that any flap with Great Britain—and the framing of an American for murder and the involvement with Jack the Ripper—might provide those people with a reason not to come in on the side of England. At the very least, it would be a tremendous distraction. But I need more time to think about this—to think about whether I should hand the diary over to Maybrick and if so, how. This was much too big a story to bury. It could catapult me to where I want to go: someplace like the *New York Times* or one of the other major newspapers in the country.

"I don't have it with me."

"I understand that, but I trust you have it in a safe place and I also trust you will come to the proper decision. But whatever you decide, may I have your promise that you won't take action before speaking with me or Mr. Findlay?"

"I can't make any promises, but I do have it in a safe place, a place that I've told only one other person about. I need time to consider what to do. So, I wouldn't try to force the issue."

"I understand you perfectly, Mr. Harper. But at the same time, I hope you appreciate my position and the position of my government. I hope to have the diary on my desk no later than Monday. My business in your country will be completed by then and I shall be returning to London. Please, take my card. It has a number where I may be reached at our embassy."

I take his card, look at it, then shove it in my pocket.

"I'll see what I can do, but if it is true that your family, your government, used that poor woman as a scapegoat, you should be ashamed of yourselves. And no amount of hush money is going to make it right."

13

The pieces of the puzzle are starting to fall into place. But I need someone to bounce things off, so I invite Maggie to lunch at the most discreet restaurant in town, the Forest Inn, which is a couple miles up Route 7, overlooking a beautiful lake. It's the first week in December and most of the trees are stripped bare and the lake is partially frozen, not enough to skate on, but enough to know that one more cold spell and it will be. It's a bleak scene, a far cry from spring, summer and fall, when tourists mob the place not only to ogle the scenery but to hike the trails, swim and boat in the lake. This time of year, most people are home getting ready for Christmas, which suits me fine because we've pretty much got the restaurant to ourselves. Only a few tables are filled, and there's a skeleton staff on duty. It's relatively quiet, the only sound coming from the murmurs of customers eating lunch and soft music coming from a radio that's been hooked up to speakers so it can be heard throughout the restaurant.

Maggie's a great listener and she's smart as a whip. She has an ability to cut through bullshit and get to the core of the matter. And, though I hate to admit it, she's more ethical and moral than I am. That's probably because she has those small-town values that somehow skipped over me. Maybe it's because I'm a city kid, through and through, having grown up in Yorkville, on the upper east side of Manhattan. I may be more pragmatic and tough, but Maggie, who still attends church every Sunday, has a much more attuned moral compass.

She's also a good listener. She doesn't interrupt, but rather allows me to tell an entire story before asking questions, questions that are always sharp, intelligent and provocative.

By the time the main course has been served I've brought Maggie totally up to speed, holding back nothing.

"I can't believe it, Jake. It's surreal. Like we're in the middle of novel or a movie. I mean, murder, international intrigue, Jack the Ripper!" She shakes her head in disbelief. "What motivates people to do such things?"

"One word, Maggie. Greed."

"Maybe I'm naïve, but it still surprises me that people will do such terrible things just for financial gain."

"In this case, it's probably more than that, Maggie. It has to do with national security and, by extension, life and death."

I think I see a tear forming in the corner of one of Maggie's eyes. I reach across the table, take her hand, and squeeze it.

"It starts small, usually with what at the time seems like an insignificant act. I took some time to look into the business aspect when I found that Stowe was involved. First, Stowe wants the contract to build the Philbin Brass Works. With the help of kickbacks, he gets the job. Then, when the war breaks out, he and his company executives cook up a scheme to get rich quick by selling inferior products to the Brits. You make every third or fifth bullet out of a composite, just a little brass mixed with some cheaper alloy, but you charge the same price. You save a lot of money, right?"

"I guess."

"Stowe makes even more cash supplying the material. What does he care if a few British soldiers suffer as a result. Even die. It isn't his country or his army, right?"

"What about the night watchman?"

"Obviously, he saw something he shouldn't have. Maybe he walked in on a meeting between Stowe and the executives. Or maybe he heard somebody talking a shipment of cheap material. Whatever it was, they couldn't let him live. So, fraud and theft leads to murder. John must have known what was going on or at least suspected something was amiss, which would explain why he suggested I look into it in the first place."

"Why couldn't he have just blown the whistle?"

"He probably had too much at stake. He was part of the community, Maggie. A lot of jobs were available as a result of the Brass Works. If he blows the whistle he becomes a very unpopular man in this town. John was much too much a part of New Milford history to risk his standing. But if the story came out in the newspaper, he could have his cake and eat it, too. Maybe even after it was exposed, he could step forward and take credit. But to do it himself? No, I think that was a risk he wasn't about to take. Tudor called it. He knew Stowe was up to no good. And he died for it."

"What a shame. But the question is, Jake, what are you going to do about it?"

"That's the question, all right. I'm not sure, but I do know one thing."

"What's that?"

"I can't sit back and do nothing."

"And what about this Jack the Ripper thing? Do you believe it?"

"There's some very compelling evidence. The dates of the diary fit. Jack did commit all those murders within the space of three months."

"But that was fifty years ago, Jake. Do you really think anyone cares anymore who Jack really was?"

"Someone does."

"But why?"

"I'm not sure, but I have a possible explanation."

"Which is?"

"I think it would be very embarrassing to the British government if it came out that Jack was a member of the aristocracy, and that an innocent woman, an American woman to boot, was blamed for a crime someone else committed. It ruined her life, Maggie. And if the British government knew about it and did nothing…well, that's morally reprehensible, don't you think? There's stuff in that diary that could be very incriminating, if it's authentic."

Suddenly, our conversation is interrupted by a voice coming over the radio.

"We interrupt this broadcast to bring you an urgent message from the State Department in Washington, D.C. At approximately 12:55 p.m., east coast time, the U.S. Naval installation at Pearl Harbor, Hawaii, was attacked by planes of the Imperial Japanese forces. The large-scale, surprise attack resulted in extensive damage to the U.S. Fleet, and preliminary numbers indicate close to one hundred U.S. servicemen dead and three hundred wounded. President Franklin Delano Roosevelt has ordered the Army and Navy onto full war footing and is expected to address Congress tomorrow morning."

The dining room falls silent. I look at my watch and see that it's about one-fifteen. I look at Maggie and all I see is shock.

"Oh, my god, Jake. What does this mean?"

"It means we're at war, Maggie. And it also means the British are our allies now. I'd better get back to the paper."

"Of course. Of course."

I pay the check, we hop on my motor bike and ride back into town. Maggie goes to the bakery, while I head over to the office.

I can't quite put my finger on it, but there's something different. It's not like there are people out on the street, weeping, or marching in anger against our new enemies. It's just something…

14

The newsroom, of course, is buzzing with activity. It's as if yesterday everything was moving in slow motion and today everything is moving double-time. The reason is obvious.

I go straight to my desk and start typing up my story. It's not the one I was originally assigned but it's one that in a personal way is just as important as the one Barrett and Doring are working on: the declaration of war between the United States and the Axis powers.

I know the story so well, I don't even have to write it from my notes, although I do have them sitting on my desk, right next to my typewriter. The words seem to flow effortlessly, from my mind to the typewriter to the paper.

I write the story in record time, at least for me. It's about Stowe and the Brass Works, the death of John Tudor and of the night watchman. I tie them all together. I even provide the headline, although I'm not sure Barrett will keep it.

"Councilman Stowe Suspected of Conspiracy to Commit Murder and Fraud."

Barrett loves the story, though he does question me for almost an hour on the veracity of what I've written. I show him all my notes, plus quotes from an "unnamed source" about the signs of a break-in at Tudor's home. I tell him, of course, who my source is: Wally Hines. Then, before publishing it, he has Al and Doring do some additional reporting. Nothing changes.

"We're going to contact the feds on this, Jake," says Barrett. Just before he publishes it. "They'll probably be all over town checking this, so I hope it's true."

"It's true, boss. I'll stake my reputation on it."

"You don't have a reputation yet, kid."

"But he will, if this is true and leads to arrests and convictions. I wouldn't be surprised if there's a Pulitzer in it for you. Keep on it, Jake," says Barrett.

I wind up sharing the byline with Al and Doring. I don't care. At least not this time.

I never tell them about the real Florence Maybrick story, because there's no way I can write it the way I'd want to. We're at war now. The Brits are our allies. A story like the one I can't write would do more harm than good.

Instead, this is what I hand in:

"Local Recluse, Elizabeth Chandler, 79, Passes Away"

"In the company of close to fifty cats, Elizabeth Chandler, of Gaylordsville, passed away last week of natural causes. Miss Chandler had little contact with the outside world, but she shared a special connection with the student body of the South Kent School, and she was buried on the grounds of the exclusive school..."

The real story, if it ever sees the light of day, is not mine to tell. I hand the story in, along with a few photographs, then leave the office. I go straight to the Post Office, where I mail a large manila envelope, holding James Maybrick's diary, to the British consulate in New York City, in care of Stephen Maybrick.

One week later I receive a letter from the consulate. I open it up to find a plain piece of paper with only two words on it.

Thank you.

Was James Maybrick really Jack the Ripper? I don't know and I probably never will. Unless, of course, the Brits decide to release the contents of the diary. But if that happens, it won't be for a while.

After all, they've got much bigger things to deal with.

A week later, I'm holding a copy of the *Gazette,* hot off the presses. The headline, in sixteen-point type, "Philbin Brass Works Shut Down by Federal Agents, Executives Questioned."

And under that, my first big byline.

Jake Harper

ACKNOWLEDGMENTS

Ross Klavan: To Mary Jones.

Tim O'Mara: To all the Usual Suspects, in particular my wife, Kate, and daughter, Eloise. Two loved ones who enjoy maple syrup as much as anyone.

Charles Salzberg: To Rusty Jacobs who came up with the idea and the impetus to write this thing.

ABOUT THE CONTRIBUTORS

ROSS KLAVAN'S novella *Thump Gun Hitched* was published by Down & Out books in 2017 in the collection *Triple Shot*. He is the author of the comic novel *Schmuck* (Greenpoint Press) and his original screenplay *Tigerland* (starring Colin Farrell) was nominated for an Independent Spirit Award, produced by New Regency and directed by Joel Schumacher.

TIM O'MARA is best known for his Raymond Donne mysteries about an ex-cop who now teaches in the same Williamsburg, Brooklyn, neighborhood he once policed. His short story "The Tip" is featured in the 2016 anthology *Unloaded: Crime Writers Writing Without Guns*, and his novella *Smoked* appears in *Triple Shot*, both from Down & Out Books. O'Mara taught special education for thirty years in the public middle schools of New York City, where he now teaches adult writers and still lives. In addition to writing the stand-alone high-school-based crime drama *So Close to Me*, O'Mara is currently curating a short-story anthology to benefit the non-profit American Rivers. For more information, visit timomara.net.

CHARLES SALZBERG is the author of the Shamus nominated *Swann's Last Song*, as well as its three sequels. He is also author of *Devil in the Hole*, named one of the best crime novels of the year by *Suspense Magazine*, and *Second Story Man*. His novella, *Twist of Fate*, appeared in *Triple Shot*. He has written numerous articles for major magazines and his non-fiction books include *From Set Shot to Slam Dunk*, an oral history of the NBA, and *Soupy Sez: My Zany Life and Times* with Soupy Sales. He teaches writing at the New York Writers Workshop, where he is a Founding Member, and he is on the board of the New York chapter of Mystery Writers of America. Find out more at www.charlessalzberg.com.

BOOKS

On the following pages are a few
more great titles from the
Down & Out Books publishing family.

For a complete list of books and to
sign up for our newsletter,
go to DownAndOutBooks.com.

Skin & Bones
Edited by Dana C. Kabel

Down & Out Books
November 2018
978-1-948235-53-2

From a host of bestselling and award-winning authors come the stories from the darkest corners of their imaginations featuring one of the most abhorrent acts of mankind; cannibalism!

Featuring stories from Lawrence Block, Stuart Neville, Jason Starr, Dave Zeltserman, Charles Ardai, Joe Clifford, Rob Hart, Richie Narvaez, Thomas Pluck, Patricia Abbot, Terrence McCauley, Tim Hall, S.A. Solomon, Bill Crider, Angel Luis Colón, Tess Makovesky, Marietta Miles, Ryan Sayles, Liam Sweeny, Glenn Gray, and Dana C. Kabel.

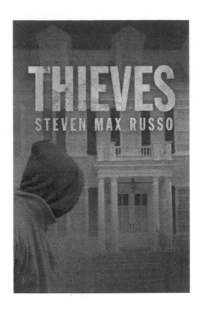

Thieves
Steven Max Russo

Down & Out Books
November 2018
978-1-948235-40-2

Dark, deadly and disturbing, *Thieves* will both horrify and delight you.

In his stunning debut thriller, Steven Max Russo teams a young cleaning girl with a psychopathic killer in a simple robbery that quickly escalates into a terrifying ordeal. Stuck in a deadly partnership, trapped by both circumstance and greed, a young girl is forced to play cat and mouse against her deadly partner in crime.

Repetition Kills You
Stories by Tom Leins

All Due Respect, an imprint of
Down & Out Books
September 2018
978-1-948235-28-0

Repetition Kills You comprises 26 short stories, presented in alphabetical order, from "Actress on a Mattress" to "Zero Sum." The content is brutal and provocative: small-town pornography, gun-running, mutilation and violent, blood-streaked stories of revenge. The cast list includes sex offenders, serial killers, bare-knuckle fighters, carnies and corrupt cops. And a private eye with a dark past—and very little future.

Welcome to Paignton Noir.

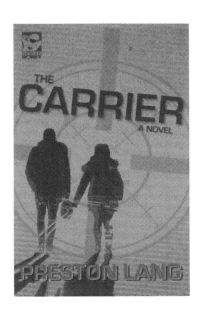

The Carrier
Preston Lang

Shotgun Honey, an imprint of
Down & Out Books
July 2018
978-1-948235-02-0

It's a bad idea for a drug courier to pick up a woman in a roadside bar. Cyril learns this lesson when the sultry-voiced girl he brings back to his motel room holds him up at gunpoint.

But he hasn't made his pickup yet, and the two form an uneasy alliance in a dangerous game to grab the loot.

Made in the USA
Columbia, SC
08 March 2020